The Unforeseen Series
Book Three

Keith McArdle

National Library of Australia Cataloguing-in-Publication data:

McArdle, Keith, 1978- author.
  Havoc / Keith McArdle ; Tim Marquitz ; Dominion Editorial.
  Unforeseen series ; v. 3.
  978 0 9925657 4 9 (pbk.)
  1. Alternative histories (Fiction). 2. Australian. 3. War stories,
      Australian. 4. Australia--Invasions--Fiction.
A823.3

Edited by Tim Marquitz of **Dominion Editorial**

Cover design by Pen Astridge of **The Mighty Pen**

Connect with Keith online:

Facebook: https://www.facebook.com/KeithAuthor
Twitter: https://twitter.com/KeithAuthor
Website: http://www.keithmcardle.com

ACKNOWLEDGEMENTS

I've been on a steep learning curve this past 12 months. It's been hard work, but fun. There's still a lot more to learn, too! I'd like to thank Tim Marquitz, my editor and Geoff Brown (also an accredited editor who gave the game away due to a small thing of buying an entire insane asylum in Beechworth, Victoria, not to mention owning and running a publishing company). Both have given firm, constructive criticism that has helped me to improve my storytelling. I'm still clambering my way up that learning curve, but I'm having a ball along the way!

Thanks so much to my Street Team for your continuing support and for putting up with my semi-polished manuscripts. You are an awesome group of people who not only keep me on the straight and narrow, but humble.

Thank you to my amazing wife, Simone. You're supportive, always, no matter what life decides to throw our way and there's no way in hell I could do this without you. It's you and I against the world, babe.

FIRST MISSION: PROTECT THE CONVOYS

CHAPTER ONE

Not long now and people will be dead. Ethan Lewis stamped his feet against the concrete.

He shoved his hands into the pockets of his jeans. "Fuckin' cold."

"Mmm." Bob Murdoc sounded distracted. "You see this fella?" Bob nodded at a tall, well-built African man at the opposite side of Queen Street Mall.

He was dressed in a black leather jacket and dark jeans with a Pindad SS1 assault rifle slung across his back. Like Ethan, his hands were hidden in his pockets. With a shaved head and heavy beard, he cast an imposing presence. The man was constantly watching the people around him, both close by and in the near distance. He seemed to be waiting for something, or perhaps someone.

"Yeah, mate, saw him a few minutes ago. He ain't just shoppin'."

"No, he's not." Bob sniffed, nose beginning to run.

Ethan nodded and glanced down the mall, allowing his eyes to pass over the men and women going about their shopping. Most of them were armed in some way. One man carried a bolt-action rifle in his hands while his wife looked over the fresh fruit and vegetables flown in by chopper three times a week. Nearby, a young couple walked hand in hand, the woman holding an SS1 slung across the front of her body.

Several of the shoppers sported SS1s, clear evidence of either a close shave with Indonesian soldiers or they had discovered a deceased enemy soldier and taken his weapon. Australia was forever changed. There was once a time when the old woman toddling towards them with a 9mm pistol holstered to her belt would have made the evening news. Police choppers might have been hovering above while officers and negotiators attempted to talk the woman into disarming herself. Now, it was commonplace for people to carry firearms.

Ethan passed a hand through his collar-length sandy hair, removed his other hand from his pocket, and grasped his rifle. His piercing, dark eyes were alert, watching for any kind of threat. Like the African man he watched out of his peripheral vision, Ethan had a Pindad SS1, although he had the weapon slung diagonally across his chest, barrel pointing to the ground. As a member of Australia's Special Air Service, Ethan had trained mainly with the M-4, and it remained his weapon of choice. But for the sake of masking their identity as plainclothes soldiers, carrying the SS1 was a necessity. Spare magazines filled the leather pouches attached to his belt.

"Word is, another bloke came in yesterday," said Bob, blowing warm air into his cupped hands.

Ethan grinned. "Serious?"

Bob looked at the younger man and nodded. "Yeah, some bloke from Three Squadron, I think his name's Troy."

"Troy." Ethan looked up at the gloomy, cloud-riddled sky and attempted to put name to face but failed. He shrugged. "That's great, another one home."

"Mmm. Only a hundred or so missing." Bob swore softly.

Ethan nodded. After the Indonesian invasion, the tiny regiment of the Australian Special Air Service was stretched thin. Small groups were sent all over the country, neutralising Indonesian communications vehicles initially. Invariably, these micro-teams found themselves involved in localised fighting, helping civilians survive against the enemy onslaught. A few were successfully exfiltrated, but the lion's share disappeared, never returning to the small headquarters elements that had been set up in each state.

They were out there, though. Some soldiers from the regiment had been confirmed killed-in-action, but he felt sure the vast majority survived, living in the scrub or tiny towns dotted around Queensland. *One hundred. That's still a shit-load of blokes.* The Army had lost forty-two soldiers KIA over a decade of fighting in Afghanistan. One hundred soldiers killed over the space of just less than a year would render one or even two entire SASR Sabre Squadrons inoperable. *And that's just one tiny unit of the Aussie Army.* Ethan clenched his jaw as anger warmed his chest.

As the other states were secured, and the

Indonesians defeated, soldiers from the small Special Forces regiment appeared in dribs and drabs. They were tired, hungry, some wounded, but all willing to continue the fight.

Within a month, it was obvious the last bastion of hope for the Indonesians lay in Queensland and, as such, what remained of two entire SASR Sabre Squadrons were deployed to help support the fight against the invaders.

Ethan cast a relaxed glance across at the African man, who had his back to them. He still looked alert and rigid, ready to act or react at a moment's notice. *Definitely not shoppin'*. Ethan tightened his hold around the pistol grip of the assault rifle, flicking the safety catch off with index finger.

"He's definitely waitin' for something," muttered Bob.

"Yeah, mate, think he knows what's about to happen?"

Bob nodded. "Possibly."

Ethan and Bob hailed from Four Squadron, a relatively new squadron of the SASR, raised less than five years before the invasion. Four Squadron was a plainclothes outfit designed to infiltrate civilian populations, gangs, guerrilla fighters, even terrorist groups, and provide inside surveillance while winning the trust of their enemy.

But as the Indonesians were driven west into the forests and mountains, Brisbane experienced its own problems, none of which was directly caused by the Indonesians. Looters, gang violence and theft, particularly of food convoys, were ever present and growing worse by the week. Most of the trouble was controlled by a combination of military police, soldiers and groups of armed civilians calling themselves The Guardian Angels.

For the first time in four hours, Ethan's wireless, skin-coloured earpiece came to life with static, followed closely by a voice, "*Stand by, stand by, convoy inbound, your loc two mikes.*"

Bob smiled. "About fuckin' time, I was getting bored."

Ethan chuckled, watching the people around him. Apart from the African man, all were relaxed, laughing and talking, enjoying a day out with friends or family. Something so ordinary and simple yet denied them for so many long months.

Among the rank amateur looters and miscreants, however, there began to appear a well-organised operation aimed at food supplies. Both fresh and non-perishable food was flown in by chopper three times per week. Loaded onto vehicles at the port, the supplies were then driven to distribution points around Brisbane, which were then disseminated to the population on a ration system. Code named *Fat Cats* by Four Squadron, the group began attacking supply columns, stealing in excess of three tonnes of food per assault. When the convoys began to sport military escorts to protect them, the Fat Cats attacked the Humvees first, usually killing all soldiers present prior to taking the provisions.

When the fifth military escort had been ambushed and destroyed, leaving only one survivor, the remnants of Four Squadron SASR, fifty-two men in total, had been deployed.

"*Approaching from the east, approaching from the east, standby.*" The static was terrible, and Ethan was forced to push the earpiece into his ear cavity to hear the voice clearer.

"Time to go," said Ethan. He walked to their car parked at the far end of the mall.

The men strolled through the mall in a relaxed fashion, glancing at stalls, occasionally greeting a shopkeeper who caught their eye, followed by a polite shake of the head, "Not today thanks," as food, pirated DVDs, blankets, or trinkets were pushed on them.

Bob glanced over his shoulder at a nearby fruit stall behind them, but Ethan knew he was checking the suspicious looking African man.

"He still there?"

"Yeah, although he's walking away, hand-in-hand with his wife," replied Bob, shrugging.

Ethan didn't turn to look. He chuckled and unslung his rifle. "Don't judge a book by its cover, I guess."

"Mmm," replied Bob, moving around to the driver's side of the faded-red old Cortina, ignoring the pair of Unimogs that roared past, leaving diesel fumes to waft around the street.

That's them…here we go. This is gonna get messy. Ethan watched the departing trucks. Lowering himself into the passenger seat, the old springs creaked under his weight. They had procured the Cortina from a young couple with the help of fifty dollars. Bullet holes adorned the doors, and one was even lodged in the centre of the windscreen, cracks spider-webbing out from the small hole, testament to the fact the car had violently changed hands at least once. The rear passenger-side seat was stained badly with what could only have been old blood, long ago scrubbed and washed so that only the stain remained.

Bob turned the key, and the Cortina spluttered to life with reluctance. The vehicle accelerated from the curb, and they were underway in rather slow pursuit of the Unimogs. It took almost two minutes, and one loud backfire, before the Cortina reached one hundred kilometres per hour.

"Can this bucket of puss go any faster?" Ethan leaned over, his lips inches from Bob's ear so as to be heard over the engine's noise.

"Wadda *you* think?" Bob shot him a glare.

"I think you're scared, you're holding back." Ethan laughed. He slapped the dash of the old car. "Come on, girl!"

They dodged slow traffic, ignoring shouts of abuse from people forced to jump out of the way, as Bob mounted the footpath to avoid both oncoming traffic and a slow vehicle in front of them.

Winding his window down, Ethan shouted, "Sorry! Don't shoot!"

Things were different now. In the past, disgruntled pedestrians and drivers could beep their horn, shout, or offer them the finger. But with recent events and an overwhelmingly armed population, it wouldn't be the first time road rage included shots fired.

In less than five minutes, the Unimogs appeared, their brake lights illuminated as the vehicles slowed and eventually stopped, parking at the side of the road.

"Shit!" Bob slammed his foot on the brakes. Gently, the Cortina slowed, brakes squealing loudly, the left working better than the right, pulling the car hard left. Bob struggled to keep it on the road.

"This is fuck'n embarrassing." Ethan looked at Bob, unbuckled his seat belt, and readied his rifle, finger gently touching the trigger.

"You know how unsafe that is?" Bob glanced across at Ethan's unbuckled seat belt, both hands gripping the steering wheel for grim death as he continued to battle the vehicle.

Ethan roared with laughter. "Fuck, you make me laugh sometimes, man."

Bob grinned, returning his eyes to the road.

The old vehicle came to a loud halt one hundred metres behind the pair of Unimogs. The occupants of the trucks disembarked, leaving one driver in each, before piling into four cars. Moments later, the cars pulled away from the curb in the direction of the approaching food convoy.

Bob remained stationary, watching the two men left with the Unimogs. Ethan rested his rifle against his thigh and brought a pair of binoculars to his eyes. One driver stood, back to them, hands on hips, talking in a relaxed manner to the second man who dragged on a cigarette and nodding.

Hayche and Mark, both Four Squadron operators, had embedded themselves with the looters, feeding back precious intelligence, including the location of the Unimogs that morning. Ethan changed the focus of the binoculars and was confident Cigarette Man was neither Hayche nor Mark. The second, however, still presented them with his back. He had the same hair colour and length as Mark so Ethan couldn't be sure. With any doubt present, they wouldn't proceed.

"Turn around, ya bastard." Ethan stared through the binoculars, pushing them harder against his face.

Cigarette Man flicked the butt towards the footpath on the opposite side of the road. He offered a passing few words to his mate, opened the door to his truck, then climbed up into the cabin. The second man turned towards the Cortina, and Ethan squinted through the binoculars. *That aint Mark. Thank Christ for that.*

"Nope, we're clear." Ethan dropped the binoculars on the dash, opened the door, and stepped out of the Cortina.

Bob crunched the Cortina into first gear and accelerated away in a mist of blue smoke and string of loud backfires.

Bucket of shit. Ethan watched the Cortina disappear amongst the thick, blue mist of exhaust fumes.

He pulled the assault rifle into his shoulder, barrel pointed towards the concrete, and strolled the short distance to the Unimogs. Both trucks roared to life at the same time, diesel fumes throwing small, dark clouds to drift across the bitumen.

He smiled and shook his head as the Cortina's screeching brakes were applied. The blue smoke began to dissipate, and he watched as Bob struggled to keep the car from veering left as it slowed.

He chuckled and watched as the old vehicle pulled alongside the lead Unimog just as it was about to drive away.

The truck jerked to a stop as the driver leaned out the open window.

"What?" Ethan heard the driver ask as he was trying to hear what Bob was saying.

Probably asking for directions. Ethan continued strolling down the footpath, keeping a keen eye on proceedings in the near distance.

"The port?" asked the driver, almost shouting over the noise of the Unimog's engine. "Oh, righto. Yeah, just keep going straight down this road…"

Ethan ignored the rest of the conversation as he stepped up onto the passenger side of the rear most truck. The driver leaned out his window, watching and listening to the conversation in front of him. Ethan brought his rifle to bear and shot the man in the head. The bullet hammered through his left ear and exploded clear of his right temple in a thick, bright red mist. The corpse slumped against the door, blood and small chunks of brain sliding down his cheek, dripping onto his shirt. A moment later, another shot echoed across the abandoned street, and Ethan knew the second driver was dead.

Moving briskly around the opposite side of the truck, Ethan opened the door, and with a persuasive tug, allowed the body to fall clear of the cabin, crashing to the street. Grabbing a foot in each hand, he dragged the corpse across to the footpath, leaving a narrow band of drying blood streaked along the street. *Jesus, heavy bastard! Ever heard of a fuckin' diet?*

Bob did likewise, and within three minutes, the Unimogs were pulling away from the curb.

Ethan lifted the radio to his lips. "In possession of Mogs. I say again, in possession of Mogs, over."

He knew Mark and Hayche, no doubt squashed into the back seat of a sedan somewhere, would be unable to answer for fear of raising suspicion, but at least they knew their comrades had upheld their end of the bargain.

"Looks like a nice area of town, never been down here before," Hayche's voice blasted into Ethan's earpiece. He could hear voices chatting and laughing in the background, unaware Hayche was attempting to give their location. In the back of the Unimog on the way in, with wind blasting through the canvas canopy and men shouting to one another to converse, it was easy to be less covert with radio communications. But seated in a quiet suburban sedan, Hayche and Mark were required to be far more careful.

"*Yeah, this area aint bad,*" replied a man, probably sitting beside Hayche, who had kept the push-to-talk button depressed.

"*Oh yeah, Larne Street, I've heard of that before. Fuck me, they could have been more original with the name of the street we're turning into, ay?*" Hayche's voice again.

"*What, Canberra Street?*" chuckled a voice. "*Yeah, I know.*"

After a click, Ethan's earpiece went silent. Applying brakes gently, he noticed Bob, driving the Mog in front, had slowed. Obviously, he'd heard the radio transmission as well and was trying to remember where the intersection in question lay. After a moment, a blast of diesel fumes indicated he had his bearings. Slamming the accelerator to the floor, Ethan geared up and followed Bob as he took a right turn, the truck's wheels squealing in protest.

"*Convoy spotted, move out,*" another voice blasted over a two-way on the Mog's dash. It must have been the commander of the Fat Cats.

Ethan ignored it.

"*You got me, Scrap? We spotted the convoy, move the fuck out!*"

Scrap? What kind of a stupid name is that? Sounds like a pet rat!

Ethan grabbed the two-way. "Gotcha."

"*Well, fuckin' answer next time! We're about to ambush 'em. Meet us at area eagle. You got that? Area eagle.*"

Shit, they're more organised than we thought. Ethan scratched his face and followed Bob as he overtook a slow moving car.

"Gotcha," Ethan threw the two-way back on the dash. "You're about to have a bad day buddy boy," he shouted at the two-way.

They turned down a side street and immediately came almost to a halt as they negotiated their way around a car parked on the narrow street. The driver sat behind the wheel, sleeping. *Well, either that or he's dead.* Ethan cringed as the left-hand wing mirror of the Mog ground along the roof of the car, leaving a deep scratch.

Oh well, I guess that's what happens when you're stupid enough to park on a street narrow enough for only one bloody horse drawn wagon to pass. Idiot.

He leaned out the window. "Don't worry, your insurance will cover it, mate!"

Ethan glanced in the wing mirror, watching the driver step out of his vehicle and shout at them, gesticulating wildly.

They turned onto a main road and accelerated fast, swerving to narrowly miss a small group of pedestrians walking on the road. They darted clear of the speeding Mogs.

"It's called a footpath for a reason!" Ethan roared as he ripped past the group. He thought he heard a distant gunshot in reply but couldn't be sure.

In the olden days, as they were now called, driving one hundred and twenty kilometres per hour in a sixty zone attracted an immediate loss of licence and vehicle impoundment. Now? People just shouted and shot at you. Ethan grinned at the thought.

How times change.

Bob's arm appeared out his window and signalled to slow down. Ethan immediately braked, bleeding off speed and distancing himself from the lead vehicle. Within a couple hundred metres, they were parked on Canberra Street with the engines shut down. Ethan swung open the door and stepped down from the truck to join Bob. They stood quietly, listening.

Neither spoke. The ambush was about to occur or was currently under way, and they needed to know in which direction to travel. However, only silence greeted them.

What the hell's going on? I hope Hayche and Mark are okay.

Ethan watched an elderly lady nearby as she screeched at her lapdog. The small animal squatted, taking a shit in the middle of the street.

Ethan caught Bob's eye and shrugged. Then the distant staccato of gunfire erupted to the southwest.

"Contact! Port of Brisbane Motorway, Port of Brisbane Motorway, over," Hayche's voice crackled in their earpieces.

Both men scrambled to their vehicles.

Ethan turned to the elderly woman. "Get your dog out the way!" He swept his arm towards the side of the road, trying to illustrate the urgency of his request. "Get the bloody thing out the way!"

With the firefight underway, neither Hayche nor Mark bothered being covert as far as the radio was concerned.

Ethan slammed the door, started the engine, and accelerated to keep pace with Bob. The tiny dog only narrowly missed being squashed by Bob's front tyre.

"I did warn you, ma'am!" Ethan offered as he swept past the stunned woman.

"You bastards!" he heard her shout and glanced at her form growing smaller in the wing mirror. She pulled a small revolver out of her handbag.

Ah shit! Now I know why Bob wanted to be lead vehicle.

Keeping one hand on the steering wheel, Ethan pushed himself low against the seat, his cheek kissing the cool leather. He heard several *cracks* and a loud whine as a bullet ricocheted off the brick of one of the buildings. Leaning back into position, he shot a glance at the wing mirror and watched the small figure of the old woman far behind them.

Too far away now to be a threat, especially with a pistol. Bloody crazy old biddy.

Within minutes, they negotiated their way onto the motorway and could see the firefight taking place in the distance. Changing lanes and accelerating, Ethan brought his vehicle alongside Bob's. *Now's the danger time.* The looters thought the Unimogs inbound were friendlies, whereas the soldiers who had dismounted from the Humvees considered them enemy and could very well fire upon them.

The convoys knew to watch for one or several Unimogs, which was the reason the Fat Cats had changed into sedans. Ethan saw two Humvees, one at the front of the convoy, the other at the rear. The group of looters had disabled the first Humvee, which was well ablaze, thick black smoke spewing from the armoured vehicle. Soldiers had taken cover behind trucks and concrete barriers, returning fire with effect.

"Hurry the fuck up, Scrap! Hurry the fuck up!" the voice sounded panicked, incessant gunfire cracking in the background.

As they barrelled closer to the firefight, Ethan took in the scene, spotting a group of looters taking cover behind an industrial bin on the far side of the convoy. It must have been moved there during the occupation for some reason.

"What's your location? Over," he yelled into the Four Squadron radio.

"We're both on the Western side, taking cover inside a small building. We're outta sight, over," crackled Hayche's

voice.

Good, that meant any looters in view were fair game and there was no fear of killing his mates. Ethan swerved slightly, planted the accelerator as far as it would go and aimed straight for the industrial bin. The Mog slammed into the large, rectangular piece of steel, crushing bodies between it and the truck. Being only half-full, the industrial bin slid along the bitumen in a shower of sparks.

Easing off the accelerator, the vehicle slowed. With a dull *thump*, the truck went over what felt like a speed bump. Checking the side mirror, he watched the bloody and broken corpse lying in the middle of the road behind him. As the Mog came to a halt, he checked the location of Bob before grabbing his rifle and exiting.

Running around to the bulbar, he searched for any sign of life and was presented with pools of blood, crushed skulls, compound fractures, and death. Not one of the five looters he hit had survived.

Sprinting 'round the far side of the steel bin, he took a knee and leaned around the corner to take in the developing gunfight. In the near distance, crouched behind a bullet-riddled sedan were four looters. Three returned fire while the fourth sat with his back leaned against the car, clasping his abdomen. His shirt was soaked with bright red blood, a stark contrast to his skin, paler now than bleached bone.

Pulling the rifle into his shoulder, Ethan put the wounded man out of his misery with the first shot. The second bullet slammed through the back of another, exiting through his sternum and lodging in the vehicle. Realising they were taking fire from another direction, the remaining two turned, saw Ethan, and fired from the hip.

Ignoring the sound of rounds hissing and cracking past his head, he steadied the scope over the face of the first man and fired a shot. His head snapped back in a spray of blood. Changing aim, Ethan ended the remaining looter.

Checking Bob's location, he watched his comrade taking cover behind one of the food trucks. With a calming wave of his hand, Ethan could see he shouted reassurance to the driver, who cowered in the cabin. The soldiers nearby, obviously deciding Bob was on their side, ignored him, continuing to take the fight to the rapidly diminishing group of looters.

The majority of return fire came from behind one last sedan. Ethan fired four shots in quick succession and moved in a crouch, running as fast as possible before stopping behind the concrete barricade separating opposing lanes of traffic.

Negotiating the concrete barrier, keeping close to the ground to remain out of sight, Ethan's thighs burned. He walked in as close to a squatting position as possible, quadriceps screaming in protest. Stopping, he carefully looked over the top of the concrete barrier and saw he still had some way to travel before he was in a position to outflank the last bastion of strength the looters held.

"*Can you flank 'em?*" Bob's voice roared in his earpiece.

"On it!" He ignored the agony in his legs and moved fast.

Hearing boots thudding in rapid succession across the bitumen behind him, Ethan rolled into a sitting position, back to the barrier, and brought rifle to bear, finger teasing the trigger.

He grinned a greeting as Hayche and Mark

hunkered down beside him, breathless.

"G'day, mate!" Hayche slapped Ethan on the shoulder. "Miss us?"

Mark moved around them, muttered a greeting to Ethan with a lopsided smile, and continued running in a half-crouch.

Thank fuck for that. Ethan pushed himself up and followed.

"Fuck! I was just getting comfortable," said Hayche.

The trio ran in a half-crouch, and before long, had taken up a position where they were able to see the looters hiding behind the bullet-riddled vehicle. A large, muddy green puddle of coolant, mixed with oil, glistened upon the bitumen beneath the engine block.

"Hold fire!" Ethan hissed. He peaked over the concrete barricade.

Five looters remained, although one lay dead, copious amounts of coagulating blood staining the road beneath his left thigh. A bullet had more than likely ripped through his femoral artery, causing the man to bleed out. *A quick death. Too good a way to die for a scumbag.*

One of the Fat Cats stood out from the rest, however. Unlike the others, he wore body armour and an ill-fitting helmet, shouting orders at the others. *Gotta be the one in command.*

"Right, we want the bloke in the body armour alive. I reckon he's the head honcho," Ethan dropped back down beside the other two. "He's kneeling beside the fella closest to us."

"No worries," Mark's quiet voice was almost inaudible over the gunfire.

"Ready?" Ethan eyed the pair.

"As I'll ever be." Hayche grinned.

The trio spread out before kneeling up together. Ethan settled the target reticule of the rifle's scope over the looter furthest from them. The man had his back to Ethan and leaned around the edge of the vehicle. He fired a few shots before darting back behind cover. *Like fish in a fuckin' barrel.*

"I've got the last one," Ethan spoke into the radio. The soldiers were spread out more than twenty metres from one another.

"I have chubby boy," Mark's soft voice crackled.

"Well, that leaves me all out of options." Hayche chuckled. *"Ready when you are."*

"Stand by, stand by, stand by. Three, two, one."

The soldiers' weapons fired simultaneously, the commander of the looters flinching as his comrades around him dropped dead.

"Put your fuckin' hands on your head!" Ethan jumped to his feet, baring his teeth, finger firmly on the trigger of his weapon.

Try something, you bastard, I bloody dare ya!

Turning towards them, unaware the soldiers had been creeping up in an enfilade position behind him, the commander took in the situation. Outnumbered and without any way to take out the three men standing behind the concrete barrier, especially as they were so far from one another, he dropped the rifle and placed his hands on his head.

"Hold ya fire," Ethan shouted at the soldiers guarding the food convoy, clambering over the barricade. "Hold ya fuckin' fire!"

Bob yelled at them, as well, until finally, not a single shot echoed out across the abandoned motorway. Ethan kept the reticule over the commander's face. He glanced briefly behind him to check he wasn't walking in front of the weapon of one of his soldiers. The pair behind him remained in positon, kneeling and using the concrete barricade to support their weapons. Ethan walked at a brisk pace, keeping rifle in shoulder, glaring over the top of the scope at his target. As he closed the distance, he could see genuine fear in the commander's eyes.

"Out here!" He pointed at an area of bitumen away from the bullet-riddled vehicle.

The man silently obeyed.

"Kneel and put your hands behind your back."

He obeyed but moved with lethargy. Ethan helped him by forcing the man onto his knees with a firm shove. When the Fat Cat commander was in position, Ethan planted his boot into the middle of the man's back and kicked him face first to the road. The looter's breath exploded out of his mouth, and he groaned.

"Fuck, what was that for, you bastard?"

Ethan ignored him. *Keep gobbing off and you'll have a lot more to complain about, trust me.* Ethan placed his rifle on the ground well away from the prisoner, leaned down over the commander, and took a hold of the Velcro holding the captive's body armour in place. He ripped the armour open and pulled the chest armour free.

"You won't need this anymore, mate."

Ethan threw it to the ground nearby. Ignoring the protests, Ethan forced the man's hands behind his back and Zip-Tied them in place.

Ethan tapped the Fat Cat commander on the shoulder. "Not too tight?"

"Yes, it fucking is! I can't feel my hands!"

"Tough luck. On your feet."

"You'll never get away with this!" The commander snarled over his shoulder.

Again, Ethan ignored him.

"My soldiers will kill you all for this!" Anger and fear glinted in the prisoner's eyes.

"Soldiers?" Ethan chuckled. He dragged the man to his feet, who squealed in pain. "You're not even a soldier's arsehole! Now get going." He shoved the man in the back, sending him stumbling forward. Bob stood in the near distance, rifle cradled across his chest, watching the prisoner approach.

"Get up in the Mog." Ethan pointed at the back of the truck.

"You're fuckin' dead." The commander turned to Ethan and glared at him.

"Hurry up." Ethan gestured towards the Mog once more.

Bob un-holstered a pistol and placed the barrel against the prisoner's head. "You'll be dead in a minute if you don't get your blubbery arse up on that truck." He flicked off the safety catch and placed a finger on the trigger.

"Alright, alright." The looter complied but stopped at the tailgate. He turned towards the soldiers. "I'm gonna need some help." He jerked his head towards his Zip-Tied hands.

Bob tapped the pistol against the man's skull to remind him. "No you won't, son, trust me. Where there's a will, there's a way. Up you get."

Stepping up onto the lowered tailgate, the prisoner leaned his weight forward to maintain his balance. As he was about to take the second step, the tailgate's hinges groaned and the looter lost his footing, crashing to the ground. He cried out as he slammed onto the bitumen.

"I'm going to need some *bloody* help!" Veins stood out on the prisoner's neck as he shouted.

Ethan gestured for Bob to give him the pistol. *Nope, all you need is some coercion.* He aimed and fired, a bullet ricocheting off the road just on the far side of the commander's head.

"Oh shit!" the prisoner squealed.

Ethan squatted and tapped the Fat Cat on the shoulder. "On your feet. Get on the truck, I'm not gonna ask again."

With some effort, and a flurry of grunting, groaning and colourful sound effects, the looter managed to clamber onto the rear tray of the Unimog. Out of breath, he sat heavily upon the bench seat and looked down at the crowd, which had gathered to watch the entertainment. Civilians from the convoy, and soldiers ordered to protect them, all stood looking up at the man who had caused them such grief and abject fear over the last few months.

"Big mistake!" said the looter at the group glaring at him. "*Big* mistake!"

"Yeah, you are." Ethan grinned. "Your father should have worn a fuckin' condom." He slammed the tailgate shut and locked it in place.

"Let's get outta here!"

CHAPTER TWO

Malik Hunter stood in the centre of the Queen Street market, hands in pockets, waiting for his wife Jayla to finish shopping. While he hated shopping, he always ensured Jayla never walked alone. They had been married only eight months. The wedding had been one of the best days of his life, alongside being presented his Navy SEAL Trident prior to marching into SEAL Team 3. Malik and Jayla arrived on the Gold Coast for their honeymoon just one week before the invasion.

Good timing. Malik chuckled without humour. His eyes swept over the people around him, watching for threats. The next eight months had been sheer hell. He ran a hand through his thick beard and closed his eyes, images flashing before his mind's eye. They had been captured by the Indonesians four weeks after the invasion. *Some goddamn honeymoon!*

He clenched his jaw as the past replayed in his mind.

"Malik!" Jayla had screamed as she was being dragged away by two Indonesian soldiers. He wasn't stupid. He knew what they would do to her. Malik opened his eyes and looked at the sky. He took a slow, deep breath. Malik had been held from behind by an Indonesian soldier as the love of his life was dragged away. He didn't regret killing the Indonesian. *Man, his neck broke like a wet branch. Never broke a man's neck before.*

He hocked and spat on the ground near his feet.

The soldiers holding his wife had hesitated as they took in what they had witnessed. That moment's pause was all the SEAL needed before he was upon them. He had disarmed the first soldier, and shot him with his own weapon before killing the second. All the endless hours of training had paid off, it seemed.

They had run as far and fast as they were able, but Brisbane in its entirety crawled with Indonesians. Within days, they were recaptured despite a prolonged firefight. Eventually, they were surrounded, and Malik was forced to drop his weapon and surrender, hoping the execution would be quick. To his surprise, however, their presumed death sentence never arrived. He often wondered if they'd been better off had they been slaughtered on the street that day. Instead, they had been dragged away to a concentration camp on the eastern side of Brisbane, near the coast.

Shaking off the memory, he approached Jayla, who browsed a small cart of assorted vegetables.

"Hey, babe, you gonna be long?"

Jayla turned and smiled.

Man, she's hot! he thought, returning the smile. *I'm one lucky man!*

"Just give me a minute. Patience!" She winked, turning back to the cart.

He sighed and looked around. He allowed his eyes to glide over the hands of the people around him. One thing he knew was a person's hands were the windows to their intention. None of the men and women around him offered threat and he relaxed…slightly. Always, he was ready to respond, knowing he could draw the sidearm holstered at his belt and fire a well-aimed shot inside one second.

His mind wandered to their dark and recent past. It had taken him three months to escape the concentration camp. Slowly gaining the guards' trust, he had won their hearts and minds. A long, incredibly slow process. All the while, people around him faded to skeletons. Sickness and fever swept the camp. Jayla had lost more energy each day, to the point where she could no longer depart the tiny concrete rectangle assigned as her bed space. His wife was dying, and he could do nothing. *She had been fuckin' dying!* Malik shoved his hands back into his pockets and glared at a tall building nearby. *I hope the guards are all dead. God help them if I ever see them again.* The memories reignited anger, fear and desperation.

He heard Jayla thank the shopkeeper and watched her move on. When she stopped at another stall, he rolled his eyes. *We're going to be here all day.* He took a deep breath and exhaled slowly. *Patience, Malik, patience.*

"Want me to grab something from another shop while you're here? That way we won't be shopping as long."

Jayla looked around at him.

He held out his hands. "It's team work!"

"No, you just stay there, I'm not going to be too much longer, anyway."

"Just a thought," he said, smiling and turning away. *You're not going to be too much longer? You said that a half-hour ago!*

It had been midnight, the moon nothing more than a sliver in the star strewn sky when they escaped the concentration camp. Ten of them made a run together, fully aware if they were caught, an on-the-spot execution waited for them. But the decisions were limited. Starve slowly to death as a prisoner or shot dead as a free man. An easy choice as far as Malik was concerned. *Die on your knees as a prisoner, or die on your feet as a free man.* He had carried Jayla on his back, as she had no energy to walk, let alone run.

By dawn, they were more than thirty kilometres from the camp and home free. Within days, they linked up with a small group of freedom fighters where Malik's expertise and experience as a Navy SEAL became invaluable.

"Ten more minutes, promise!" Jayla's voice broke him from his thoughts. She flashed him a smile, then turned back to the stall.

"That's code for another half-hour," he muttered.

"What's that you say, babe?"

"Just talking to myself." *I said that's code for another half-hour!*

Inside one month, the small group of guerrillas had become a serious thorn in the side of the Indonesians occupying Brisbane. They'd ambushed nineteen convoys, destroying vehicles, and killing an estimated one hundred enemy soldiers. Stealing food supplies and hundreds of kilograms of weaponry, it wasn't long before the occupiers were being killed with their own assault rifles. Malik smiled at the memory. *Instant karma.*

"Okay, you ready?" she asked, snapping him from his reverie once more.

"I was ready three hours ago," he replied, helping her with the bags full of groceries.

"Smart ass."

He grinned, taking the lion's share of the shopping, leaving her with only a couple of bags. It was only a short walk home, which was an abandoned, half-destroyed apartment on the ground floor of a high rise. Electricity was yet to be restored so heating came in the form of a kerosene heater, which seemed to keep them comfortable enough during the night.

Malik led the way as they walked home. His eyes swept the environment around him, looking for wires on the road that might indicate an IED. He watched the roofs of the buildings around him for armed assailants. Habits he'd learned during seven deployments to Afghanistan and something he still carried out walking down the streets of Coronado, California.

He'd tried to break the habits when at home with Jayla, but it was difficult. Luckily, it was something he hadn't managed to shake, a handy behaviour to have in the middle of the invasion of a foreign country.

He heard a vehicle and turned to see a dark blue Ford Falcon sedan turn into the street behind them. He observed the vehicle, but nothing about it seemed suspicious. Malik stared at the driver, but he seemed relaxed, one hand on the wheel, the other resting on the window sill. He craned his neck to see the street sign as if he was lost. The woman beside him had her eyes cast down as if reading a map. Malik squinted, focusing his eyes to the back seat where two more men sat, one talking as he glanced out the window, the other laughing. No threat there. Why then did Malik's gut tell him otherwise? *You're being paranoid.* He turned away and continued walking. Less than one minute and they'd be home.

Not far. Malik repositioned the bags to gain a better purchase. *Almost there.*

It was then he heard Jayla's voice. He turned to see her bent over and leaning in to the passenger side window of the vehicle. She spoke to the woman.

"Careful, babe." He turned back and stood rooted to the spot, adrenaline sweeping through his body.

"I think it's just down past the next intersection,"

she said, pointing beyond Malik towards a set of traffic lights, which stood in hibernation, power to them cut long ago. He took a deep breath and let it out gently. *They're just a bunch of people who are lost, man. Relax!*

Then as if in slow motion, he watched the rear door closest to Jayla swing open and, within moments, a man much larger and stronger than she, grabbed her around the waist. Jayla dropped her shopping bags and screamed before she was pulled into the vehicle.

"Jayla!" He dropped the bags. The door slammed shut and the Ford accelerated away from the curb. Malik's right hand dropped to his belt and came back up clasping a Browning 9mm. As the sedan screamed past, he brought the weapon to bear and shot the front passenger in the temple. Adjusting his aim, he fired two more shots, the first striking the driver, the second driving a hole through the driver's window.

Feet pounding on the concrete, Malik broke into full sprint. He was tempted to stop and take aim, but with the vehicle departing fast, he was worried about accidentally shooting Jayla.

"Fuck!" he roared in frustration, watching the sedan scream around a corner, before it disappeared behind a building. The last thing he saw was Jayla leaning forward, her wide, terrified eyes pleading with him to save her.

Fear and fury surged through him. He screamed, the swirling emotions erupting from his mouth and echoing from the buildings around him. He fell to his knees and looked up at the sky. Malik roared again, tears cutting lines down his cheeks and tendrils of spittle hanging from the corners of his mouth.

* * *

"Trish!" Dozer screamed, glancing at his dead girlfriend beside him. He wiped his face with a sleeve, trying to clean blood spatter and small chunks of her brain from his cheek. The bullet that had killed Trish had ripped past his face, just in front of his nose. Dozer's left arm hung uselessly beside him, a bullet having passed through his bicep and possibly lodged into the bone of his humerus. That's what it felt like, anyway.

He kept his right hand on the wheel of the Ford Falcon. Their prisoner struggled in the back, although Bones and Wedge held her in place. He felt a powerful kick in the back of his seat, followed by a high-pitched shriek.

"Shut that black bitch up!" Dozer glared at the woman in the rear-view mirror.

"She's feisty, I'll give her that!" laughed Bones.

"Reckon she'll be a good bargaining chip?" Wedge spoke through clenched teeth as he attempted to control the panicked prisoner.

"She'll do to start with," replied Dozer, taking a corner at speed and struggling to hold the wheel with one hand.

"Waddaya mean?" Bones this time, all humour departed from his voice.

"We'll need more, you fuckwit!" Dozer snarled. "One won't be enough. We want those bastards to stand up and take notice."

"You wanna kill us all, Dozer?" Wedge shouted. "We capture one chick and one of us is already dead." He gestured at Trish slumped in the front seat, her blood-soaked head resting against the passenger side window.

"Yeah, it was a fuck up, I get it!" He swung around

in his seat to look at Wedge. "Okay? I get it!" he roared, slamming a hand onto the dashboard. Trish had meant a lot to him, not to mention, she had been an integral part of the operation.

"Just watch the bloody road, man!" Bones pointed at the windscreen. "Fuck'n sit still, you slut!" He punched the woman in the face. Her struggles stopped for a moment as she passed out. A second later, she regained consciousness but was lethargic, confused and compliant, her eyes searching the faces of those around her.

"Where am I?" her words were slurred.

"She's American!" said Bones. "Even better! We could even get money out of the US for her!"

"Maybe." Dozer nodded.

"You're in a safe place, sweetheart, a safe place." Wedge patted her shoulder.

Bones chuckled.

"The next time, we'll pick our target more carefully," said Dozer.

"Did you see how fuckin' fast he moved?" Bones shifted forward in his seat to be heard from the front.

"Haven't seen someone react that fast in a long time," Wedge agreed.

"Definitely some kind of training," Dozer said, looking across at Trish before returning his gaze to the road. He shook his head. "Probably a cop or soldier in a previous life."

"We need to be more careful next time." Bones stared at Trish's limp form and looked away with a sigh.

"Oh, you *think* so, you dickhead?" Dozer slammed his hand against the steering wheel. "You think so? Fuck me!" His knuckles turned white as he grasped the wheel.

"I'm just saying." Bones held up his hands. "Don't

bite my bloody head off!"

"Who are you?" murmured the woman.

"We're your guardian angels, sweetheart." Wedge grinned, patting her leg.

"Where's Malik?"

"Malik? So that's the mystery man's name?" Wedge crossed his arms. "That's a…ah…unique name. Don't worry, he's in a safe place. You'll see him soon."

She seemed satisfied with that reply. Nodding, she looked at her feet.

"Knocking her the fuck out was the best thing you could have done," muttered Dozer, hissing against the pain in his left arm. Looking down at the wound, he saw his left sleeve soaked with blood.

"You alright, boss?" Bones tried to get a better look at the wound his superior sported.

"Yeah, sweet as." Dozer glanced at Bones in the rear-view mirror. "It's just a scratch." He grinned.

* * *

Malik sprinted back to the market, eyes wild, thoughts racing through his mind. He ran to the last stall Jayla had been standing and barged through the customers, ignoring the angry comments.

"My wife was just here," he said to the stall keeper, who was mid-transaction with a customer.

"Yes?" she said, confusion and fear on her face as she looked into Malik's panicked eyes.

"She's just been kidnapped! Have you got a car I can borrow, *please?*"

The woman hesitated, unsure how to proceed. "I'm sorry, love, I need my car. It's taken me nearly six months to get one." She glanced at his hands as if expecting him to be holding a gun.

"Please, ma'am, I'm *begging* you! My wife's been taken, they'll rape her." He squeezed shut his eyes and clenched his jaw, reliving the moment Jayla was kidnapped. "They'll probably kill her."

Silence surrounded the stall as the many and varied customers stood listening to the exchange.

"Anyone!" Malik turned to the people around him. "Has anyone got a car? I'll return it to you, I promise."

No one responded, and Malik pushed through them, running to the next stall, pleading once more. He couldn't believe the reaction he received, especially after everyone in the mall that day had survived the invasion. Something that would go down as the most horrific loss of life in Australia's history. He assumed people would be more than willing to help each other out given the events of the recent past.

Malik's hands dropped to his side with a soft slap and he hung his head. "Please, God, please!"

"I'll come with you," said a large man at the rear of the crowd gathered around the fourth stall he approached.

He pulled the keys from his pocket and the pair ran to the man's car, waiting more than a block away.

It's too late! Too dang late! Malik cursed inwardly. *She's long gone.*

"What's your name, mate?" panted the man, obviously out of shape.

"Malik," he replied. "You?"

"Geoff."

"Geoff, thanks for this, man!"

"You're not a local. American, Canadian?" Geoff held up his hands. "Sorry, I find it hard sometimes to tell the difference between the accents."

Malik waved his hand. "Don't worry about it. I'm American. We were over here on honeymoon when the invasion happened."

"Jesus Christ, I'm sorry to hear that, son! That's some shitful timing."

Malik nodded. "Sure is."

They arrived at the car, a Hyundai Excel. *Definitely not a pursuit vehicle but better than going on foot. I'll never forget this generosity.* He glanced across at Geoff, leaving the thought unspoken.

"You drive, Malik, you know where you're going," Geoff said, throwing the keys.

Catching them with one hand, Malik unlocked the driver's door, which in turn unlocked all the vehicle's doors. He pulled away from the curb, accelerating hard. Within a minute, he turned down the same street Jayla had been taken. The shopping he left abandoned was gone, he noticed, apart from three empty bags. Times were tough, and he couldn't blame the thieves for taking advantage of the opportunity. If the invasion had taught Malik one thing, it was that if someone was pushed hard enough, if almost everything was taken away from them, a perfectly reasonable, average person was capable of doing anything.

Turning down the street the Ford had taken, he encountered another empty street. *Fuck, I'm just guessing now! Jayla, I'll find you, baby! I'll find you!*

"They went down here," Malik muttered.

"Which way did they go from here?"

"That's the thing, man," he looked at Geoff, "I don't know."

"Ah shit, mate, we aint got a chance in hell, they could be bloody anywhere by now."

"I know." Malik slammed a hand onto the steering

wheel. "I know!"

"Alright, mate, alright, we'll get your girl back."

Malik glanced at Geoff and saw the man was looking at him in the corner of his eye. Geoff swallowed and looked away.

He's scared of you. Good work, Malik! Good work, man.

"How 'bout we try down here?" Geoff pointed down a wide street.

They drove around the area for almost two hours before Malik pulled over and buried his head in his hands. He sobbed. "I can't believe I allowed this to happen to her again!"

"*Again*, what do you mean, mate?"

Malik explained.

"Jesus, she's been through the wringer!"

"She sure has." Malik sniffed and wiped his nose with his hand. "I've failed her again. This time she might be gone forever!" He snarled and slammed a hand against the steering wheel again.

"Look, Malik, let me drive, mate. I'll take you back to the markets, you never know, you might see someone you recognise. Do you know the description of the car the blokes who took her were driving?"

Malik nodded and wiped his eyes. They swapped places, Geoff made a U-turn, and they were soon on their way back towards the Queen Street markets. Within ten minutes, they were walking along the old Queen Street Mall, passing pop-up shops and stalls. The stores of the original mall were long decimated, some nothing more than rubble, others still standing but burned out. With night falling, large generators were groaning in unison the length of the mall, feeding power to large overhead lights providing illumination to the evening shoppers browsing for groceries, gifts, or trinkets.

Geoff stopped and turned to Malik. "So, before we split up and start asking around, let's get this right, mate. The car is a dark blue Ford Falcon, and the bloke who snatched her is a tall, skinny, Caucasian fella with shoulder length brown hair?"

Malik nodded. "Spot on, Geoff. He was wearing a white shirt and jeans, too."

"Right. It's alright, son, we'll find her." Geoff patted Malik's shoulder.

"I appreciate your help, Geoff."

"No worries, mate. Happy to help."

Malik moved away towards a nearby stall where five people browsed the goods on display.

"Excuse me, have any of you seen a dark blue Ford Falcon driving around this area recently? The men driving it kidnapped my wife. She was taken earlier today, and I'm desperate to find her."

Some offered their sympathies but were unable to assist. Another couple steered their child away from Malik, the mother casting a nervous glance over her shoulder at the newcomer. There had been a gunfight out near the Port of Brisbane the day before, which probably had people on edge. A number of looters had been killed, and rumour had it the mastermind was captured by some unknown group. According to word on the street, the military personnel escorting the food convoy thought the civilians assisting them might have been Guardian Angels, but they couldn't be sure. The events of the previous day were more than likely the reason most people were wary. Their guard was already up, and although many offered condolences, they were afraid. Malik could smell it on them.

Standing in the middle of the mall, he looked up at the night sky and took a deep breath, letting it out slowly. *Where are you, baby?* But aside from the relentless ebb and flow of his own mind, there was no answer. His Jayla was gone.

Gone! The word swirled through his mind. He clamped shut his eyes and fended off tears. *God damn, how could this happen?* Opening his eyes, he noticed Geoff in the near distance, taking to a group standing near a pop-up shop. He was in deep conversation with one man, but after a time, the shopper offered his apologies and turned away.

Half an hour later, and with no success, Malik decided to walk down the far end of the old Queen Street Mall where a large, burned-out shop had been turned into a public bar. Trying to relax, he kept one hand on the pistol grip of the 9mm Browning. With the market stalls long behind him, the people down the opposite end were starkly different to the families going about their weekly or daily shopping. More often than not, the men and women down here were cut from a decidedly darker, less innocent cloth. On average, the far end of Queen Street Mall boasted at least two people shot dead on a monthly basis when an argument spiralled out of control and weapons were drawn.

A large group of intoxicated people strolled passed him, laughing at some innocuous story one of them was spouting. They barely glanced in Malik's direction, causing him to relax slightly. Sweeping the street, he allowed his eyes to focus on dark, vacant buildings, long ago destroyed, or flicking a glance at piles of rubble. Always, he was prepared for a threat. Several young women passed him, one offering a greeting and a harmless wave of her hand. She looked to be recovering from malnourishment, and he knew she had probably only been liberated from a concentration camp months, maybe only weeks, before.

"Hey," he said, with a nod and smile.

Within five minutes, he stood outside the pub, which had been setup without ceremony. The bar itself had been created out of wooden pallets, patrons either standing in groups or sitting on plastic chairs in groups around pallet tables. He knew she wouldn't be there, why would she? But the hostage takers might be. He allowed his eyes to pass over the groups of people, analysing each face. None tweaked his memory until his focus turned to the group of men standing near the pallet bar. One in particular stood out. A man of average height with dark eyes and sandy brown hair. He'd seen the man in the mall the day before yesterday, which as it happened, was the same day the firefight took place at the port. What made it all the more coincidental was the fact this stranger, and the man whom accompanied him, had taken a dangerous interest in Malik. He had pretended not to notice, but in his peripheral vision, he had watched the pair scanning the crowd, always ensuring they were aware of Malik's location in relation to them. He knew they either saw him as a threat or were scanning for a potential kidnapping. Had their interest in him that day meant they were gauging his threat level in case they attempted to apprehend Jayla?

Fuck this, he thought, clenching his jaw. *There's only one way to find out for sure.* He strode towards the bar with purpose, but was soon surrounded by three security staff, obviously alerted by his rapid movement and purposeful glare.

"Gun first, mate," one of them demanded, holding out an open hand.

"Excuse me?"

"You're welcome to have a beer, mate, but no one

carries in the bar. New rule," he said gesturing to a large weapon rack some distance from the pub's entrance.

Malik noticed the rack was at least half-full with weapons, mostly handguns, although there was the occasional bolt action and assortment of assault rifles. Once he'd handed over his weapon, Malik was given a hardened plastic card with a number stamped on it. His side-arm was placed in a small metal locker on the front of which was etched the same number as the card he'd been issued.

"No trouble mate, hey?"

Malik turned to the security guard. "I'm not here to cause trouble if that's what you think. I'm just here for a beer."

The guard held up his hands. "No worries mate, just a reminder we give everyone. Have a good night."

Malik pushed the card safely into a pocket and strode into the bar.

* * *

Ethan Lewis downed the last of his beer, placed it on the bar top, and ordered another. The others nearby were listening intently to one of Bob's stories. The man was quite the raconteur, telling of a near miss he had once experienced with a yowie as a rural firefighter in Victoria, long before he joined the Army. Bob never let the truth step in front of a good tale. Even though the others knew truth had taken a decided back seat, they still chuckled as Bob regaled. A boy, no more than fifteen years old, sat nearby, mouth slightly open, eyes wide and listening intently.

"I thought yowies were a myth," the boy said.

Ethan grinned and turned away, having heard the

story several times before.

* * *

Hayche burst out laughing. *This fuckin' kid is as gullible as a puppy.*

"A myth?" Hayche asked, his jaw hanging open. "Yowies are as real as I'm standing here, son," he said, keeping a straight face.

"Yeah?" The teenager shifted in his seat, obviously uncomfortable at the thought.

Hayche almost snorted the cocktail through his nose. "Fucking *yes!* What am I speaking, Swahili?"

"No," said the boy, shrinking away.

"How the fuck do you know?" Hayche's eyes narrowed. "You speak Swahili, do ya?" He gulped the last of his cocktail before placing the empty glass upon the bar. "Do ya?" he roared.

"No, no!" said the young man, stepping back, eyes wide with fear.

"Only jokin', son," Hayche grinned and slapped the boy on the shoulder. "Now shut up and listen to Bob." He turned back to the bar and caught the eye of the bartender. "Yeah, give me another Adios Motherfucker. Thanks, mate."

A man shoved into Hayche. "Cocktails are soft, mate. Cocktails are for poofs."

What the fuck? Without missing a beat, Hayche swivelled on his chair, grabbed the newcomer by the throat and pushed him into the bar.

"There is nothing intelligent about a bogan drinking shit beer and talking tough."

"Oi!" Ethan stepped forward to try and break the two apart.

But before his boss could reach him, Hayche continued. "Cocktails are sophisticated and complex."

The man gulped against the forearm pressing into his throat, choking him. But Hayche hadn't finished. "In fact, my cocktail has more alcohol in it than your beer so you're the pissant dickhead who needs to be drunk to be brave. Now, fuck off before I make you wish you made a will."

Hayche released his grip as Ethan reached them. The man gasped for air, clutching his neck and stumbling away. Moments later, several security guards arrived at the altercation.

"Everything alright, Hayche?" one asked.

"Yeah, mate, just some dickhead trying to make trouble." He nodded his thanks as the bartender delivered his cocktail.

"Sorry about that. You enjoy your night, Hayche, we'll take care of it."

"No worries, Chris, have a good one, mate."

"Right, mate. You've had enough, let's go!" The security guards grabbed the man by the collar of his shirt and escorted the troublemaker off the premises.

* * *

"*You!* I know you," an American accent said from behind him.

Jesus, here we go again! Can't we just enjoy a drink and have a laugh? Ethan turned to face a tall, well-built African.

That's the same man from the mall! I thought he was African, but obviously he's an American. Stay on the ball Ethan, he's still a threat until proven otherwise.

He pushed his hand into his pocket and allowed

fingers to close around the pistol grip of his sidearm. He flicked off the safety catch, the perks of knowing the security guards.

Ethan smiled. "How can I help you, mate?"

CHAPTER THREE

Twenty-eight members of Four Squadron found themselves scattered throughout Brisbane on various tasks and missions. The remaining twenty-four deployed to selected areas of Queensland, working in four man teams. It was a tiny unit, but potent in its capability.

"Shut up!" Ethan held up a hand. "Shut the fuck up for a moment!"

He sat with twelve other members of Four Squadron in a large circle of their operations room, which was a decrepit mansion in the middle of the inner city. All voices went silent.

When the voices quieted, he continued. "What if this is legit? If this Malik bloke is telling the truth, is his wife the only one who's being held hostage?"

"To me, sounds like perfect ambush," Skippy spoke in a thick Russian accent. His comment was followed by grunts of agreement from several around him. Skippy was a tall, well-built soldier, tattoos covering his arms, a horseshoe moustache lending menace to his dark green eyes. The clean-shaven scalp completed his look.

"Elaborate." Ethan turned to the Russian-Australian.

"Well, just look at facts." Skippy shrugged. "We capture their head honcho. We kill shit load of their people. You even admitted Malik looked suspect when you saw him in the mall that morning." Skippy fell silent and turned away, pushing hands into his pockets. "What better way to bring us to one area at same time? They could knock us off in one hit."

"It's a possibility." Ethan nodded.

Skippy glared at his superior. "More than possibility," he muttered.

"So, what, we just sit on our arse and do nothing?" Hayche piped up. "Because I'm not bloody okay with that. We're many things, but we're definitely not the type to lie around on our laurels while other people do the heavy lifting."

"I'm not suggesting we do nothing." Skippy pulled his hands out of his pockets and held them up to assuage Hayche. "I just saying we need to proceed with extreme fucking caution."

"Agreed." Ethan paced to the far end of the room. "But I think this Malik fella is tellin' the truth."

"Yes?" asked Skippy, raising his eyebrows. "Willing to bet our lives on it?"

Ethan took a deep breath and let it out in a rush. "Mate, I'm not saying that. I'd never stake anyone's life on the line unless I thought we could win the fight and the outcome was worth fighting for. I think we need to put feelers out, keep our ears to the ground, and wait."

Skippy fixed his boss with a piercing stare, leaned back in his chair, and crossed his arms. "A good idea. I like."

"Bear in mind, we still got three blokes embedded with that mob," Hayche reminded them. "They're due to report in day after tomorrow. We might find out more then."

"Quiet." Bob's loud voice cut through the conversation like a knife. He held up a radio, pulled the headset from his ears, and unplugged the earphone jack from the socket. The radio presenter's voice immediately filled the room.

"Yes, good morning, Michael. We can indeed confirm that following the breaking news of the capture of the commander of the looters, now calling themselves The Pirates, one woman has been taken hostage. She was last seen being dragged into a dark blue Ford Falcon sedan. More than that, we don't know. Authorities have yet to clarify whether they have received a list of demands. What the authorities have said, however, is to remain alert. If you are out on the streets with your friends or family, stay in a group. Always know where everyone in your group is. Following the occupation of Brisbane, one would hope we could have come together as a community to rebuild. But it seems it won't be quite that easy. Michael, back to you."

Bob flicked the radio off.

"Happy?" Ethan looked at Skippy.

The large man, who appeared more like a biker than a soldier, nodded. "Yes, now I am. Let's get her home safe."

"That's the plan." Ethan paced from the far side of the room back to the group of men. "That's the plan."

* * *

Holding up his Army ID, the guard at Brisbane's Federal Police compound scanned the card before taking it from Ethan to have a closer look.

"You don't dress like a soldier," observed the guard.

Oh, really? Fuck'n genius! Ethan stared deadpan at the guard. "In case you hadn't noticed, we've been invaded and for the past several months have been left to fend for ourselves by the international community." The guard made to reply, but Ethan held up his hand. "So, you'll have to frigg'n excuse me if I haven't had a shave or polished my boots in a while."

"Yeah, righto, no need to be a smart arse about it. Just doing my job, mate."

Barely, mate. Fuckin' barely. Ethan grunted.

After he'd signed in, he made his way into the compound where he was ushered into the main office.

"What can we do for you this morning?" A female police officer smiled.

"G'day, I'm here to ask the leader of The Pirates some questions."

Without missing a beat, and holding her smile in place, the officer shrugged. "Afraid not, sorry. He's locked securely away and no one aside from authorised personnel can gain access to him."

"I was with the group that brought him in." Ethan placed his hands on the desktop.

"Oh, well that changes everything." She grinned, moving towards another door. "Right this way."

"Okay," he started following. *This is more like it.* But she turned back to him.

"No, not really. How stupid do you think I am?" Her grin disappeared and her brow creased in a frown. She glared at him. "I have no idea who you are. No one gets access to that scumbag who hasn't been authorised. Now, if you'll excuse me, I have paperwork to finish."

"I'll get my boss to ring you."

"Brilliant." She didn't look up from a form she was filling in. "You have your people talk to my people and maybe we can organise a lunch or something."

Not quite as easy as I thought it'd be. Shit!

***

Two days later, and after calling in several favours,

the dirty, cold, tired, starving leader of The Pirates sat in front of Ethan. He'd requested they be allowed to use a small office room and for the temperature of the reverse cycle to be turned up to thirty degrees. They hadn't even started yet and the prisoner's eyes were already heavy.

"What's your name?" Ethan sat across from the man. He opened a notepad he'd brought with him, holding a pen at the ready.

"Huh, why?" The prisoner's bloodshot eyes fixed on Ethan through thick eyelids.

Ethan ignored him, staring down at the notepad. After close to five minutes, the prisoner's forehead rested on the tabletop, eyes closed and snoring softly. Ethan allowed him to sleep for several minutes before quietly standing and moving behind the sleeping man. Leaning down beside him, he slammed a hand upon the table's surface hard. The noise sounded like a gunshot.

"I asked, what's your fuckin' name?" Ethan roared inches from the prisoner's ear, small globules of spit settling upon the man's cheek.

"Barry Taylor!" shrieked the prisoner, terror strong in his voice. "Jesus, mate, scared the fuck outta me."

Ethan nodded and sat back down. "Answer the question next time. Now, what's your date of birth?"

"What the fuck, bloke? What ya need that for?" Barry shifted in his seat and scratched his head.

"Ah, look doesn't matter, mate." Ethan waved his hand, dismissing the question. "Forget I asked."

Barry grumbled something incomprehensible, sniffed, and sat quietly. "What's this about, anyway?"

Ethan remained silent, writing notes on the paper in front of him. In truth, he was penning gibberish, but the prisoner need not know.

"Hey, mate, what's this about?"

Ethan stood up and moved to the door, ignoring the prisoner. He knocked a few times and waited until a guard opened it. He nodded his thanks and stepped through.

"Just give him five minutes, and I'll go back in."

The guard nodded. Knowing the soldier had only been in the room a matter of minutes, he seemed confused by Ethan's request but remained silent. After several minutes, he turned back to the guard.

"Okay, let me back in. Do it quietly, please."

The guard gently slid the lock clear before opening the door.

Ethan walked into the room. Barry was asleep again, his head resting on the table, his breaths coming in soft snores.

Moving around beside the prisoner, he launched a kick, which sent the sleeping man off his chair and crashing to the floor. Ethan stormed forward, grabbed Barry by the shirt collar, and pulled him to within inches of his face.

"What's your fuckin' date of birth?" Ethan felt the veins in his neck bulge through the skin.

Barry stammered the numbers.

"Thank you." Ethan's voice became soft once more. He smiled, writing the birth date on his notepad. "Not so hard, was it?"

Ethan watched as Barry sat up, eyes wide with adrenaline. It seemed the initial shock and pain of the kick began to dissipate.

"Pick your chair up." Ethan pointed with his pen at the chair lying on its side.

Barry did so, unaware he was now becoming a subject to his interrogator's will.

"Sit down."

The prisoner grunted as he lowered himself onto the chair. Ethan instinctively wanted to apologise for kicking the man, it was part of his nature. In the past, he'd been told it was a weakness, but he preferred to think it as a strength. Hurting an unarmed man was not a strength, certainly not in his opinion, anyway. However, he did not apologise, for doing so in the current situation would indicate weakness and provide the prisoner a psychological upper hand.

Ethan remained standing so he looked down at Barry. "Where do you live, Barry?"

"Oh come on, mate, why do ya need to know that?"

He shrugged. "I'm just told to ask these questions, Barry, don't blame me."

"Look, I get it…sorry, I didn't catch your name?"

Ethan remained silent, curious to see how the prisoner would fill the silence.

"Whatever." Barry looked away when he realised he wasn't going to learn his interrogator's name anytime soon. "I get you're just trying to do your job. But do you really need to know where I live. I mean, why?"

He shrugged. "Now you mention it, I don't know. Hang on, mate, I'll be right back."

Ethan walked to the door once more and knocked to be let out.

"Where can I get a bucket of cold water?" Ethan turned to the guard once he'd closed and locked the door behind him.

Within ten minutes, Ethan stood back inside the interrogation room. Barry lay sprawled upon the floor, dead to the world, mouth open as he slept peacefully. Padding over, Ethan promptly emptied the bucket over the prisoner's face and body.

"Wakey, wakey!" He knelt beside Barry, who now gasped for breath, body shivering with cold. "Right. Now, where…do…you…*live*?" he yelled the last word.

Barry spluttered, wiping his cheek, eyes wide, he licked his lips and shrunk away from Ethan.

"What's your name?"

"I already told ya! Jesus, mate!" Barry rubbed his arms in an attempt to warm up.

Ethan moved to the door and knocked once more.

He leaned into the guard so as not to be overheard by Barry. "Turn the reverse cycle to cold and screw the temperature down as low as it'll go. Also, have a bucket of warm water ready, please." The guard nodded and closed the door, re-locking it.

In a relaxed fashion, he walked back to the prisoner and stood over him, hands in his pockets. He poked a boot into the prisoner's ribs. Barry did not respond. Pushing the boot harder into his flank, Ethan waited until the prisoner flinched and looked up at him.

"What's your name?"

The warmth suddenly left the air as the massive air-conditioner kicked in.

"Barry Taylor." Barry's shivering became worse as his wet clothes and cool air robbed the warmth from his body. "Please, I'm freezing man, how long will this take?"

Ethan shrugged, hands still in pockets. "That's up to you Barry. As long as you answer my questions truthfully, you can go back to your warm cell within five minutes. Keep fucking me around and we'll be here all night. You really think I give a fuck if you die in this piece of crap shit box?" Ethan looked around at the small concrete room with chilling calmness.

"You wouldn't let me die," said Barry with false

bravado, trying to chuckle, but all that came out was a serious of squeaks.

"Is that a dare, mate?" Ethan laughed and crossed his arms, turning away from Barry and pacing to the door. Turning back, he glared at the prisoner, a smile creasing the corners of his mouth. "I like dares."

"You know what I mean." Barry looked at the floor. "You have a duty of care."

Ethan sniffed. "Mate, I spent months fighting the Indonesians while men like you skulked in the shadows, hiding from danger. Now the enemy has been pushed out of the cities, you, and fuckwits like you, prey upon people who have gone through enough. And to think you're a bloody Australian, as well! You think I care about any duty of care towards you? You think for a second I give a shit what happens to me in two weeks, months or years, when I'm hauled before some court and sentenced to prison for your death?" He glared at Barry, teeth clenched. "You *really* think I give a shit what happens to you tonight?"

Ethan saw the shift in Barry as the prisoner realised he was not dealing with someone bound by rules and restrictions to guard him from being harmed. Whether Barry thought of him as a loose cannon or not was irrelevant.

Let him think that.

"My name's Barry Taylor," he said, teeth chattering. "Please! Barry Taylor."

"Good work, Barry, I appreciate your cooperation." Ethan looked at his watch. "Listen, mate, hold that thought. I'm off for a coffee. I'll be back in say…forty-five minutes to ask you some more questions."

"Forty-five minutes? I might *die* before then!"

Ethan turned back as he was about to reach the door. "Possibly. Hey, where do you live?"

"What, why?"

Ethan chuckled and turned away. "Suit yourself."

"Wait! I'll tell you, please, I'll tell you!"

Ethan stepped through the door and the guard slammed it behind him, leaving Barry to scuttle into a corner where he sat and pulled his legs up against his chest to try to keep in warmth.

True to his word, Ethan made himself a coffee, sipping the warm drink from a polystyrene cup.

International dirt. Better than nothin', though. At least it sort of tastes like coffee.

"This is completely against our policies and procedures, you know that, right?" The guard watched Ethan enjoying the coffee.

Ethan shrugged. "I'll be gone once I find out what I need to know."

"You must have seen the camera in the interrogation room? It's a live feed to the main headquarters. It'll only be a matter of minutes before they shut this interrogation down. Look, I don't give a shit what you do to him, the man's a scumbag, but if you need to find out information, I suggest you change it up a gear." The guard held up his hands. "That's all I'm sayin'."

"Appreciate it."

When he downed the last of the drink, he binned the empty cup, picked up the bucket of warm water, and allowed the guard to open the door for him. He stepped through and saw Barry sitting in a tight ball in the corner of the room. He was dozing, but his lips were tinged a light blue. Hypothermia was beginning to set in.

I've softened him up enough. If he doesn't talk now, he

might never spill his guts. Ethan looked at his watch again, then up at the small cameras in the corners of the room, idly recording all in their path. *I don't have the time to push any harder. It's now or never. Christ, Ethan, a woman's life rests in the balance here. If he doesn't talk now, they'll kill her. No pressure, mate.*

Striding over to the prisoner, Ethan dumped the warm water over him. Barry woke with a gasp, blinking water out of his eyes.

"Where do you live?"

"Oh, my God, that's good!"

"Shut the fuck up," Ethan roared. "Where do you live?"

"Our crew live in a large industrial building on Lytton Road, Hemmant, Brisbane, Queensland."

Obviously, Barry had thought long and hard and realised there was no easy way out of the interrogation, which had been conducted in a decidedly different way in which the Federal Police usually ran them.

Thank fuck for that. It's a start.

Ethan knelt before the prisoner. "The warm water," he gestured towards the soaked man. "It'll soon become cold, and you'll be freezing your tits off in no time. But I can turn the heater on again. Would you like that?"

"Oh Christ, yes, please!" Barry's teeth already began to chatter.

"You need to earn it first, mate." Ethan stood and walked away, shoving his hands in his pockets once more. "There's one last bit of information I need before I leave you alone." He stopped in the corner and looked up at the ceiling, remaining silent for a long time.

"What bit of info?" Barry's voice filled the silence. He spluttered the words through numb lips.

"Hmm?" Ethan turned back to him as if he'd been lost in thought. "Oh yeah, sorry, mate. Now, this industrial building you're shacked up in. Where on Lytton Road is it located?"

"Near the intersection of Lytton Road and Luke Street. I don't know the number, I'm sorry."

"That's quite alright, Barry, quite alright, mate. I'll get the guard to turn the heater on mate, you've earned it."

The prisoner relaxed, relief washing over him.

"Oh but before I do," Ethan stopped before he reached the door.

Here we go.

"I almost forgot. Your comrades kidnapped a woman recently. Where would they have taken her?"

"Initially to the warehouse, definitely. From there, I don't know. I'm sorry."

"Good enough, Barry."

Shit! Better than nothing I guess.

Ethan knocked on the door. "Heater on full, please."

As he was turning back to the prisoner, the door burst open again and three Federal Policemen barged into the room.

"Just what the bloody hell is going on here?" demanded the first.

"Nothing, I'm finished. He's all yours." Ethan brushed past the men.

"We can have you charged for this!" one directed at Ethan's departing back.

"For what?" He turned back to the feds.

"For mistreating our prisoner. It's called assault or didn't you know?" the officer's voice was thick with sarcasm.

"Obviously my interpretation of assault is vastly different to yours."

"We'll check the recordings first, but this isn't over yet, mate. We'll be in touch."

"Okay, no worries." Ethan shrugged. "Good luck with that." He turned away. While the cameras had captured events taking place in the room, the recording equipment had been disabled. No record of the day's events would ever surface. The guard grinned and nodded at Ethan as he passed.

"Thanks for your help."

"Anytime. It's 'bout time that piece of shit got a taste of a real interrogation instead of the pansy-arsed shit they carry on with in this joint." The guard's voice was soft, almost a whisper.

"Thanks again," Ethan said, shook the man's hand, and left.

* * *

"This fuck'n city!" Skippy growled as he drove along the highway, dodging between light traffic. "Sick of it. *Sick* of it!" He leaned forward so both forearms rested on the steering wheel. Each time he overtook a slow moving vehicle, he grumbled a few choice words under his breath. "Oh, check out hedge!" The big Russian pointed at a distant house, the front of which was hidden by a thick, well-tended hedgerow.

"Jesus, mate, watch the frigg'n road." Bob grabbed the sides of his chair.

"Lilly Pilly." Skippy still looked at the distant hedge.

"What?" Ethan leaned forward from the back seat.

Skippy glanced at his superior in the rear-view

mirror. "Syzygium smithii."

"I don't know what kind of fucked up language you're speaking, but can you watch the bloody road?" yelled Bob, a vein threatening to burst from his temple.

Skippy sniffed and returned his eyes to the road, narrowly missing a small car.

"This place is arsehole of world," Skippy glanced at Bob. "You agree, Bob?"

"Yeah, whatever you say. Just please watch where you're driving, mate. I'd prefer not to end up with the bloody engine block in my lap."

Arsehole of world. Sooner we grab woman, sooner we get back to Perth. Skippy smiled as he weaved through the traffic. *Perth, nice place.*

The smile left his face. "This is Arsehole of world," he muttered.

When they neared the intersection of Lytton Road and Luke Street, the sedan slowed to a stop, allowing Ethan and Bob to exit the vehicle.

Skippy wound his window down. "You let me know when to move up. I keep engine running."

Ethan glanced over his shoulder as he walked away. "Yeah, mate, no worries."

* * *

The building in question was almost one kilometre away. But it grew ever closer as the pair walked in a casual fashion, chatting. Ethan had his hands in his pockets. He looked relaxed, but his right hand gripped tight to a 9mm Browning.

"When we find a good target, we'll call for Skip to move up." Ethan glanced at a car that drove by slower than usual. More than likely a Sunday driver, as neither the driver nor passenger were particularly interested in the pedestrians.

"No worries, boss," Bob said.

"That must be it," Ethan spoke softly as he stared at a large warehouse in the distance. "It's right near that intersection."

"This is Skippy, radio check, over." Skippy's voice crackled over the radio Ethan held in his other pocket.

"Loud and clear, Skip, over."

"Likewise, out."

Within ten minutes, they stood outside the industrial building in question, talking to one another while looking out at the highway. To anyone driving past, it would seem like two mates chewing the fat.

"Think she's still here?" Bob looked at his boss.

"Not likely. She's probably been moved on elsewhere by now in preparation for their demands. If they're worth their salt, anyway. From what we've seen so far, these fuckers aren't amateurs so I can only assume she's long gone."

Bob nodded but remained silent.

A black BMW sedan purred past them and pulled up outside the warehouse. Ethan deliberately pointed towards the water in the opposite direction of the building as if he was talking about something out at sea.

"Okay, we got four exiting the vehicle." He tapped Bob on the elbow, sweeping his other arm across the distant water as if talking in depth about some nautical theory. "One head honcho, definitely." He watched the men out the corner of his eye. The man in the centre was dressed in a suit and strode, back ramrod straight, chin jutting out and arms swinging without a care in the world.

"Those four include the driver?" Bob asked, staring

out towards the empty ocean towards which Ethan continued to gesture.

"Yeah."

He knew what Bob was thinking. If there was a driver left with the vehicle, they could easily hijack him. Moments later, the newcomers disappeared through a doorway on the far side of the building, which promptly slammed shut behind them.

Ethan dropped his hand by his side.

"You blind, boss, over?" the radio crackled to life.

"No, Skip, I'm not blind, mate. Just waiting for an opportunity. Patience my man, over." Obviously, Skippy had been watching the proceedings through binoculars.

Bloody impatient Russian.

"You had perfect opportunity, over!"

"Four on two, yeah good on ya, idiot," Bob observed.

Ethan swore under his breath. "Just sit tight, mate, out!"

I'm going to throttle him in a minute.

For all the hundreds of hours of training to which Australian Special Forces were subjected, Ethan knew all it would take was a punk with a gun getting a lucky shot that could kill him.

He knew Skippy was astute to know that much, but the big man was impatient. He was probably hanging out for a smoke and a snack.

The door through which the group had recently disappeared, opened, and a single man exited.

Probably left a phone or something else in the car. There won't be a better opportunity any time soon. This is our bloke.

"We're on," Ethan nudged Bob.

The pair strolled towards the black beamer.

"Go! I say again, Go! Over," Ethan spoke into the

radio with discretion. He glanced over his shoulder to see the distant vehicle begin to move. He knew Skippy would take at least thirty seconds, at best, to cover the one kilometre of road, especially from a stationary position.

"Roger."

"Excuse me, mate," Ethan called to the man who had now unlocked the car and was opening the driver's side door. "Sorry to interrupt you." He smiled. "We're not from `round here and were wondering if you could point us towards Queen Street Mall?"

"You're fuck'n way off, pal." The man sneered. "It's over that way." He waved his hand off behind the pair.

Ethan turned and looked towards the direction the man gestured, noticing Skippy was about halfway to their position.

Like clockwork so far.

"Oh, I see. Thanks, mate. I've got this map," Ethan pulled a paper map out of his pocket and unfolded it to its full A3 size.

"Oh, for fuck's sake, pal, I don't have time."

"I'm so sorry to hold you up." Ethan walked around to stand beside the man. "Can you just show me where the mall is and we'll be out of your hair. I promise." He used his most apologetic voice.

Bob turned to face the door from which the man departed, hand in pocket, tightly clasping his sidearm.

"It's on Queen Street, you idiot! Hence Queen Street Mall," he spoke the last three words slowly, as if talking to a fool.

Ethan glanced at the map, watching Skippy's approach from his peripheral vision. "Like I said, we're not from around here." Ethan kept his voice light and non-threatening. "If you could just point to the street, we'll be outta here." He smiled again.

What a rude moron.

The man cursed, stepped closer to Ethan, and pointed towards the map. Ethan slapped the man's hand away, stepped behind him, and in less than a second, had an arm around his throat. Dropping the map, he used his other hand to force pressure on the arm around the man's throat, occluding both carotid arteries, starving the brain of oxygenated blood.

Night-night, you arrogant prick.

As Skippy came to a halt beside them, the man lost consciousness, slumping in Ethan's arms. Bob ran to the vehicle, opened the rear door, then helped Ethan carry and push the unconscious man into the rear seat. Ethan slid in beside the motionless man. Bob scooped up the map and sat in the front passenger seat. Moments later, Skippy was pulling away from the curb.

Within moments, it seemed as if the man had never existed.

Clockwork.

"Good work, fellas," Ethan offered as he placed a seatbelt on their captive.

"I still think you could have taken one from first group. Just as easy."

Ethan shrugged. "If you say so, mate. Doesn't matter now, it's over and done with."

The prisoner began to regain consciousness just as Ethan Zip-Tied his hands together.

"Give it a rest, Crazy Ivan," Bob glared at Skippy. "We got the target, everything went well."

"No problem, old man, I give it rest."

Bob swore under his breath and fell silent.

Ethan held back a chuckle.

"Where am I?" the prisoner asked, he looked around the car confused, trying to regain his bearings.

"We're taking you for a tour of the city," Ethan informed him. "Free of charge, of course."

"Why are my hands tied together?"

"For your own safety, son. Now be quiet and enjoy the ride."

"Yes, give it rest, boy." Skippy glanced in the rear-view mirror at the prisoner.

Bob glared out the window and clenched his jaw.

CHAPTER FOUR

Without the constraints of the Australian Federal Police, the men of Four Squadron could deal with the prisoner any way they wished. Considering time was of the essence, they tended towards a hard hand than a softer approach.

Hayche barged into the room in which they held the prisoner.

"What's your name?" He stormed towards the man sitting in the corner, naked except for a pair of underpants. Eyes as wide as saucers looked up at the soldier. He had his hands Zip-Tied behind him.

"Tony Bell."

"Date of birth."

Tony's shoulders slumped, and he looked down at the ground. "I've told you that about a hundred fuck'n times."

The dickhead's still got a bit of arrogance in him.

Hayche wrapped a blindfold over the prisoner's eyes and unceremoniously pulled an empty sand bag over his head.

You'll soon change your tune, fuck knuckle.

"Okay, okay! It's seventeenth of March, nineteen seventy-two."

Hayche ignored Tony and pulled him to his feet, remaining indifferent to the gasp of pain. He pushed the prisoner out of the room, forcing Tony into a trot. Steering him around a corner and pushing him forward. Unbeknown to Tony, Hayche had guided him several times around the ground level of the house they were using as their headquarters element. Sometimes retracing their steps, moving backward and forwards through the same doorways, keeping their prisoner confused, and making him think the prison in which he found himself appear much larger and more robust than it was in reality.

On the third pass, Hayche shoved Tony around a corner and pushed him up onto a set of stairs.

"Watch your step," Hayche offered.

Tony tripped, tried to gather his feet, but the soldier pushed him on. When they reached the second level, the prisoner was pushed through another doorway, and then forced onto a wooden chair.

* * *

Ethan sat before the blinded prisoner. He tutted and drummed a staccato upon the table with a hand. "When will you learn, Tony? You're such an idiot."

He fell silent and allowed the quiet to grow. When several minutes passed, he indicated for Hayche to join him in the corner.

Cupping hands around his mouth, he leaned into Hayche's ear and whispered, "What are we having for dinner?"

"Chicken curry."

"Fuckin' ace." Ethan grinned.

The conversation seemed odd given the surroundings, but they knew all Tony could hear was distant whispering as his interrogators discussed something. Possibly his execution.

Ethan walked slowly back to his chair and sat before Tony.

"Now, Tony, I've talked with my colleague, and he wants me to give you one last chance. You're fuckin' lucky, *pal,* believe me. I was going to shoot you myself." Ethan stopped talking and allowed his last words to sink in for a few minutes.

Ethan slapped his hand on the table, watching the prisoner flinch at the sudden sound. "What's your date of birth?"

Before Tony had a chance to answer, Hayche strode forward, leaned over so his mouth was beside the prisoner's ear and roared, "Answer the fucking question!"

Tony answered the question as fast as possible, his voice quivering with fear.

"That's good, Tony," said Ethan, keeping his voice light and conversational. "What's your name?"

"Tony Bell. Please what are you going to—?"

"Shut up!" Hayche's voice echoing off every wall in the small room, silenced the prisoner.

We're getting there. This bloke is all but broken. He leaned back in his chair and yawned. *A few more days, and he'll spill his guts. Have we got that long, though?* Malik's face came to mind. *Has Malik's wife got that long?* He clenched a fist, knuckles turning white.

The room remained quiet for almost twenty minutes before Ethan eventually nodded.

$$* * *$$

Hayche stepped forward, grabbed hold of Tony, who flinched, and pulled him to his feet. He shoved him out the door and forced him down the stairs. Tony lost his footing and starting tumbling forward, but Hayche grabbed his shoulders and pulled him back.

After another thorough, methodical investigation of the lower level, Hayche shoved Tony into his cell, nothing more than an empty bedroom, the window having been secured with steel bars on the inside and planks of hardwood on the exterior. He forced the prisoner into a kneeling position facing him into one of the room's corners. Tony had been placed about one metre down from the corner.

Hayche leaned down beside Tony. "You're so fuckin' lucky, mate. So lucky." Hayche fell silent and waited to see if Tony was stupid enough to speak. Wisdom prevailed. Hayche shoved Tony between the shoulder blades. "Lean forward so your head's almost touching the wall."

Tony did so. He'd be quite comfortable for the first few minutes, but then the muscles of his thighs would begin to hurt, becoming worse, and eventually unbearable as time went by.

"Stay in that position until I come back for you, got it?"

Hayche walked to the door, opened and then slammed it shut, remaining in the room, silent and still as a gargoyle.

How the fuck do you prey on your own countrymen? Hayche snarled as anger swept through him. *Some other country invades us, and the last person you'd expect to turn on you are your own people.* He glared at the motionless Tony. *He's nothing but a grub. Probably hid in terror until the Indonesians were pushed out of the area. But now you're the big man, aren't ya? Think you're so tough.* Hayche felt like punching Tony in the face, but self-discipline held him in check.

He watched the prisoner. Two minutes later, Tony leaned forward and rested his head against the wall to relieve the stress in his legs.

"I told you to stay in fuckin' position, you piece of shit!" Hayche stormed forward and planted a boot into the prisoner's side, kicking him to the floor.

Tony cried out. "Please, don't hurt me!"

"Shut the fuck up!" Hayche grabbed hold of him and pulled him back into the kneeling position. He pushed Tony's head forward until it again hovered close to the wall.

Reaching to his belt, Hayche's hand came back holding a 9mm Browning pistol, he cocked the weapon.

Time for a bit of a scare, sonny boy. He grinned.

The working parts slid forward, slamming into place with a deafening metal *thunk* in the small, silent room. Keeping his finger well away from the trigger, Hayche pushed the barrel into the soft, fleshy spot at the back of Tony's skull.

"If you move, if you even *think* of moving, I'll fuckin' end you right here!" he said through gritted teeth.

He stood there for close to five minutes, holding the pistol's barrel against the prisoner's head. When Tony pissed himself, Hayche thought he could probably back off a little.

Woops, better not let Ethan find out about that.

"I'll be back shortly. Meantime, you stay put," he said, striding to the door, opening and slamming it shut once more. Again, he remained in the room, watching Tony.

This time the prisoner remained in place, his head beginning to quiver as the muscles of his legs began to scream in agony.

"Good work, Tony!" Hayche spoke, Tony flinching at the sudden words. "This time I will leave the room…perhaps."

The door opened, Hayche stepped through and

slammed it shut. But he remained standing outside the room so the prisoner did not hear him walking away. After almost half an hour, Hayche barged into the room and pulled the door closed behind him. Tony was still in place, but his head had slid down the wall so his forehead rested on the ground.

He tried to kneel back up into the original position, but groaned as the muscles of his lower back froze. Hayche assisted him by placing a knee in the middle of his back, grasping his shoulders, and pulling back violently. Tony involuntarily cried out.

"I said stay in position," Hayche shouted next to the prisoner's ear. "What don't you understand about that?"

"I'm sorry. Oh please, God, I'm sorry!"

"Too late fuck-head!" Hayche pulled the man to his feet and pushed him back out the door. They toured the lower floor as before, and then negotiated the stairs before Tony found himself planted back onto the wooden chair with which he was becoming familiar.

The smell of chicken curry filled the room.

* * *

"Tony!" Ethan exclaimed in pleasant surprise, chewing on his meal. "I didn't expect to see you again so soon. What happened?"

"He fucked up! Didn't ya, son?" Hayche slapped the back of Tony's head.

"Ah, okay. Slow learner, huh?" Ethan washed the food down with cold beer, savouring the taste.

"That's putting it politely." Hayche growled.

"Take the sandbag and blindfold off." Ethan gestured at the prisoner.

Tony was left blinking against the sudden light, watering eyes squinting.

"Hungry?" Ethan asked, showing Tony the plate from which he ate. He nodded. "Thought you would be. You haven't eaten now in…what?" Ethan looked at Hayche.

Hayche shrugged. "Probably twenty-four hours." The soldier cracked a beer and took a swig.

"Can I have some?" croaked Tony, looking at the half-finished plate of food.

Ethan paused and stared at the prisoner. "That depends on you, mate. Tell me what I want to know and you can have as much as you like. Fuck me around and you get nothing. Pretty simple really, isn't it?"

Tony nodded, his shoulders slumped in exhaustion and defeat.

"Tony Bell, seventeenth March, nineteen seventy-two," he blurted the words out as fast as possible.

"You haven't been asked to answer anything yet, idiot!" Hayche shouted, pulling the man to his feet and forcing him into a corner, before pushing him to his knees and into the same stress position. He pushed the barrel of the Browning into the back of Tony's head. "You last three minutes, we'll give you one final chance. You don't make it?" Hayche chuckled. "Then I'll fuckin' blow your brains all over that wall in front of you."

Jesus, Hayche! What are you doing? He's losing the bloody plot!

Ethan placed the knife and fork down. "Put the handgun away, mate."

Hayche threw a glare in his superior's direction. "Why?"

Friggin' hell, Hayche, we can't be seen to be squabbling in front of the prisoner. Christ!

Ethan glared back at the soldier. "Put…it…down," he mouthed.

Face red with fury, Hayche turned away and holstered the Browning. "Fuck!" he shouted.

Tony was shaking, whether from muscle fatigue or abject fear, it was difficult to know.

That little disagreement may have worked in our favour.

"Damn, this is nice," Ethan muttered through mouthfuls of his dinner. "It's got just that right amount of heat." He looked up at Hayche. "You know? Not too hot, but not too mild either. Bloody beautiful."

Hayche grunted, but did not reply. "That's two minutes down, one to go," he said to the back of Tony's head. In reality, almost five minutes had passed. The prisoner's muscles quivered as they strained to hold him upright. His breathing came in loud gasps through pursed lips as he struggled to maintain his posture.

"That's it, mate, just one more minute to go," said Hayche when another minute ticked by. "Doing well, Tony, me old boy."

Ethan clenched his jaw. *We want to break him, not turn him into a drivelling mess. What's gotten into you, Hayche?*

He gained the soldier's attention with a wave of his hand. Hayche glared at him. "Stop!" he formed the word with his lips.

Hayche cursed and turned away. He grabbed the prisoner beneath his arms and pulled him to his feet. "That's time!" he shouted. "Good work. We'll give you one last chance, okay?" Hayche steered Tony back to the chair.

He nodded, flopping into the chair but remaining silent.

"But this is the last time. You fuck this one up," Hayche tapped the barrel of the 9mm against the prisoner's head, "and you're done. Got me?" he asked, leaning so he whispered directly into Tony's ear.

Ethan used every nuance of his being not to roll his eyes.

He nodded once more, remaining silent.

"Good," muttered Hayche.

"Now that we're back on track, you want some?" Ethan pointed to his plate, which had a few scraps of food left on it.

"Yes, please."

Ethan nodded. "Good manners there, mate." He scooped up another mouthful and chewed on it. He stared thoughtfully at the wall behind the prisoner. "Now, there was a young woman taken hostage by your group. You know who I'm talking about?"

"What, the black bitch? Yeah, I know who you mean."

"So I suppose we can add racist to your extremely short repertoire?" Ethan pointed a fork at the prisoner.

"Waddaya mean?"

Hayche slapped Tony's head hard. "Have some respect, you shit heel!"

"Sorry!" The prisoner flinched, cowering in his chair.

"That's okay, Tony. It's your first and final warning, though. Okay?" Ethan smiled pleasantly. He ate another mouthful, leaving almost nothing on the plate. "But the longer you take to answer my questions, the less food you'll have to eat. As I said, this really can't get much simpler." He played with the last forkful of food. "Do you understand?"

"Yes!" Tony said, staring with longing at the last, succulent piece of chicken smeared with Indian Curry.

Ethan noticed the prisoner staring at his plate. "It's

Vindaloo. Ever eaten that before?"

Tony shook his head.

"It's quite a hot dish, but very tasty. Certainly not for the faint-hearted. You're not faint-hearted are you Tony?"

"No, not me! Never."

"Well, from what I've seen, I disagree, mate." Ethan Chuckled.

"Fuckin' right there!" added Hayche.

Tony wisely remained silent.

Using his fork, Ethan skewered the last piece of chicken and held it up for inspection. Tony's eyes followed the morsel of food.

"Now, let's start again, shall we?" Ethan sat forward in his seat and glared at the prisoner. "Your circus of an outfit took a young woman hostage. Do you know who I'm talking about?"

"Yes." Tony's eyes glued to the chicken.

"Much better!"

Okay, here we go. Now or never.

"You took her to your warehouse. Was she moved on at any stage?"

"Yes, yes she was."

The soldier nodded. "Good. Now this may be the most important question of your life, Tony. Where was she taken?"

Tony remained silent for a long time. He shifted in his chair, obviously uncomfortable.

"Tony?" Ethan leaned back in his chair, his eyes glinting with controlled fury. "Time's ticking, mate. This chicken's going to be cold before long."

"I…" Tony looked at the ground and clenched his eyes shut. "I can't say. Please! They'll kill me!"

Ethan remained silent, staring at the prisoner.

Finally, Tony looked up, his eyes glistening with tears. Ethan ate the last morsel of chicken, watching Tony slump in defeat.

"Not bad." Ethan nodded as he chewed on the last of his meal. "Now, who's going to kill you?"

"The people I work for."

"Oh? And who's that?"

"Oh, sweet Jesus, I can't say! You don't know how bad these people are. They'll gut me like a fish if they find out I talked."

"They're not as bad as you think," said Ethan, a hard light entering his dark eyes. "We killed an entire group of your colleagues the other day. We also captured your head honcho."

He watched realisation enter Tony's eyes as the prisoner finally understood with whom he shared the room.

"I heard about that," muttered Tony.

"Did you? That's good. You're all nothing but a bunch of fucking rank amateurs." Ethan snarled, standing to look down at the prisoner. "You had your chance!"

The prisoner tried to shift away from him. "No, please!" his voice was a squeak.

"Get this piece of shit out of here!" said Ethan, storming out of the room, slamming the door behind him.

* * *

"Gladly," said Hayche, grabbing Tony by the jaw and pulling his head back. Tying the blindfold tightly in place, he dropped the empty sandbag over his face.

"Stand the fuck up!" he roared.

Ethan's being too fuckin' soft on this piece of shit!

Hayche shoved him out of the room and pushed him down the stairs. When he lost his footing, the soldier pulled him back so he could regain his balance.

"How long is this going to go on for?"

Ignoring him, Hayche pushed him on until they were on the bottom floor. After the scenic tour of the house's lower level, the prisoner was guided into the centre of his room.

"Kneel," said Hayche. After a moment of hesitation, Hayche kicked the back of the prisoner's knees, forcing him to his knees.

"Chin to your chest. Now stay there."

He walked out, slammed the door, locked it and departed for his dinner.

Taking the stairs two at a time, he barged into the interrogation room where Ethan still sat, nursing a beer and looking thoughtful.

"Fuck me, what are you contemplating? How to bend space and time?" asked Hayche, falling into a chair.

"Hey?" said Ethan, blinking. He chuckled. "Nah, mate. You think he'll talk?"

"No, no I fuckin' don't!"

Ethan's eyebrows rose. "Really? And why's that?"

Want me to paint a picture?

"You know why, boss! You're being too soft on him."

Ethan's eyes darkened. "No, Hayche, I'm not. We might have been invaded, and our country might be in tatters, but we still have to abide by the Geneva Convention. We're professional soldiers, not third-world country insurgents."

What the fuck?

"Are you questioning my professionalism?"

Hayche's voice took on a dangerous tone.

"When you pull a nine mil and threaten to blow the back of our prisoner's head out? Yeah, I bloody am. Get a hold of yourself, mate."

"Get a hold of my—" Hayche fell silent. "Fuck you, boss. Seriously!" Hayche jumped to his feet and stormed clear of the room.

* * *

Ethan sighed. He took a gulp of his beer and leaned back in the chair. The door opened and Skippy wandered in, an unlit cigarette clenched between his lips. He was fumbling around in his shirt pocket, looking for a lighter.

"You eaten, Skip?" He watched the big Russian.

The soldier nodded. "Good food, boss," he said, the cigarette jiggling up and down as his lips moved. His hand reappeared from a pocket clenching a lighter. "I heard disagreement."

Jesus, who fuckin' didn't? Lucky this street is half-abandoned or every man and his dog'd know what's going on here.

Ethan took another swig of beer, but remained silent, watching the Russian.

"You want me to talk to him?"

Might be an idea.

He placed the empty glass on the table and pushed it away. "Good idea, mate."

"This his dinner?" Skippy pointed at a plate of untouched food sitting on the table.

Ethan nodded.

"See you soon." Skippy picked up the plate with one hand, lit his cigarette with the other, and departed the room, a puff of smoke drifting over one shoulder as he closed the door behind him.

* * *

Skippy found Hayche on the lower level sitting on the ground, leaning against a wall.

"You eat dinner." He shoved the plate of food in Hayche's face.

"Thanks."

Taking a long drag on the cigarette, Skippy exhaled the smoke through his nose and sat down next to his comrade.

"The boy will talk," Skippy said.

"Yeah, eventually," Hayche mumbled through a mouthful of food. "He just needs some more softening up."

We soften him up more, he'll break.

"A thin line, my friend. We want him to talk, but we need truth. If we push harder, we run risk of him saying anything and everything to make it all stop. You understand?"

Hayche's head snapped around, and he glared at the Russian. "Yeah I understand, Skippy. I'm not stupid."

Could have fooled me. The Russian suppressed a smile.

"I meant no offence, Hayche. We just need truth, and fast, or that woman is dead."

"Do we have the time? That's the question." Hayche finished the food and placed the empty plate beside him.

"He hasn't eaten in twenty-four hours, he hasn't sipped water in twelve. He slept maybe ten minutes the entire time he's been here. The boy is scared." Skippy pushed the spent cigarette upon the ground, extinguishing it. "And cold," he added. "He'll talk, mate, and sooner than later, too. But we need to interrogate, not torture."

Hayche sighed and swore softly. "Yeah, I know, Skip. I know, mate. I'm just frustrated and angry. This scumbag and his mates have been preying on our people when we should've been banding together against a common enemy." He rubbed his face. "I overreacted, I guess. Now his dickhead friends are holding an innocent woman hostage." He held out his hands. "Shit, who knows. She might even be dead by now."

"I agree, Hayche, but no lopping fingers off. We soldiers, remember? Not terrorists."

Hayche closed his eyes, leaned his head against the wall and nodded.

"That self-doubt whether he'll even survive his stay here will play on him. If he thinks giving info will prolong his existence, he'll fuckin' squeal. That is all the leverage we need."

"True."

I leave him to think on it. He's coming around.

"I go watch over prisoner." Skippy grunted as he pushed himself to his feet, striding to the prisoner's door. The bikey-looking soldier unlocked the door and threw it open. Tony knelt in the centre of the room, chin to chest. More than likely the position Hayche had left him in.

"Well done, boy," said Skippy.

Tony flinched at the new voice. Skippy knew that as much as Hayche had terrified the prisoner, he was the man with whom Tony had developed a rapport, and what was familiar, was safe. Skippy's presence had thrown a spanner in the works.

"Don't get up, please, don't trouble yourself! Not

for me." Skippy burst out laughing, walking around in front of Tony. "Just joking, mate."

The prisoner remained silent and still, to his credit. Pulling out a cigarette, Skippy lit it and inhaled deeply.

"Ah, much better! Nothing like cigarette after good meal. Am I right?"

The prisoner nodded.

Clenching the cigarette between his teeth and squinting as the smoke drifted up into his eyes, Skippy pulled the sandbag off the prisoner's head and threw it into a corner. Untying the blindfold, he discarded it in a similar manner.

He pointed towards a wall. "Go sit down, mate. Make yourself comfortable."

Tony hesitated, eyes shining with fear, unsure whether it was some kind of trap.

Skippy took a drag of the cigarette and gestured at the wall again. "Go, Tony. Sit down. How you say? Take a load off. You've gone through enough. No tricks, Tony, I promise."

The prisoner stood with a groan. Moments later, he leaned his body and head against the wall, looking up at the ceiling. With hands secured behind his back, Tony likely still experienced some discomfort, but nothing in comparison to his previous experiences under Hayche's careful watch.

"Now I level with you, boy," said Skippy, sitting against a corner of the room. One leg stretched out in front of him. His other leg was bent up, foot flat on the floor, knee pointing towards the roof.

"I am like a loyal dog, I easy going and friendly. But you poke me with stick or fuck me around, I tear your fucking throat out." Skippy exhaled smoke out at the ceiling. "Follow me?"

Tony nodded.

"Good." Skippy flicked the spent cigarette away. "Good." He fell silent and stared at the prisoner. Tony held the stare for a few seconds before looking away. "I tell you this, boy." Skippy looked at the ceiling as if in thought. "The blokes upstairs," he pointed up with his index finger. "They not fucking around, Tony. They serious, believe me. If you don't give them information they need, they going to kill you. You understand?"

The prisoner's eyes, round as saucers, stared at his potential new ally.

"Tony, this is important. You understand?"

"Yes." The prisoner cleared his throat and blinked out of a reverie. "Yes, I do." His voice quivered.

"I just trying to forewarn you, mate. The last thing I want to see is fellow Australian executed. I've been fighting Indonesians for best part of a year. They've killed enough of my countrymen for my liking. I don't want to see another Australian murdered under my watch."

Skippy deliberately allowed emotive words to enter his vernacular, to reiterate to Tony he might die if he did not answer their questions to their satisfaction. The soldier stopped speaking and ran a hand down his horseshoe moustache. He allowed the silence to grow. Looking at the concrete floor, he was aware Tony was staring at him, almost willing him to continue speaking.

Time to reinforce our friendship.

"Listen, this against regulations, but I'm going to allow you to sleep. I'm not going to be relieved for another two hours." Skippy lit another cigarette. "Want one?" he offered it to the prisoner.

Tony nodded.

Skippy pushed himself to his feet and gave the

cigarette to Tony before resuming his seat. He lit another and took a long drag, before exhaling the smoke through his nose.

"I know you've been through a lot, Tony. I want to be fair to you because I know you haven't had much of break while you've been here."

Skippy fell silent as he enjoyed his smoke.

He's on the verge of talking. Skippy glanced at the prisoner. *Not long now and we'll know where the woman is.*

He pushed the cigarette between his lips, squinting against the smoke drifting into his eyes. *We treat Tony's friends not so nicely.*

He chuckled, looking forward to the altercation. The prisoner stole a sidelong glance at the amused Russian.

If they shoot woman, we kill them all. Skippy burst out laughing. *We kill them all anyway.*

He noticed the prisoner watching him with fear-filled eyes.

"Is no problem," he reassured, Tony. "Just thinking of old joke. No problem."

Tony looked away. Several minutes later, they finished their cigarettes.

"Now, you sleep, mate. I'm afraid I can't free your hands, but try and make yourself as comfortable as possible. Okay?"

Tony nodded, relief seeming to glow from every fibre of his being. He lay in a lateral position, knees pulled up to his chest.

"I let you sleep, mate. Just before the next bloke takes over, I wake you up. Fair?"

"Thank you," muttered Tony. "Yes, more than fair."

"No problem, boy," said Skippy, relaxing against

the wall.

The soldier waited in silence, watching Tony. The prisoner's breathing deepened. When he began snoring softly, Skippy stood quietly, moved over to him and nudged him with a boot.

"Tony!"

The prisoner groaned.

"Tony! Wake up, boy. Up you get." Skippy nudged him with a boot, this time less gently.

Exhausted, he sat up, dark bags beneath bleary eyes. "Has it been two hours already?"

"Afraid so," said Skippy. "They want you upstairs. Up you get." He helped the prisoner to his feet, prior to replacing the blindfold and sandbag.

Now it's crunch time. Let's find out where this hostage is so we can get her home safely.

Within five minutes, Skippy guided him to the chair placed before Ethan.

"Wait outside," Ethan said, looking at Skippy. He deliberately made his voice sound gruff.

* * *

He watched the big Russian head towards the door.

"I'll be right outside, Tony, okay?" Skippy said.

"Please, can you stay in the room?"

"No!" Ethan slammed a hand down on the table. "You don't get to dictate to us, son."

Skippy turned back to Tony. "Remember what I told you downstairs. You'll be fine. Got it?"

The sandbag bobbed as Tony nodded.

Skippy gave Ethan thumbs up and slammed the door behind him.

Ethan stood and walked to the prisoner, ripping the sandbag away and untying the blindfold. He returned to the small table and poured himself a fresh glass of water before taking a long drink. He finished the glass and placed it back on the table. Noticing Tony stared at the tall, frosted bottle of water, Ethan shook his head. "Oh, sorry, how rude of me. Would you like some water?"

"Yes, please," Tony croaked.

Ethan sat down and placed his hands on the table. "I'll get you one in a minute. *If* you decide to cooperate. Do you understand?"

The prisoner nodded, licking dry lips.

Ethan launched himself to his feet and pushed his face within centimetres of Tony's ear. "I said, do you understand?" he roared.

"Yes, oh shit, yes, I understand," he babbled.

Ethan sat down. "I'm just going to start where we left off. Where was she taken?" Ethan's piercing eyes bored into the prisoner.

Tony shook his head, "I-I just…I'm not allowed to—"

Ethan's hand disappeared beneath the table and reappeared holding a 9mm handgun, which he placed gently on the table with a soft *thud*. "Tony, I'm not sure you appreciate the danger in which you currently find yourself," he said.

Allowing the silence to grow, he waited. The door barged open, and Hayche strode in, picked up the pistol and walked round behind Tony.

"Tony, do you understand what's about to happen?" Hayche stared down at the back of the prisoner's balding head.

"Hayche!" Ethan jumped to his feet. "What the

fuck are you doing?"

"What does it look like, boss. I'm getting shit done." He shot an acid glare at his superior. "You know what I'm about to do, Tony?"

"Yes," blubbered the man, weeping openly.

"Hayche, for fuck sake, put that fuckin' weapon down *now!*"

The soldier ignored Ethan.

"I'm going to give you one last chance. This *is* your last chance," Hayche's voice was cold and calm.

Shit he's going to shoot him. Ethan watched the scene in slow motion. He began moving around the table to stop Hayche. *Hayche is going to kill him.*

"*Where* was she taken?"

Hanging his head, shoulders shaking as he sobbed, Tony took a deep breath and looked up at the ceiling. "It's a house."

Ethan hesitated and glared at Hayche.

"Good, that's a start," said Hayche. "What's the address?"

"Twenty-four Woodcliffe Crescent, Woody Point."

Ethan strode forward and snatched the sidearm from Hayche. He didn't say anything to his subordinate. *Now's not the time.* "Not so hard now, was it, mate?" he said, pretending Hayche's loss of control was part of the plan.

The prisoner looked at the floor. "You'll never get close, though. They have it guarded like Fort Knox."

"Do they indeed?" Ethan chuckled.

He poured Tony a glass of water and held it to the prisoner's mouth. When the glass was finished, he called for Skippy.

The giant Russian barged through the door. "What's up?"

Ethan told him the address. "Go and have a squiz, make sure old Tony isn't telling fibs."

"No worries, boss, back to you shortly." Skippy strode from the room.

Within the hour, Skippy returned with news the target house was legitimate.

"Well it seems you were telling the truth, Tony," Ethan said. He pushed a small plastic plate of left over chicken Vindaloo towards the prisoner. "Eat up." He placed a plastic cup of water beside the plate.

Tony didn't care he had no knife or fork, he dug into the meal with his fingers, pushing as much food into his mouth as was possible. Soon, he was coughing and reaching for the water, sweat beading upon his forehead.

"Tomorrow, we'll pay your friends a visit." Ethan grinned, but the humour failed to reach his eyes.

CHAPTER FIVE

Jayla sat against the wall, resting her head back. One eye swollen closed and sore. Her cheek throbbed where one of the captors had punched her in the face when she did not answer a question to his satisfaction. She looked at the ceiling through her remaining functional eye, although she noticed her vision was slightly blurry.

Where are you, Malik? What happened to you? I need you! She stared at the locked door as if he might barge through and carry her away. But the door remained locked and silent. Squeezing her eye shut, she inhaled a sharp breath through clenched teeth as pain spread across her face. Relaxing, she sniffed and looked at a cobweb in the corner. A single tear cut through the thin film of dirt on her cheek as all hope fled.

* * *

Malik Hunter launched from his seat to stand over Ethan, his eyes wide. "You found her?"

Ethan nodded.

"Are you sure, man?"

"Yeah, mate, we're sure."

The big African-American lifted Ethan to his feet and crushed him into a bear hug. "Thank you!" He pushed Ethan away and took a step back, doubt and fear entering his eyes. "Is she still alive?"

"As of a few hours ago, Malik, yes."

Thank God, you're safe, baby! We're gonna get your outta there, sweetheart, just hold on a little while longer.

Relief washed over him, shoulders relaxing, he dropped his head, closed his eyes and took a deep breath. "Thank God." He glared up at Ethan. "So, what now?"

"We get her out of there."

"When?"

"Today, Malik. We'll have her out of there today."

"And how are you going to do that? I don't want her killed during the assault!"

Ethan's eyes narrowed and he pushed his hands into his pockets.

Probably wondering if I have military experience. I've already let slip I know they'll make entry with force.

He crossed his arms and waited for Ethan to reply. *I guess a civilian would assume negotiation might be the first port of call.*

"Mate, I'm not going to go into that, but we'll let you know when we know more."

"I understand, Ethan." Malik shrugged. "You don't want to talk about your method of entry."

Ethan remained silent, eyes locking on Malik.

Now he knows I'm military. Well, either that or he thinks I've watched too much TV.

"You want to maintain opsec, I get it," Malik added.

"That's the one, mate. You served in the armed forces?"

"Yeah, man, spent six years in the Marines and have been a SEAL now for the last ten."

Ethan nodded and appeared to accept the information with a healthy level of doubt. He all but rolled his eyes.

Malik clenched his jaw. "I want to help, Ethan. Please, let me come along with the assault force, I can be an extra set of hands."

* * *

Ethan considered the well-built American standing before him. *Yeah and a fuckin' hindrance if you aren't what you say you are, which you probably aren't.*

"No."

Anger flashed across Malik's eyes for a moment, quickly extinguished and replaced by a solemn sheen. "Please?"

Malik's internal struggle displayed self-discipline and control.

Ethan sighed. *Just tell him no and be done with it.*

"Tell you what, mate. I'll talk to my team, see what they think, and then get back to you. Alright?"

Malik nodded but looked disappointed.

* * *

"Thoughts?" asked Ethan, leaning back in his chair.

He sat at the head of the table, surrounded by the soldiers of his team. Hayche muttered a string of expletives, arms crossed. Bob looked out a nearby window. Skippy, smoking a cigarette, cleared his throat. "No, boss, bad idea. Very bad idea."

"So, he says he's a SEAL?" Mark leaned forward, arms resting on the table. "You believe him?"

Ethan shrugged. "I have no reason to believe him."

"Has he been cleared Top Secret?" Mark glared at Ethan. "He been cleared Top Secret with Positive

Vetting?"

They were rhetorical questions.

You already know the answer to that, smart arse. Ethan sighed and lifted a glass of water to his lips.

"To be honest, I'm surprised you're even asking us this, Ethan. You want to risk the operation by bringing in an untried, untested outsider on what he says he *might* be?" asked Hayche.

Ethan placed the glass back on the table. "No."

"Right." Hayche nodded and stood. "Then let's get crackin', time's ticking. Even if he is a SEAL, do you think he's in his right mind? Do you think you could do your job properly if Sally was in that house being held hostage?"

Raising his eyebrows and exhaling through pursed lips, Ethan looked out a window as he thought of his wife, Sally, and his daughter, Ashlyn.

No way in hell. My focus'd definitely not be on the job.

He had been deliberately blocking them out, but with the mention of his wife's name, memories came flooding back. He hadn't seen them now for close to two months. On the day he had deployed to Queensland, they had hugged and kissed him, told him not to worry.

"I'll be fine," Sally said as he replayed the memory in his mind's eye. *"But you better come back to me. You hear?"*

"That's *exactly* what I mean," said Hayche, watching Ethan.

Snapping out of his reverie, Ethan looked at Hayche. "Fair call, mate. Even if he is what he says he is, he wouldn't be in the right frame of mind to be effective."

"Well then," Skippy extinguished the remnants of his cigarette into an ashtray, "let's get arses in gear."

* * * * *

Skippy drove the lead vehicle, Ethan beside him, Hayche sitting on the back seat crammed in beside a mountain of equipment, weapons, and ammunition.

He looked around at the soldier. "You look real comfy there, mate."

Hayche frowned. "Oh yeah, boss, as snug as a bug in a fuckin' rug."

Ethan chuckled and looked beyond Hayche through the rear window, watching the vehicle driven by Bob, following behind them. Bob kept at least one hundred metres between himself and the lead vehicle. Ethan could just make out Mark sitting in the front passenger seat.

One kilometre from the target building, the vehicles came to a halt.

"Go," Ethan spoke into the radio.

Hayche, Bob, and Mark departed the cars with their personal weapons and gear. The vehicles remained parked, although Skippy kept the engine running. Ethan watched as his soldiers broke into a fast jog. The trio remained silent, concentrated on their breathing, while their sneakers made a soft staccato upon the footpath.

* * * * *

Between a vacant lot of land and the target building sat a large multi-story block of units. Hayche and Bob disappeared into the building, having said farewell to Mark some streets before.

Hayche liked the look of the building. *This looks promising.*

"I'll set up in this one."

Bob nodded. "Good luck," he whispered before heading to another block of units next door.

Hayche took the stairs two at a time, thighs and calves burning by the time he reached the second level.

Where's the bloody elevator when you need one?

He hadn't spotted another person and hoped the units were vacant. He tried the door of one unit, but it was locked. Moving to the next one returned a similar result. The third was unlocked, and he strode in.

Good room. This would have been a nice place to visit before the Indos turned up. Shame about that.

Moving to the sliding door, he knelt before gently pulling the curtain back a centimetre or two. Placing his weapon and gear on the floor, he delved into a bag and found a pair of binoculars. He brought them to his eyes and carefully scanned the target building in the near distance. The windows of the building were closed but not blocked by curtains, cardboard, garbage bags, or anything else.

A slight smile played on Hayche's lips. *Good.* But the room into which the window led was vacant. There was no movement and nothing of interest to see.

Patience, my son, patience. He kept the binoculars to his eyes, waiting and watching for movement. Scanning slowly, he saw nothing untoward. *Fuck it!*

After putting away the binoculars, he re-located to another unit down, but found a tree blocked out most of the target building. *Having a bloody win here.* He cursed softly and exited the room.

He moved again, the third unit along returned more promising results. Hayche knelt statue-still, staring through the binoculars again. In the first window, he saw a man walking across the room with a cup of coffee in hand before sitting on a couch and reading a newspaper.

Coffee! White and two, please.

The second window revealed a vacant room, but as he was about to refocus back to the first window, a door on the far side of the room opened and two men entered. They were talking and laughing with one another. Disappearing from view, they soon reappeared in the room next door and joined the first man on the couch.

Hayche made a mental note of the door. With three potential targets in sight, he decided this would be his position.

Don't mind me, fellas, I'm just stalkin' ya. Hope you don't mind? He grinned.

"Hilton One, radio check, over," he spoke into the radio.

"HQ loud and clear, over," Ethan's whispered voice crackled in response.

"Hilton One, in position, out."

Time to get to work. He unpacked his sniper rifle, pushed a fresh magazine into the weapon, and cocked it.

***

With a sports bag slung over his shoulder and an MP10 submachine gun clasped in his hands, Mark ran along the far side of the block of units into which Hayche and Bob had disappeared. He scrambled down the large, gunmetal grey rocks on the shoreline until his shoes hit sand and continued at a more relaxed pace.

When he'd walked along the beach far enough that the block of units was behind him, the target building emerged. Mark stopped, knelt, and removed his backpack. Releasing the magazine, he cleared the weapon prior to placing it in the bag. Slinging the pack, he lay on his guts and leopard-crawled along the beach towards the target building. Within minutes, his shirt and jeans were soaked through, fine grains of sand having worked their way between his skin and belt. He ignored the discomfort and continued. From the target building, Mark's progress along the beachhead would be invisible.

Pushing himself into a kneeling position, he still couldn't see over the rocks along the shore. Standing, he could see the roof of the target building nearby. Ducking into a crouch, he managed to rapidly cover the last fifty metres. In less than a minute, the MP10 was slung across his front, a magazine in the breech, the safety catch disengaged. He rummaged around the sports bag and removed a large, rectangular black object the size of a house brick labelled C4 Explosive. Into the upper surface was pushed a small detonator with a tiny antenna. The explosive could be detonated remotely via a WIFI signal from Ethan's laptop.

Gotta love technology.

Climbing up the grey rocks, he stopped when he could see the target building. Remaining frozen in place, Mark watched for movement suggesting enemy presence. As nothing was evident, he crept further up until he knelt behind the rear fence, out of sight. He crawled along the fence until he reached the corner, then began moving slowly towards the road in front of him and along the length of the building. When he was what he thought was halfway along the fence line, Mark placed the explosive down. Making his way back, he renegotiated the rocks until he was once again standing safely on the beach.

Pushing his hands back into the bag, he came out with a small headset, which he placed on his head and activated.

"Beach boy, radio check, over."

"HQ loud and clear, over," Ethan's reply was instantaneous.

"Beach boy, standing by, out."

A moment later, he heard Bob call he, too, was in position. Both snipers were ready. He hadn't assaulted a building by himself before. In the past, he'd have at least another three or more soldiers with him. But numbers, not to mention resources, were limited.

Only a matter of time now and it'll be on. For the first time, Mark smelled the fresh beach air. He missed Perth and the beautiful beaches near the city. With a bit of luck, it wouldn't be too long and he'd be back in Perth enjoying the amazing weather.

Stay focused, son. He stretched his neck, grunting as he felt it *click. Stay focused.*

* * *

Ethan stared at the laptop's screen.

Incredible to think I can control the entire assault from this one small device. At least in theory, anyway.

At the top right of the screen were two large dots, one red, the other green. These were linked wirelessly to the triggers of both sniper rifles. When the sniper's finger touched their trigger, it indicated a viable target was in their scope and they were ready to engage. The assault would only proceed when both snipers could engage.

Right now, both lights were red. Skippy had the driver's window down, cigarette in hand. When the assault began, he would drive to the target building like a thousand startled gazelles and both men would assault the front while Mark assaulted the rear.

The large explosive Mark had placed acted only as a distraction to the occupants. The massive explosion would take the inhabitants' attention away from both the front and rear of the dwelling.

One green…one red.

"Come on," Ethan whispered, glaring at the two dots, willing the other to turn green.

Two red.

"Fuck!"

"Don't worry, boss." Skippy flicked a spent cigarette away. "Only matter of time. How you say? All in good time."

Ethan grunted in response, his eyes remaining glued to the computer screen.

One green, one red…two green.

"Standby, standby," Ethan spoke into the radio.

One green, one red.

"Disregard, I say again, disregard."

* * *

Mark knelt on the beach, MP10 slung so the weapon lay across his chest. In his right hand, he clutched a *nine-banger* flashbang grenade. He would throw this into the room prior to entering the rear of the building. The flashbang had multiple stages, including several bright flashes and nine deafening explosions designed to shock and incapacitate the occupants for a short duration.

"Standby, standby," he heard Ethan's command and scrambled quietly up the rocks, ensuring he was out of sight from the house.

"Disregard, I say again, disregard."

Mark remained in place, squatting on a rock and

trying to gain a position of comfort. Within minutes his thighs burned, but he ignored the pain, alert eyes glaring at the block of units in the near distance. The entire assault relied upon the snipers gaining viable targets simultaneously.

***

Hayche stared through the sniper rifle's scope. His mind was distant, numb, cold. What few thoughts managed to make themselves present, moved like mud and, as such, he was not distracted by them. Breathing slowly, he relaxed and allowed the crosshairs to find their target. The sliding door of the unit in which he had setup was open less than one centimetre, a gap wide enough for the bullet to pass. He lay well back from the door, cloaked in darkness.

One target sat on the couch, leaned back, placed hands behind head and sighed. The crosshairs of Hayche's rifle hovered over the chest of the bearded looter. Firing from an elevated position required the marksman to adjust his point of aim just below the point of impact. However, shooting through a glass window meant the bullet would naturally deflect slightly downward once it punched through the glass. Taking this into account, Hayche adjusted his point of aim a fraction upward and allowed his index finger to apply gentle pressure on the trigger. He felt the tiny *click* that would send a wireless message to Ethan's laptop, indicating to the assault commander that one sniper had eyes on target.

"Standby, standby, standby," Ethan's voice crackled over the radio.

Hayche continued deep, rhythmic breathing, and

was completely relaxed. The weapon's butt pulled firmly into his shoulder, finger still depressed upon the trigger.

****

Without taking his eyes from the laptop's screen, he gestured for Skippy to start driving towards the target building.

The car lurched forward and, in what seemed moments, they must have been travelling close to one hundred kilometres per hour.

Two green.

"Standby, standby, standby."

Still two green. Here we go.

"Go, go, go!"

****

Mark leapt up and sprinted towards the house, two deep *thuds* echoed from block of units indicating the snipers had engaged. Throwing himself behind the rear wall of the property, he only had to wait a few seconds before the explosion he'd planted at the side of the property rocked the ground.

Dirt, chunks of grass, and fragments of concrete and glass rained down around him.

Shit! Probably used too much explosive. Better than not enough, though. He chuckled.

Mark vaulted the fence, sprinted round the pool, brought his weapon to bear in his left hand, and fired several rounds into the glass sliding door at the rear of the house. The door shattered. Pulling the pin clear, he threw in the nine-banger and ducked for cover. The flashbang sailed unimpeded through the destroyed door.

The grenade roared to life, deafening in its effect. Mark pushed himself out of the alcove, and with submachine gun pulled into his shoulder, staring down the metal sights, moved fast into the rear of the house. Stepping through what remained of the glass sliding door, he ignored the nine-banger. An Indonesian assault rifle appeared through a half-open door and several bursts of un-aimed shots added to the flashbang's crescendo. All he could see of the enemy was the hand holding the weapon. Mark shot two rounds, the first hammering into the man's hand, severing a finger, the second slamming into the rifle itself and ripping it from the looter's grasp. A scream rent the air as the bloody hand disappeared behind the door.

Mark fired several rounds through the door and the high-pitched scream changed to a deep groan. Continuing to advance, he pulled the door open and saw the looter in the foetal positon on the ground, bright red blood soaking into the carpet around his abdomen. A single shot to the head ended the man's agony. Stepping over the corpse, Mark walked briskly forward, hearing the distant *thud* of gunfire from the front of the building. Skippy and Ethan had commenced their assault.

* * *

Jayla screamed as the nearby explosion rocked the house, shattering the window beside which she sat, tied to the chair.

"Lamont, they're comin' for her!" she heard the ugly man closest to the door shout. "Kill the black bitch!"

"Please! No, please!" she cried, tears streaming from her uninjured eye. She looked up at him, but

Lamont's face was cold. His lips formed a flat line, nostrils flared and jaw clenched.

"The fuck you waiting for?" yelled Ugly as the sound of gunfire grew closer by the second.

Oh, please, Malik, baby, help me! Help me!

Lamont cocked his rifle, flicked off the safety catch, and held it to Jayla's head. She wailed, moving her head from the muzzle, but with her hands tied behind her and rope around her waist binding her to the chair, she could not move far. Lamont simply moved the weapon until it was pointing at her forehead once more. A smile played upon his lips.

He's enjoying this, the evil dog!

"Please, God, no! You don't have to do this. Listen to me, you don't have to do this," Jayla pleaded of Lamont.

His finger touched the trigger. "I know I don't." His smile widened into a grin. "But I want to. You fuck'n hear me?" He snarled. "I want to shoot you, you black, American bitch!"

Lamont's face exploded and his lifeless body dropped to the ground, followed immediately by a dull *thud* that seemed to come from the block of flats beside the house.

Jayla flinched and shrieked. If her hands had been free, she would have covered her face. *Oh, God, what's happening?*

"Holy shit, Lamont. Lamont?" shouted Ugly, looking at the faceless mess that lay at Jayla's feet.

He took a breath and staggered backwards, a soft scream issuing from him. He stared out the window, and then ducked to the floor, out of sight. A fraction of a moment later, a large hole appeared in the wall where Ugly's head had been, followed by another dull *thud*.

Malik! My Malik's coming to save me! Oh, baby, I hope you kill them all. Kill…them…all.

Jayla suddenly felt empowered. As tears slid down her cheek she smiled through clenched teeth. If Malik wasn't currently inside the house, he wouldn't be far away. For the first time in what felt like a lifetime, she smiled as relief began to ebb throughout her.

"You're all fucking dead!" screamed Jayla, glaring at the cowering man. "You're gonna die, you hear me?"

"Shut up, bitch. I'll fuckin' shoot you myself."

"You're all gonna die!" She bared her teeth in a half-snarl, half-grin, more animal than human.

She watched Ugly's eyes widen in fear as he saw his captive in a new and dangerous light. He brought his weapon to bear and aimed at Jayla's chest.

"I'll bloody show you who's gonna die!" he roared, finger taking up pressure on the trigger.

* * *

Ethan tested the front door and found it unlocked. *Ha,* he thought, *idiots.* Stepping aside, he opened it a crack, allowing Skippy to throw in a flashbang grenade. Following the mighty noise, Ethan pulled the door fully open and stepped over the threshold, weapon pulled tight into his shoulder. Moving briskly into the living room, he spotted two men, one running away, the other standing up from a nearby couch. He fired a short burst, which ruptured the second target's sternum and hammered through his throat. Skippy opened fire a moment later, and the running looter was dead before he hit the ground.

Quickly checking the kitchen, Ethan found it empty and moved on. Another flashbang coming from the rear of the house, followed by gunfire, suggested Mark had now entered the back entrance.

Ethan stopped at a corner and craned his neck only so far that one eye could see down the corridor. A looter knelt facing him, weapon in shoulder. Ethan ducked out of view as the enemy opened fire, bullets cracking through the air where Ethan's head had been a moment before.

That was a bit too close for comfort.

He took a flashbang out of his pocket, pulled the pin, and tossed it around the corner, following behind it after a second's pause. The grenade exploded with a massive, ear-shattering sound combined with a bright, blinding flash. Ethan negotiated the corner, stepped to the opposing wall, weapon still tight into his shoulder. The looter was blinking and rubbing his eyes with one hand. Ethan opened fire.

The pair stepped over the corpse, Ethan hugging the right wall, and Skippy advancing behind him, pushed left, so that if need be, he could shoot past his comrade to provide covering fire. The corridor opened into a larger rumpus room, a large, bullet-riddled LCD television hanging on one wall. Lying on the couch nearby was a dead woman, the large hole in her chest giving light to the sniper's bullet that had taken her life.

Wrong place, wrong time, love.

More shouting. Ethan stopped outside the door beyond which the shouting had issued. He signalled to Skippy he was going to breach. Flinging the door open, he spotted the hostage tied to a chair near the window. By her feet lay a corpse, and lying on the floor beside the body, in a supine position, was a looter, weapon pointed at the captive woman. Ethan killed him with two short bursts that peppered his chest and skull.

Ethan walked with calm fluidity and knelt by the woman. She had been beaten badly, one eye swollen and closed. Skippy turned back to the doorway and knelt, weapon to his shoulder.

Jesus, they've flogged the shit out of her! Malik ain't going to be happy.

"Package secure. Extracting," Ethan spoke into his radio to let the other members of the assault know what was happening.

"We're getting you out of here, love. Okay?"

She sobbed but did not reply.

Withdrawing a clasp knife from a back pocket, he flicked open the blade, and with a few deft slashes, cut her hands free. A moment later, the rope fastening her to the chair lay in a messy coil at her feet.

He grasped her under one arm. "Okay, take a breath. Time to stand up." He supported her to her feet, allowing her to gain her bearings. The last thing he needed was for her to faint after being seated in one position for so long.

"My name's Ethan," he said quietly as he guided her forward.

"Jayla," she replied through a sob. Wiping tears from her cheeks, she shook her head. "I thought I was going to die."

Ethan did not reply, continuing to guide her out of the house. Skippy walked quietly ahead of them, weapon ready.

"Moving to your six," Mark's whispered voice crackled in Ethan's earpiece.

Glancing over his shoulder, he saw Mark behind them, facing rearward, the rifle-stock held tight into his shoulder as he walked.

"Relocating," Hayche's voice boomed into Ethan's

ear.

"Covering," Bob replied, letting the assault know at least one sniper remained in overwatch.

"In position," Hayche sounded short of breath, and for good reason. To be in position so fast meant he would have sprinted from his overwatch location in order to provide surveillance and cover for their vacant vehicle out the front of the target building.

"Vehicle secure. Go!"

They picked up the pace, Ethan's tight grip on Jayla kept her from tripping twice.

"I'm sorry," she offered, wiping tears from her cheeks.

"Nothing to apologise for, Jayla."

She appeared weak, emotionally exhausted, and with the temporary loss of sight from one eye, she must be having a hard time adjusting. However, now was not the time to console her. Everyone, even Jayla, needed to stay focused.

"Okay, Jayla, a little faster, love," Ethan whispered, pushing her into a slow jog. "That's it, good work. You're doing well."

Less than a minute later, they were outside and making a beeline for the car. The street was empty, much to Ethan's relief. He helped Jayla onto the back seat, Mark sitting beside her. Ethan climbed in behind the steering wheel, and a moment later, Skippy slammed his passenger side door.

"Good to go," Skippy muttered, a cigarette dangling from between his lips.

The car pulled away from the curb. Ethan scanned the road ahead and glanced often in the rear-view mirror. Skippy remained silent, watching their flanks, allowing his eyes to pass down side streets and rake across rooftops. Both men were experienced enough to know it wasn't yet over. An ambush was still possible. Apart from the quiet sobbing of Jayla, the occupants of the vehicle remained silent.

"We're mounted up and moving," Hayche's voice again.

Almost in the clear. A small weight lifted off Ethan's shoulders. All members of the assault were vehicle borne and departing the area.

Jayla continued to cry softly on the rear seat, Mark talking softly to her in an effort to comfort her. After a few minutes, she began to calm herself. Ethan adjusted the rear-view mirror and saw she stared out the side window, occasionally sniffing or wiping her cheeks. She'd started to acknowledge the hell was over. *That's good. Poor woman's still got a long road ahead of her.*

"Chin up, Jayla." He continued to watch her in the mirror. "You're safe, love, okay? You're safe."

She nodded but continued to stare out the window. A hint of anger had entered her eyes, Ethan noticed. *There's still fight in her, yet. She's far from broken.*

They'd take her back to their headquarters building to shower, change, and eat, before taking her to Malik.

Readjusting the rear-view mirror so the road behind came back into view, he saw only a vacant street and began to relax. *Another successful operation.*

"Good job," said Skippy. "Now, who wants beer?"

* * *

Malik was asleep on the makeshift couch. Several thick pieces of foam over a few pallets served the purpose well. Although it wasn't the most comfortable thing he'd ever sat on, it was better than the floor.

There was a sharp knock on the door, and his eyes

snapped open. *Who the fuck is this?* In some absurd way, he was hoping it was the same people who'd taken Jayla hostage. He rolled to his feet, pistol in hand. He shook his head to clear the sleep and approached the door, weapon raised. He could dole out justice to the entire group inside five seconds.

"Who is it?"

"It's Ethan, mate. I've got someone here to see you."

Heart skipping a beat, Malik holstered the sidearm and swung the door open.

"Oh, sweet Jesus!"

Jayla ran to him. He embraced her and buried his face into her hair. "Oh, my baby, you're okay!" He crushed her to him, allowing her to cry, feeling a warm wet patch develop on his shirt. "You're okay," he whispered.

"I'm okay, Malik. I thought I was going to die." She sobbed into his chest. "They were going to kill me."

Anger warmed him. He clenched his jaw but remained silent. They stood, holding each other for some time before he heard Ethan clear his throat. "Well, I'm off." Ethan smiled and began to turn away.

"Thank you so much, sir," said Malik. "You don't know what this means to me." He looked down at his wife. Her face still buried in his chest. "To us."

"Ethan." He turned back to face Malik. "Please, call me Ethan, mate. I work for a living. And you're welcome."

"Thanks, Ethan," Jayla said from Malik's embrace, and she turned to face him. "Thank the rest of your crew, too. They're straight up bad ass." She chuckled through her tears.

"Will do." Ethan winked and departed.

It was then Malik saw her face, and he held her at arm's length.

"What have they done to you?"

Fresh anger swept over him. His voice quivered. He looked at her bruised, puffy face and the black eye she sported. He pulled her gently to him and hugged her.

His dark eyes glared at the still open front door. If Ethan's soldiers had left any of the abductors alive, he intended to pay them a visit.

"I'll fucking kill them all."

Jayla breathed out deeply, held him a little closer. "Just hold me, Malik. That's all you need to do now."

Ethan lay on the bed, staring at the ceiling as the sun climbed in the eastern sky. He allowed his mind to wander but, invariably, it always strayed back to Sally, his wife. In just a few months it would be their seventh wedding anniversary.

Damn! Seven years. Where does the time go?

Yawning, he rolled out of bed, stretched and walked into the kitchen. After a short search, he found the satellite phone. There were two phones. One for work and one for the soldiers to call their loved ones. It was plugged into a long cable, which lead up to a solar panel placed on the roof of the house. He unplugged the charger and dialled the familiar numbers.

After close to twenty seconds, a connection was established and the dial tone began to ring. When he thought it was about to ring out, there was a click.

"Hello?" Sally sounded sleepy.

He cursed inwardly as he remembered Perth was

two hours behind so it would be sparrow fart over in West Australia at the moment.

"Hey, babe. Sorry I rang so early, but it's the only chance I could get to drop you a line."

"Hello?"

There was a delay of two seconds, sometimes longer, before what was said reached the receiver. It sometimes led to overlapping conversations.

"Oh, Ethan! How are you? It's so good to hear your voice." Her voice became thick with emotion.

"Good this end, although I miss you heaps. Don't know how much longer we'll be. How are you there?"

He couldn't say too much as anyone could be listening to the conversation. Sally knew the drill. She had been married to him now for long enough. She was used to him departing at short notice for prolonged periods.

"I miss you too, sweetie, but I'm much better now. They restored power to Perth last week. How good is that? It's just Perth at the moment, but they're hoping to have the whole state back on the grid in two or three months."

Ethan allowed her to speak, listening to and enjoying her voice. It had been almost two weeks since he'd talked to her.

Ethan's thoughts turned to his three year-old daughter. "How's Ashlyn?"

"Good. She's still sleeping, thank God. Otherwise I'd put her on."

Ethan smiled. "Is she sleeping all the way through now?"

"The day before yesterday was the first time she's slept through since…" her voice trailed away. "Since, you know…before the invasion."

"That's good, babe. Sounds like Ashlyn's starting to settle a bit. Gives you a break, too. Is she still having those nightmares?"

There was silence on the other end of the line. "Babe?" he lifted the satellite phone away from his ear and stared at the small LCD screen. There was still a connection. He placed it against his ear again. "Babe, can you hear me?"

He heard his wife sigh and realised she was struggling against tears. "Yes," she whispered.

Ethan cursed inwardly. "Sorry to hear that, babe. I wish I was there to help." He felt useless as he listened to his wife sob quietly.

"I wish you were here, too!" she blurted. "You're always away. I'm sick of it! *We're* sick of it. Ashlyn asks every day when you're coming home."

"I'm sorry, Sally. I really am. With a bit of luck we'll be home sooner than later." He clenched shut his eyes and swore under his breath. "How often does Sally have the nightmares, sweetheart?"

"Almost every night."

"Shit, okay. I thought they might have started to pass by now."

He heard Sally sniff and blow her nose. "Me too."

"Is it still the same one?"

"Exactly the same one. Happens almost the same time every night as well. She usually starts screaming around eleven pm. I could almost set my watch by it."

"Shit." Ethan breathed into the satellite phone.

He could hear Sally's voice in his ear, but with eyes closed, her words were nothing more than background noise as his thoughts turned to his little girl. The recurrent dream usually centred upon, in Sally's words, a bad soldier breaking into the house and killing both Sally and he. Then the bad man ran into Ashlyn's room and cut her throat. *My poor girl. Three year-old girls should be dreaming of ponies or dolls. Not being murdered in their sleep.* There was no doubt the Indonesian invasion had, in large part, affected his daughter. Time would tell whether the damage might be permanent or not.

"I hope not," he whispered.

"Sorry, Ethan, did you say something, sweetie?"

"Hmm? Oh no, babe, no. Sorry, go on."

He remained quiet while he listened to his wife as she brought him up to speed on her day-to-day life and the rapid way in which Perth and greater Western Australia was recovering. Although the west had not been hit quite as hard as the Australian eastern seaboard, the state had its fair share of struggle.

When Sally eventually trailed off with no further news from home, Ethan talked sparingly about Brisbane, focussing mainly on the markets, day-to-day life, and harmless tales at the expense of the other soldiers, which left Sally laughing.

"Well I've gotta run, babe." Ethan checked his watch.

"I know, sweetie. Great to hear from you. Ring when you can."

"I'll try and ring in a few days."

"That'd be great, Ethan. Try and make it a bit later in the day. Ashlyn would love to hear your voice!"

"Will do, babe. Love you heaps."

"I love you, too."

He kept the satellite phone to his ear and waited for Sally to hang up. When the connection ended, he walked back into the house, feeling happier he had spoken to his wife and that all was well at home. *Well, for the most part.* He plugged the satellite phone back into the charger.

"Skip, how are you, mate?"

The Russian sat at the table, chewing idly on a piece of toast.

"Any better, I'd be illegal." Skippy chuckled.

"Good to hear."

"We got any jobs, boss?"

Ethan poured himself a coffee. "Not at the moment, no. You want one?" he gestured at the metal pot sitting over a gas stove.

"What? Coffee or job?"

"A fuckin' coffee, smart arse."

"Love one!" the Russian boomed, grinning.

Leaving the steaming cup in front of Skippy, Ethan wandered over to the kitchen window and took a sip of the hot, dark liquid.

Ah! Nothing like coffee first thing in the morning. He savoured the taste. Lifting the cup back to his lips, he looked out at powder puff clouds adorning the deep blue sky. *It's going to be a great day.*

Up until Operation Fat Cats, Ethan's team had been quiet, sitting around playing cards for almost a full week between jobs. *It'll be good to have a quick rest.* A cloud drifted clear of the morning sun, and Ethan closed his eyes as the gentle heat warmed his face.

He turned back to Skippy. "Might not have another job for a week or two."

Skippy grunted and downed the last mouthful of his coffee. "Hope not." The Russian pushed himself to his feet. "I'm already bored!"

Considering whether he should have some toast for breakfast, Ethan paused as the satellite phone marked 'Work' began to ring.

"It's not the first time I've been wrong!" He

walked to the phone.

Skippy gathered up his cup and plate. "Won't be last, either," he stated.

"Steady on, ya cheeky bastard!" Ethan chuckled, pressed the accept key and brought the phone to his ear.

* * *

Wedge brought the vehicle to a stop with a jerk and ignored the hiss of pain from Dozer in the passenger seat. Dozer gently clutched his wounded shoulder.

Wedge cursed. "Sorry, man, forgot about your wound."

Dozer nodded but remained silent.

If that wound gets infected, he's fucked for real. Wedge looked away and out the window at the holding house. The building was turning a pale sheen of gold in the light cast by the setting sun. Stepping out of the car, Wedge slammed the door and stood waiting for Dozer to negotiate his way clear of the vehicle. With only one functioning arm, it took time and patience. *Come on, you slack prick. It can't hurt that much, surely?* He watched Dozer as the man grunted, groaned, and swore. Eventually, he pushed himself clear of the vehicle and slammed the door behind him. He moved to stand beside Wedge. *About fuckin' time. It's like working with a bloody sloth!* Wedge grinned at his own wit.

"Shit!" Dozer brushed past.

"What's up?" he looked at the departing man. He looked beyond his comrade and noticed the front door of the holding house was open wide.

"Oh fuck!"

No, no! Fuck! FUCK! Wedge drew his sidearm and

the pair proceeded towards the house.

"Anyone there?" Wedge called. He stared down the metal sights of the Glock, finger hovering over the trigger. "Hello?" Silence met him. *This is bad, man.* He swallowed and glanced across at Dozer beside him. *This is* real *bad.* He stepped over the threshold, listening. Nothing.

Dozer made to step forward, but Wedge shoved a hand onto his chest and pushed him back. He shook his head. "Stay there, man. Let me go first."

You're fuckin' flat out getting out of the car. What good are you gonna be here, dick bag?

"I'm alright!" Dozer said through clenched teeth.

Wedge turned on him. "No you're fuckin' not, man! Now stay back. Let me go first and stay outta my way."

"Bloody hero," Dozer muttered.

Too right, man. 'Bout time you realised that. A tight smile spread across Wedge's face.

"Bones? You there?" he shouted. Silence greeted him. "Oi! Bones!"

What the fuck's goin' on? Where are they all? Somethin' definitely ain't right.

Feeling Dozer advance behind him, Wedge moved further into the house, and within a few steps, found the first dead body.

"Oh, mother of fuck!" He looked down at the corpse.

Wedge pushed the prone body over with his boot and winced as the sickly-sweet smell that exuded from the disturbed corpse reached his nostrils. It was Steve. He'd been shot in the chest and several small holes were drilled into his forehead.

"We're in the shit," whispered Dozer.

Wedge scowled. "Oh you fuckin' *think*?" He squeezed his eyes shut and tried to think. "Bloody hell!"

The pair moved through the house with care. They found corpse after corpse. By the time they'd finished, they discovered every one of their team had been killed.

"Where's the black bitch?" asked Dozer staring at the empty chair beneath which lay the rope used to secure her in place.

Wedge's shoulders slumped. *Oh, fuck me. How dumb can you be?* He closed his eyes and took a breath. "Clearly not *here*."

"Just what the fuck do we do now?" He said the words more to himself than Dozer.

"We can start by—"

"Shut the fuck up," Wedge cut the man off mid-sentence.

"Hey, how about some friggin' *respect*?" Dozer snarled.

"Dozer, shut up man. I'm trying to think."

"Just who the *fuck* are we dealing with?" asked Dozer.

"I can tell you who we're *not* dealing with. These ain't no amateurs. This is a pro hit."

"That bitch's boyfriend had something to do with this!" Dozer sat heavily on the floor. "I can feel it. You saw how he reacted the day we took her! He's probably a cop or somethin'."

Wedge nodded. "Maybe."

He turned to Dozer and saw his face was pale. The bandage wrapped around his shoulder was bleeding through again. *Not good. If infection don't kill him, blood loss will eventually.*

"You alright?"

"Yeah, I'll survive," Dozer replied. "I think."

"Might need to get that checked again."

"Oh yeah, no worries. I'll just nip down to the local doctor's clinic, shall I?" Dozer clenched his jaw against the pain.

"You know what I mean, ya fuckin' twat waffle."

"Help me up." Dozer reached out.

Wedge stepped forward, clenched a tight grip, and pulled Dozer to his feet.

"I don't feel so good."

You don't look so good either, man. You're probably dying.

"I'm sure you'll be right, mate." The lie came easily. "Let's get outta here."

Dozer nodded but remained silent.

"In less than a week, half our crew has been killed," said Dozer, passing a hand through his hair. "It's taken us a couple of months to build up to where we were and five days to ruin us. Who the fuck are these guys?"

"I dunno, mate," muttered Wedge. He sighed and holstered his Glock. "I don't fucking know. But something tells me we ain't seen the last of them yet."

"You think?" Dozer asked, his eyes widening.

"I'm bloody certain."

Dozer pushed past him. "Let's get outta here."

"Hang on!"

Wedge turned towards the rear of the house. "You hear that?"

Dozer stopped and turned. "Huh?"

He held a finger to his lips to stop Dozer from talking further.

I swear there's someone back there! He took a pace forward and froze. *There it is again!* It sounded like footsteps.

"What's got into you, dickhead?" Dozer blurted.

"Shut the fuck up, numpty."

Fuckin' dumb arse is going to get us killed.

He walked towards the rear of the house to investigate.

* * *

"I don't want to talk about it."

"Come on, baby." Malik sat beside his wife and wiped a tear from her cheek. "I know you find it difficult to talk about, but you have to try."

"No, Malik, I don't." She pushed his hand away.

"Please? Try and remember where you were kept hostage, it's important."

She curled her legs beneath her and dabbed a tissue against her nose.

"Babe?"

She looked away and ignored him. "Just let it go, Malik."

"I can't." He clenched his fists. "I've tried, and I can't. I have to know where you were taken."

She looked at him, her one good eye bloodshot from crying. "Why?"

Because I'm going to kill them all!

He sighed. "I don't know. Curiosity, I guess. What if it happens again?" He held up a hand as Jayla took a sharp breath. "I'm not saying it ever will, but if in the one in a million chance it did, I'd know where to go at least to start with."

She touched the skin around her swollen eye, wincing against the pain. "That's not why you want to know."

"Of course it is! What do you mean?"

"Malik, I know you better than that!" She stood

and walked to a window, staring out at the street. She folded her arms and swore under her breath.

"Okay, Malik." She hung her head and began to sob.

He was by her side in seconds, holding her tight. He kissed the top of her head and stroked her back.

"I'll tell you what I can remember."

He continued to console his wife, listening carefully as she spoke. He burned descriptions of landmarks into his mind and made special note of street names. Jayla's voice faded into the background as he created a three dimensional mud map in his mind's eye, analysing it from every angle. The captors had made the fatal mistake of not blindfolding their prisoner.

God damn amateurs. You gonna pay for that, let me tell you!

After Jayla had finished describing the house in which she'd been kept against her will, he gently turned her to him.

This is so damn hard for her. But she's a trooper! She always has been.

He drew her into a tight embrace and kissed her neck.

"That's all I wanted to know, baby girl. You did so well. *So* well. Come over here and sit down."

He guided her back to the couch, and they sat together. She sobbed against his chest while he stroked her back and cradled her face with the palm of one hand. Malik remained silent, allowing her to grieve. It was almost like squeezing a pimple. He just needed to allow the crap to come out.

How much time had passed, Malik had no idea, but eventually, Jayla faded to silence. She occasionally sniffed, or wiped her face, but she remained snuggled against him. When her breathing began to deepen, and he felt her relax against him, he gently pried himself free from her and stood. He looked down at her as she slept. Her injured eye was still swollen and looked sore. He had purchased some Paracetamol and Nurofen, which seemed to take the edge off most of her pain. He'd already gently pried her injured eyelids open and checked her pupil. It reacted to light and although slightly blurry, she could see. That was important and a promising sign.

He walked to the door turned the handle and pulled it open. The hinges squeaked their protest.

"Where are you going?"

He turned back to her. Jayla was sitting up on the couch, watching him.

"I'm heading out to get something for dinner, okay? I won't be long."

Without refrigeration, they were required to purchase meat on a daily basis unless they chose to eat an entirely vegetarian dish. Which, much to Malik's joy, was not often.

"Okay, baby."

"Under no circumstances are you to leave the house."

"I won't."

"Under *no* circumstances —"

"I heard you the first time, baby. Go." She waved her hand at him, a half-smile playing on her lips. "Go!"

He noticed a gleam had re-entered her eyes. He hadn't seen that strength emanate from her in a long time; probably since the beginning of the invasion.

That talk did her more good than I thought it would.

Malik smiled and winked at her. He closed the door behind him and checked the door was locked several times before he was satisfied.

* * *

Twenty minutes later, he'd broken into a Holden Commodore and hotwired the vehicle. In another ten, he made a slow pass of the house in which Jayla thought she'd been held. It looked vacant, although the front door was open. Parking the vehicle two hundred yards up the road, he exited, walked through a yard, gate-vaulted the rear fence, and in less than a minute, was strolling along the beach towards the house in question.

Keeping low, he clambered up the rocks, unwittingly using the same path as Mark days before. Peeking over the edge where boulders met level ground, the rear of the house came into view. Again, nothing. The glass door had been shattered. Squinting, he saw a lifeless arm protruding from around a corner on the far side of the rear entrance. He couldn't see any further without advancing closer, but he was willing to bet a dead body lay there. Malik grinned.

The Australian soldiers did a good job!

Drawing his sidearm, Malik crept closer, skirting the swimming pool, which was green with algae. Stepping through the shattered door, he took his time placing the weight upon his lead foot to reduce the amount of noise it created as it bore down upon the small pile of shattered glass. Advancing slowly, he noticed a spent flash-bang lying on the floor near the lifeless arm. Moving to the corner, he glanced around and saw the corridor was vacant. Only then did he proceed. He looked down at the corpse at his feet. The several bullets that had killed the man grouped close together over the centre of his chest.

So long, fucker. Malik smirked to himself and proceeded. He paused as he heard a quiet voice ahead.

There was a hissed response, and then silence. He remained frozen, extended arms holding the Glock before him so he was staring down the metal sight. A creaking floorboard, another soft voice, then nothing but the quiet burble of the ocean's song in the distance. A man appeared around the corner. He was holding a weapon by his side, relaxed, not expecting any kind of resistance. When his eyes locked onto Malik's, he began raising his weapon, finger dropping to rest upon the trigger.

Malik shot him in the forehead and again in the chest as the corpse began to fall. Taking a step back, the Navy SEAL disappeared around the corner.

* * *

"Ethan Lewis here." He pushed the satellite phone hard against his ear, struggling to hear the voice at the other end.

"Yeah, g'day, mate, Whitey here. I understand you finished the mission that came up at the last minute?"

Whitey was the nickname everyone used for Captain Michael White, commander of the 4 SQN detachment in Queensland.

"The abduction? Yeah, over and done with. What's up?"

"I have another mission for you lot."

Didn't take as long as I thought it would.

"A-huh, go on." Ethan took a notepad and pen out of his pocket. "Wait. Say that again?" He looked over at Skippy sitting at the kitchen table, watching idly.

I can't have heard that right.

"Whitey…yup…yeah I got that, mate. Just hit the rewind button. You want us to fly into Jakarta and capture the Indonesian president?" He dropped the pen onto the notepad and turned away, striding across the room. "You must be fucking joking? And whose genius plan was this?" He fell silent for a moment, listening.

Skippy remained nonchalant. He watched Ethan with calm, calculating eyes.

"Righto, stop right there, Whitey. Briefing, your office, fifteen minutes." Ethan walked to a window and glared out. "Bullshit, mate! Fuckin' watch me. We're on our way, put the bloody kettle on!"

Skippy stood, placed an unlit cigarette in his mouth, and patted down his shirt pockets in search of a lighter. "I have time for cigarette?"

"Yeah." Ethan slammed the phone onto the table, dark eyes wild with anger. "Oi! Downstairs, now!" he roared, looking at the ceiling.

Within several minutes, the entire team were milling around the kitchen.

Hayche barged through the door and approached Ethan. "Jesus, mate. What happened, you drop your ice cream?"

"We're heading to Whitey's office. Just so we're all clear, a mission from higher has come down to be disseminated to the next available patrol," Ethan explained. "And guess what?" he jerked a thumb at his own chest. "That's us."

Mark shrugged. "Yeah…and?" he asked in a quiet voice.

"They want us to head into Jakarta and capture the Indo president."

Hayche burst into laughter, sitting down at the kitchen table. "Nice!" he chuckled, eyes glinting with mirth.

Ethan glared at him.

"You're fuck'n serious, aren't ya?" the grin rapidly departed Hayche's face.

"Yup, so let's go hear this grand plan and see how much thought higher has actually put into this cluster fuck, shall we?" Ethan headed for the door, grabbed the handle and pulled the door open, allowing it to slam against the wall.

"Sounds good, boss." Skippy stood. "I could do with laugh."

* * *

Malik crouched, keeping the weapon pointed at the blind corner around which the second assailant would appear should he choose to advance.

He's probably shitting himself. He just watched his buddy get blown away. Come on, fucker, walk `round the corner. I dare you!

Silence greeted him, although he strained to hear the sound of soft footfalls that might foretell the presence of the remaining enemy.

"Wedge?"

The voice was a whisper.

"Wedge!"

No response. Nor would there be if that was the name of the man whom Malik had shot.

"Fuck, Wedge!" the voice hissed. "Fuck!"

Then the sound of footfalls.

Do it, boy! Come join Wedge.

Malik took up the trigger pressure and stared down the metal sights, expecting the second man to appear any moment.

But the footfalls became fainter as the man left. Shortly afterward, Malik heard the front door slam shut.

He let out a breath of relief, dropped the weapon to his side but kept a finger on the trigger.

Malik snarled. "I'll be back for the rest of you." He stood and relieved Wedge of his weapon. "It isn't over yet."

* * *

"No, no, fucking no," said Ethan after he listened to Whitey's briefing of what was planned for his patrol.

"What, you're refusing to do the job?" Whitey moved in his chair, a hint of anger entering his voice.

"No, but I would if I thought it'd place the lives of my men in jeopardy. We'll do the tasking, but only if it's done our way." Ethan glanced at his soldiers and saw their support glinting in their eyes.

"What, the plan's not good enough for you?"

"No, quite frankly, Whitey, it's not." Ethan jumped to his feet, his chair falling backwards onto the floor. "Those fuckers sitting in their office, staring at their bank of computer monitors have placed almost no thought into this. We'd be compromised inside the first day. And we'd probably be either captured or dead inside the second."

Whitey leaned back in his chair, stared at the ceiling, and allowed a deep sigh. "Alright, Ethan, give me a rundown of your thoughts and we'll see what we can do."

"Yeah, mate, again, not bloody good enough. 'We'll see what we can do,' is nothing but lip service. It gets done our way or doesn't get done at all. I'm not sure I can make it any clearer."

"Alright, alright, for fuck's sake. We'll do it your way. Give me your plan and I'll pass it up the chain."

"First and fuckin' foremost, the French have to know friendlies are in the area." Ethan righted his chair and sat back down. "It's almost embarrassing I have to mention that."

French battlegroup Aéronaval, led by the flagship aircraft carrier *Charles de Gaulle*, had been patrolling the Indian Ocean just south of Christmas Island for months, simultaneously sending in strike groups to bombard strategic targets deep within Indonesia. Many of the targets were in and around Jakarta.

"I don't see why, but alright."

"You don't see why?" Ethan leaned forward, resting his forearms on the table. "Are you serious, mate? What if it all turns to shit and we need air support? Or extraction at short notice?"

"You won't, though. It'll run smoothly. You're planning it after all, remember?"

Bloody smug arsehole.

"In addition," Bob cleared his throat, "not only should the French know about our presence, but to some extent, they should be involved in the operation."

"I agree," Mark chipped in.

Great points, fellas.

"Alright," nodded Whitey. "How?"

"They'll insert us."

Whitey looked up at Ethan, and then back down at the large notepad before him. He was madly scribbling. "Yup, okay. Any other thoughts?"

The fucker seems to have toned down a bit now. Good!

Ethan shifted in his chair and smirked. "Yeah, plenty."

* * *

The French aircraft carrier *Charles de Gaulle* cut west through the Indian Ocean at a sedate ten knots. To the east, the morning sky brightened in hues of pink and deep orange. It would have been peaceful and calming had it not been for the four Rafale fighter-bombers catapulted airborne in quick succession. The aircraft had been working ceaselessly all night. Ethan and his soldiers had barely slept since being dropped off onto the French carrier by Blackhawk helicopter the previous evening. Sleep deprivation had been for no other reason than the constant thump of the catapult as aircraft were sent outbound, or the dull *crump* and brief muffled screech as aircraft landed.

For the men and women of the carrier, it was part of life and they were well adjusted to life on the mighty ship. As for the five soldiers of Four Squadron, they would be happy to walk on terra firma once more.

The soldiers were sat around a table in one of the scran halls having finished eating breakfast. They were careful to keep their conversation focussed on the mundane.

A sailor approached their table and waited for the conversation to stop and the soldiers to look at him. "Excuse me, if you please?"

"G'day, mate." Ethan appraised the young sailor. *What does this nob want?*

"Good morning," the sailor said. "Your aircraft is on deck and will be departing in thirty minutes."

"Cheers," Ethan thanked him. "We appreciate that."

"Thank you. Good morning." The sailor smiled and nodded before moving away.

Hayche watched the departing French sailor. "Jesus, he sounded like a walking airport PA system!"

"Speaks English better than you, boy," said Skippy with a chuckle.

Hayche burst out laughing. "Shit, if that isn't the pot calling the kettle black."

"Righto, get your shit together and… Oh, for fuck sake." Ethan looked at Mark, who'd returned to the table with a fresh piece of toast.

Mark looked surprised. "What?" he asked, stuffing the butter and jam lathered meal into his mouth.

"No, you're right, mate, take your time." Ethan casually pulled the sleeve of his uniform back and glanced at his watch. "We've got all day."

Mark grinned. "It's French bread, mate. Tastes beautiful!" He took a gulp of coffee and stuffed the last piece of toast into his mouth. "Right!" Mark stood, mouth full, cheeks bulging. He looked at the others still seated around the table. "You comin' or what?"

Ethan laughed and stood. "Let's fuck off."

* * *

Although they had checked their equipment the night before, they rechecked it for peace of mind. Their weapons, cleaned prior to breakfast, sported a magazine containing live rounds attached. The working parts weren't cocked and would remain in that condition until Ethan gave the order which, normally, would be just prior to insertion.

They walked in single file along the narrow corridors of the aircraft carrier, stepping over the lips of open watertight doors, hugging the walls to allow French sailors to pass, occasionally offering a nod or greeting. Trotting up Spartan metal stairs, the soldiers stepped out of hatches onto the new deck before renegotiating constricted corridors and repeating the process until the noise of the deck started to become deafening.

Pulling on their helmets, the roar of aircraft engines was immediately dampened to a dull, muffled groan. Ethan twisted the wheel of a closed airtight door and the team stepped through to a view of the sea. Cool, clean ocean air wafted around them. The flight deck was only one level above them, and the noise of the aircraft, despite the protection of their helmets, had increased in volume.

They walked along the deck, the steel wall of the carrier on their left and four horizontal steel cables, thick as a man's thumb, one beneath the other, serving as a barrier between the soldiers and the ocean far below.

Taking the metal steps two at a time, Ethan walked onto the flight deck and was immediately brought to a halt by a French sailor wearing hearing and eye protection, a bright yellow vest pulled over his uniform. Looking around, Ethan saw teams of French sailors wearing different coloured vests. Much like their US counterparts, each colour denoted a separate job on the flight line.

The man in yellow unleashed a sentence in French.

Ethan shook his head and held out his hands. "English mate, English!"

"Anglais?" the sailor asked.

Ethan nodded.

"Apologies. You wait here for few minutes." He wanted to say more but struggled with the words, instead turning to point at several fighter-bombers lined up ready for the catapult.

Ethan understood. "Yeah, mate, no worries. Once they're gone, we're right to go." He nodded.

"Your helicopter there." The sailor pointed to a Panther chopper already turning and burning. The loadmaster closest to them was standing on the deck. He wore a helmet with tinted visor down. Although he could not see his face, Ethan knew the man was watching them.

Probably cursing us, thought Ethan, corners of his mouth curling upward.

Ethan felt a tap on his shoulder and turned to face Mark.

"Sorry if we're late!" the soldier shouted, although the twinkle of humour in his eyes suggested he wasn't.

"Hope that bloody toast was worth it!" Ethan shot back, grinning.

Mark gave a thumbs up and a wink.

With a loud *thump* that passed across the flight deck and through Ethan's body, the catapult launched the first fighter-bomber airborne, afterburners glowing red as the powerful engines roared. Within thirty seconds, the next Rafale was sent streaking across the deck of the carrier and skyward, following the first. In less than four minutes, Ethan and his crew were given the all clear to approach their chopper.

The loadmaster raised his arm and gestured them towards him, signalling to keep well clear of the rear rotor. He counted the soldiers in before stepping up into the helicopter behind them. Using a similar hand signal to *don packs*, the loadmaster requested them to strap into their three-point harnesses.

Hayche sat back and ignored the harness. A moment later, a hand tapped him firmly on the shoulder several times and the loadmaster gave him the same signal.

Not a request then. Ethan smiled as he watched Hayche's response. He couldn't hear what Hayche said, but his lips seemed to form the words, "Fuck me. Alright, alright, keep your bloody knickers on!"

Minutes later, Hayche was strapped in and they were lifting off the deck. As they ascended, Ethan looked out the window and watched as three more Rafales were brought onto the top deck via massive lifts. It seemed a non-stop operation.

Jakarta must be getting hammered!

The *Charles de Gaulle* disappeared from view as they accelerated away. Over the next few minutes, they passed over the top of several destroyers. The ships were within close proximity to the carrier. The pilot maintained a low profile, keeping the aircraft close to the water's surface. It was difficult to calculate the speed, but Ethan guessed they must have been flying close to three hundred kilometres per hour.

If everything went to plan, they would be met within several minutes of being dropped off. He checked his watch.

15:17

They were making good time. Ethan pulled the sleeve down over his watch and looked around at his crew. Skippy had his head back, eyes closed, relaxed. Hayche glared out the window, either running through his mind what was to come or still pissed off at the loadmaster. It was difficult to tell. Mark was taking in the environment, looking around the cabin and occasionally leaning forward in his seat to better see through the front windscreen of the cockpit. Bob rested back in his seat, hands behind his head, his weapon, muzzle down to the floor, clasped between his thighs. He was looking idly out one of the windows.

Ethan checked his watch again.

15:21

Come on. He wasn't nervous, he just wanted to infiltrate, get on with the mission and be extracted as soon as possible. He had a bad feeling about this mission. In the past, he'd had similar feelings, which had amounted to nothing. But that heavy feeling in his gut was still something he had never chosen to ignore. They'd need to be extra careful on this mission. However, on a positive note, it was much more thoroughly planned than it would have been had they decided to go with the stupid, dangerous plan higher had laid out for them. They wouldn't have lasted twenty-four hours. Ethan knew it, and his men knew it. But still, there was an uncomfortable niggling feeling at the back of his mind.

Feeling eyes on him, he looked around to see Bob staring.

A hand slapped him on the arm and he shifted to look at Bob. "You alright, boss?"

Ethan nodded and gave a thumbs up. When Bob seemed satisfied and had looked away, Ethan's smile disappeared. *Is it too late to cancel the mission?*

CHAPTER SEVEN

Ethan relaxed back into the helicopter's seat as he looked out the window of the side door. He watched the ocean glide by close beneath them. Occasionally, they flew near a fishing vessel, or at least a large boat made to look like its prime use was fishing. Each time they passed such a ship, Ethan watched with interest as the door gunners tracked it with their mini-guns as if expecting to return fire at any moment. But at three hundred kilometres per hour, the vessel fast became a small speck in the ocean. Ethan positioned his right foot on the floor just beneath the side door's release handle. If they were to crash into the ocean, more than likely, there wouldn't be much light. The weight of the engine made the aircraft top heavy, meaning once submerged, it would become inverted within a matter of seconds. Sliding his hand along his thigh, and down the shin of his right leg, would give him a rough landmark as to where the release handle of the door was situated. He rested his head back, closed his eyes, and relaxed. The grim feeling in the pit of his stomach had eased and he felt more confident with proceedings.

"Let's go for a swim!" said Sally, running away from him across the beach towards the breaking waves.

He tried to push himself to his feet, feeling sluggish. Ethan attempted to call out to her to slow down, but his mouth would not open. With a grunt, he finally managed to stand, but his feet began sinking into the sand. Meanwhile, Sally waddled into the ocean, diving beneath the waves and disappearing from sight.

He tried calling to her again, but his mouth remained clamped shut. The sand was up to his calves, and he was sinking fast. With all the strength ebbing from his body, he was powerless to pull himself clear. When the sand was at his hips, fear began ebbing through his body.

Fuck! I'm going to die here.

He screamed for Sally, but only a growl sounded in his throat. She reappeared in the ocean, turned towards him, treading water, and waved. Realising his predicament, she swam back to shore and ran to him. He was neck deep in sand. Sally knelt above him and tapped him on the head. 'Oi!' she said, smiling. 'Oi!' she tapped him again, this time more forcefully.

'Help me!' Ethan tried to say, but again, nothing.

'Oi!' Sally shouted, smacking him across the cheek, the cheery smile never leaving her face.

"OI!" Hayche roared, slapping Ethan across the face.

Ethan sprang awake, heart thundering in his chest, eyes wide, bringing his weapon up. Hayche grabbed the barrel of Ethan's assault rifle and forced it back to the floor of the chopper.

"Five minutes, boss!" he held up five fingers.

Shit, that went quick!

Ethan shook his head clear, gave thumbs up, and took a deep breath, letting it out in a rush. He checked his watch.

16:25

They'd be touching down near a town called Sindangbarang on the southern coast of West Java right on time. Their contact would pick them up at 16:35.

Feeling eyes watching him, he turned to see Bob staring at him.

"All good?" his soldier shouted, his voice almost inaudible over the noise of the engines.

"Yeah, mate! All good."

Bob seemed satisfied and looked back out to the ocean gliding close beneath them.

Ethan pulled his sleeve back and glanced at his watch.

16:28

The loadmaster grasped the side door handle, unlatched it, and pushed it open, locking it fully open. Humid air rushed into the cabin. A moment later, ocean disappeared to be replaced by beach, which faded into farmland and patches of forest. The helicopter flared, bleeding off speed and descending simultaneously. A violent jolt, and the chopper touched down. The soldiers unclipped their harnesses, following one another out the door in rapid succession, allowing the chopper to immediately ascend and accelerate south.

Less than a minute later, the silence was deafening. The soldiers, dressed in civilian attire, slung their Indonesian assault rifles and sat down in a huddle. Instinct screamed at them to push into all 'round defence, but if there were Indonesians nearby who came to investigate the noise of the helicopter, the men would look less threatening were they sitting together chatting than weapons at the ready.

Skippy lit a cigarette and took a deep drag, exhaling the smoke slowly, staring up at the sky, seeming to be deep in thought.

Ethan's PRC-112 vibrated. He pulled the radio out of his pocket and checked the LCD screen.

7° 27' 32.8212" S
107° 7' 48.2988" E

Right on time.

Ethan punched the coordinates into his GPS. The pickup point was less than four hundred metres away. So far, the mission was proceeding seamlessly, although it was only early days. He tapped the keypad of the PRC-112 and sent a secure reply to the sender.

Moving.

Ethan stood. "Let's go." He unslung his weapon and broke into a jog.

"Steady on, boss!" Skippy swore, racing to finish his cigarette. "Did not know it was foot race." He tapped the ash clear, made sure it was extinguished, and placed it away in a pocket.

They covered the uneven terrain fast and minutes later were hidden amongst thick forest, where Ethan slowed to a quick walk. Apart from insects and birds calling to one another high in the forest canopy, and the soft crunch of shoes on leaf litter as the men passed through the area, silence reigned. They pushed on, instinctively sweeping their arcs, watching for threats, but the forest was devoid of people, much to their relief.

As they walked, the soft grumble of a vehicle was heard in the distance, growing ever louder as they closed the distance. Looking down at the GPS, Ethan checked they were still on target. Happy they were making good time, he put the GPS away and made directly towards the noise of the engine.

Here we are.

The forest suddenly ended and Ethan slung his weapon prior to pushing himself over a poorly-crafted three-rail fence, which almost gave way under his weight.

Within a minute, the car arrived and came to a noisy stop nearby, the driver wrenching on the handbrake.

"Fuck!" Ethan hissed, looking over the roof of the car at a house on the far side, where a local was leaning against the doorway, watching proceedings with indifference. Allowing his eyes to refocus upon the car, he saw an old, red Daihatsu sedan. Climbing down a small embankment, he sprinted round the far side and opened the front passenger door, slipping onto the badly worn seat.

"Ethan," he said by way of introduction to the driver, a lanky man in his mid-twenties, with short-cropped dark hair and coke bottle glasses.

"Greg." the younger Australian man held out a hand.

Ethan ignored the offered hand. "Picked a nice fuckin' place here, mate. Are you *trying* to get us compromised?"

"What! No, of course not. Why?"

Hayche, Skippy, and Mark piled onto the back seat, slamming the door behind them.

"Bob, you're in the boot!" Hayche yelled, grinning.

"Fuck me!" Bob's voice was muffled to those inside the car.

"See him?" Ethan pointed at the local, still leaning against the doorway, watching them. The local spat into the dust, scratched his face, and then disappeared inside.

"Oh, Samarang? He's a nice fella. He doesn't even know there's a war on!" Greg burst into laughter.

Ethan relaxed a little, inwardly breathing a sigh of relief.

Okay, we're still good. It's not a complete fuck up. Relax, Ethan! Relax, mate.

There was a rattle from the rear of the vehicle, a

bang as a hand slammed upon the vehicle's skin, and then Bob's voice again. "Oi! Open the fuckin' boot, you dick'ead!"

"Oh shit, better let him in." Greg exited and moved round to the back of the Daihatsu.

Ethan turned in his seat to watch the proceedings.

"There's a bit of a knack to opening it," said Greg by way of explanation.

Bob simply stared at the young man, incredulous. "A knack? Really? This has gotta be some kind of joke."

Greg shrugged. "I was never much of a comedian, mate. Sorry, can't help ya."

"I'm not your mate," Bob spoke through clenched teeth.

Greg slapped him on the shoulder. "Oh, come on, mate. Don't be like that!" The younger man chuckled.

Ethan winced. *Bad move, Greg!*

Bob slapped the hand away. "You touch me *one* more bloody time and I'll knock your block off. Got it, son?"

Greg held up his hands. "Just trying to be friendly. You know, team bonding and all that?"

Bob ignored him. "How fuckin' unprofessional is this?" He gestured at the old car. "Who the fuck you work for?"

"If I told you, I'd have to kill you." Greg chuckled. He jiggled the button, but the boot refused to open. The young man looked at Bob, his grin vanishing as he saw the stern look Bob was giving him.

"Like I said, there's a knack." Greg returned his concentration to the boot.

"Yeah, you said that already."

"It can be a little stubborn. You want to have a go?"

"Get the bloody boot open…now!" Bob clenched his jaw and looked away.

Ethan was struggling not to laugh at the exchange.

Finally, it opened with a loud *squeak*.

"Okay, got it! In you get," Greg gestured at the empty space.

Glaring sidelong at the young man, Bob stepped in and pushed himself into a foetal position to fit. "Well this is fuckin' comfortable!" He snarled.

"You can get out and walk if you carry on like that." Greg winked.

Ethan burst out laughing. *You smart arse! I like you. But Bob will make you pay for that later.*

"Listen here you little shit, if you say one more—"

Greg slammed the boot shut, silencing Bob's outburst.

"Right, let's get going," Greg said when he returned to the driver's seat.

"Mate, you pushed your luck there." Ethan grinned.

"What do ya mean?" The young man looked confused.

"Knock it off, son. You're not that stupid. Bloody funny, though!"

"Glad I could be of service."

"Oi! What's going on?" Bob's voice erupted from the boot.

"Time to go," muttered Greg.

"It's all good, mate." Ethan stared out the window, noticing the Indonesian man had taken up his prior position, watching them with bored disinterest. "Your friend's back. What you say his name was again?"

"Samarang!" Greg waved at the man.

Samarang moved his wrist slightly in

acknowledgement and took another puff of his cigarette.

"He's certainly livin' the dream," Hayche observed. "Needs to get a bloody hobby."

"Or a job," added Mark, chuckling.

Greg started the engine and pulled away, accelerating down the narrow road, wide enough for only one vehicle. If another car approached from the opposite direction, they would have to pull over to allow safe passage.

Skippy cleared his throat, shifted forward in his seat and smacked Greg on the shoulder. "You picked interesting choice of car, boy."

"Yeah, we have a modern people mover back at base, but we're in a lower socio-economical area here. This is exactly the kind of car you want to be driving around in these parts. Even owning a shitty car like this, people perceive me as being rich. Almost everyone around these parts own scooters."

"Fair call," said Ethan.

They hit a pothole, the car bottoming out, and Bob's muffled voice immediately exploded from the boot. They couldn't make out the words, but the soldiers knew Bob wasn't a happy camper.

"Sorry!" Greg called out over his shoulder.

"Get fucked!" Bob's muffled voice roared.

They heard the words that time.

"I don't think he likes me very much," said Greg quietly, smiling.

"He'll be right, mate," said Ethan.

No, he fuckin' won't. Ethan stopped a chuckle from breaking free. He looked over at Greg, struggling to keep a straight face. "Bob's pretty chilled out, won't take him long to cool off."

As if!

Greg glanced across at him. "I'll take your word for it."

"You alright?" asked Ethan, noticing Greg's face take on a pained expression.

"Yup, I'm fine."

You bloody don't look fine. You look like you're about to blow a valve.

"Oh shit, I've gotta stop. I'm sorry Ethan, I've gotta stop, mate."

He braked hard, stopping the vehicle in the middle of the road.

"What's wrong?" Ethan asked.

"Wait here!" Greg said, his voice tinged with what sounded like fear and desperation. He threw open his door, pushed himself out, and sprinted down the middle of the road, holding the seat of his shorts with one hand. A moment later, he made a sharp turn and disappeared into the forest.

"Boss, what's going on?" Mark asked in a quiet but concerned voice.

"Not sure, mate. Everyone at instant, prepare to dismount and take cover."

"Roger," muttered Hayche.

Several clicks followed as the safety catches of their weapons were flicked off. Doors opened and the soldiers prepared to depart the idling vehicle.

"Fuck's goin' on?" Bob called from the boot.

Ethan exited the vehicle and moved to the rear where, after some fiddling, managed to open the boot. Bob immediately climbed out, rubbing his back.

"Fuck me!" Bob said.

Ethan explained the situation and the look of consternation immediately left Bob's face.

"I think our friend has the shits, but in case I'm

wrong, it's best to be prepared."

Bob chuckled. "Right you are, boss. Serves the asshole right."

A sound much like a garden hose spraying the ground, followed by a distant, "Oh thank God. Oh shit that feels good," suggested Ethan was correct.

"Be right with you!" yelled Greg.

"Take your time, boy." Skippy lit a cigarette and took a deep breath. He let it out slowly. "Take your time."

There was silence for a moment before the garden hose started again. "Oh, sweet Jesus!" Then silence once more.

Greg sprang clear of the forest. Still securing his shorts in place, he sprinted towards them.

The young man skidded to a stop beside them. "That's better! Right, let's go." Bent over, he'd placed hands on knees as he attempted to regain his breath.

"You good?"

Greg straightened and looked at Ethan. "Yeah, all good now."

"You got the shits?"

"Yeah, mate, sorry. Can't help it."

"I know you can't. It's better out than in. I just hope you don't spread the joy around."

"Yeah, you better fuckin' not," Bob grumbled, glaring at the young man.

"Oi! Who let you out of the boot!" Greg noticed Bob. "Time to get back in, buddy."

Buddy? Oh shit, son, you're pushing your luck.

"Steady there, chief," Mark warned, taking a step forward in an attempt to slow the young man.

But Greg had already darted to the rear of the vehicle. He jiggled the button, and with a groan, the boot yawned open. He was unaware of Bob standing nearby, fists clenched, knuckles white.

He grinned at Bob. "In you get, Bobby."

Bobby?! Jesus, Greg, you're gonna end up dead in a ditch in a minute.

Ethan strode around to the back of the Daihatsu and stepped between the two. Greg seemed to have no idea how close he was to becoming a corpse.

He placed a hand on Greg's shoulder. "Just a second. Wait until Skippy's finished his cigarette."

Ordinarily, Skippy would extinguish his smoke when it was time to move, but Ethan used the excuse to relax the tension of which Greg was blissfully unaware.

"Just relax, Bob. We'll be there before long," he whispered.

Bob snarled but remained silent.

"Huh?" asked Greg, pushing his glasses further up the bridge of his nose. "What's that?"

"Nothing, Greg. We'll just wait for Skippy to finish, hey?"

"Oh, sure!"

Skippy finished his smoke, stamped it out, then placed the spent butt in his pocket.

"Okay, everyone ready to go?" Greg said. "Bobby?"

Ethan placed a hand on Greg's shoulder and guided the young man from the rear of the vehicle and away from certain doom. He offered a warning glance to Bob and a slight shake of his head.

"I'll go and jump in the driver's seat, shall I?"

Ethan grinned. "Sounds like a good idea, mate."

Greg rubbed his hands together with enthusiasm and walked away.

Bob stood rooted to the spot, tense, eyes wide with

fury, glaring at the back of the young man.

"Just jump in the boot, mate." Ethan approached Bob.

"I swear to fucking Christ, if he so much as—"

"Bob," Ethan placed a hand on the man's shoulder. "You want me get in the boot? I don't mind. You can have a break."

"What and sit beside that halfwit?" he gestured at the young man sitting behind the wheel, whistling to himself. "No thank you!"

Ethan held out his hands. "Alright, mate, alright. Point taken. In that case, jump in." He tapped the vehicle.

Bob released a string of profanities under his breath, but climbed in, the rear suspension of the vehicle squeaking under his weight.

"Comfy?"

Bob looked up at him. "No, not really!"

"Fuck you can whinge hard, mate." Ethan grinned and slammed the boot as Bob began shouting.

Ethan wedged himself into the front passenger seat and looked at Greg. "Just get us to Jakarta."

"He doesn't sound happy though, does he?" Greg jerked a thumb back towards the muffled ruckus exploding from the boot.

"What, Bob? Nah, he's ecstatic, mate! You should see him when he's cranky. Holy shit!"

Greg swallowed but remained silent. He reached down and turned the key. The engine roared to life. The young man sat rigid staring into the distance.

Ethan's anger began to mount. "Whenever you're ready, Greg."

"Just give me a sec," the young man said, holding up index finger.

"You're playing with fire there, boy," Skippy warned from the back seat.

"Greg? What are you doing?" Ethan glared at the young man who sat silent and still, index finger still raised in the air.

"Oh God. I think I'm gonna shit myself."

"Oh, for Christ's sake." Ethan sighed.

"What the fuck's going on out there?" Bob roared from the boot. "We just sitting here all figgin' day?"

"Just hang on!" Ethan shouted.

"Oh God," muttered Greg, pushing himself clear of the car and sprinting from view.

"Greg needs to shit!" Hayche informed Bob.

The car shifted up and down for a second as Bob manoeuvred himself. "What? He just shat like a fucking fire hose a couple of minutes ago!"

Moments later, Greg was back.

I better not get the shits! Ethan gritted his teeth. Approaching the infiltration, the last any of his crew needed was to become sick.

"I'll turn some tunes on. Sorry, it's only in Indonesian." Greg began fiddling with the vehicle's radio.

"Shut the fuck up and drive, you little shit!" Bob's muffled roar erupted from the rear of the vehicle.

"Okay, okay. Jesus, talk about uptight," said Greg, shifting into first gear with a loud *crunch* and accelerating away.

Greg looked at Ethan. "I wrote a book once, it was a short fiction novel. I even sold one to an American, so I guess you can call me an international author."

Ethan nodded, but remained silent.

"It was hard to write at first, but as the months went by I found it —"

Bob's muffled, booming voice interrupted him. "Shut up, ya fuckin' dick'ead!"

"Just drive, mate," said Ethan, glaring at the younger man. "That's the best advice I can give you. Just bloody drive."

Greg glanced at Ethan and nodded, concentrating on the road.

"Well, that went well," Greg muttered.

* * *

Malik knelt in the rear tray of a Toyota Hilux utility with two others from the Guardian Angels. One, a young man sporting a Mohawk and bolt action rifle, the other an older woman clutching an Indonesian assault rifle. He couldn't remember their names, but if shit became real, he was sticking with the female. He could see the young man was inexperienced and scared.

The Toyota was parked down a side street, facing the ocean.

"Yo!" Malik called to Mohawk, knelt staring over the roof of the vehicle's cabin.

The boy looked around at him.

"It's going to be okay, man, just chill, alright?" Malik spoke in a reassuring voice. "Chill."

The young man nodded and turned away, although the worried look never left his eyes.

Little fucker's going to get someone killed.

"It's Sammy's first day out for real, isn't it Sammy?" the woman shuffled over to pat the young man on the shoulder.

He nodded.

"Well, just chill, man. Nothing to worry about, just concentrate on your job and fall back on your training and rehearsals.”

“Training?” Sammy asked. “What training?”

Malik looked at the woman. She shrugged. “We don’t have much time to train the newbies. Their training is usually on the job, so to speak.” She chuckled, showing a missing tooth.

Malik struggled not to roll his eyes. *For real? This is worse than I thought.*

“You ever shot a rifle?” Malik nodded at the weapon clutched in Sammy’s hands.

“Never.”

Malik closed his eyes and grimaced. “So that thing isn’t zeroed, huh?”

“Zeroed? What does that mean?”

“You want this boy to die?” Malik asked softly, watching the woman.

The woman stopped grinning. “Now listen here, yank, no one’s dying today.”

“And just how do you know that? Anything can happen in a fight.”

“We’ll take care of him. Won’t we, Sammy?” She patted the young man again.

She stopped and shot an angry glare at Malik. “Anyway, what do you know?”

“I’ve seen my fair share of fights. I know what to expect, am well trained, and unless something goes very wrong today, I know I’ll be walking away from this. Can you say the same?”

She swallowed and looked away. “I’ve seen my fair share of combat, too, Malik.”

Well, shit! She remembered my name!

“After all, Australia was invaded.” She looked back at him. “Remember?”

“How could I forget?”

"So you were here from the beginning?"

Malik nodded, and over the next half an hour, explained what his new bride and he had been through since the arrival of the Indonesians.

"Wow!" Sammy piped up. "That's some story!"

"It isn't a story." The woman's voice was soft, but berated him all the same. "I'm sorry to hear of your wife's suffering, Malik," she added.

"Not your fault." He shrugged.

"Still." She moved over to him and laid a hand upon his shoulder. "I'm sorry all the same. It's terrible what she has been through. Let's make these fuckers pay."

Malik smiled and nodded. "That sounds like a plan."

I'm beginning to like this woman. She's tougher than an old boot.

"I'm sorry, I've forgotten your name already. I'm terrible with names. Got a photographic memory for a face. But a name?" Malik chuckled. "No chance!"

"No worries, mate." She smiled and turned back to him. "It's Shaz."

Malik nodded, committing the name to memory. "Shaz," he said softly. The American watched the young man. "And Sammy."

The well-built SEAL relaxed and sat on the tray of the vehicle. "Now, let's kill some of these fuckers."

Shaz laughed.

"I feel sick," Sammy said in a soft voice. He looked pale.

Malik rested his forearms on his knees and nodded. "That's normal. It'll get worse, particularly after you make your first kill, Sammy. But it'll pass in time."

Shaz shot him a warning glance. "It's okay, Sammy,

don't worry, we'll be right." She wrapped an arm around him.

Malik shrugged. "You can't mollycoddle the boy, Shaz. This isn't a fucking game, make no mistake. We're at war here, and people are going to die."

"No shit, Sherlock." Her gripped tightened around Sammy. "But you don't have to scare the living shit out of him!"

Better now than in the middle of a firefight. Poor kid is so unprepared, he'll probably die today. Malik sighed.

It was Monday, and as such, supplies were flown in by a squadron of Chinook helicopters to the Port of Brisbane. From there, they were loaded onto Unimogs, where the food was driven into the city to be distributed. Supplies were flown in Monday, Wednesday, and Friday. The convoy was protected by a small host of armoured Humvees, but as seen with the ambush in recent days, the fact a military escort was present did not seem to deter the more organised of looters.

"Here they come!" the driver shouted out the window of the Hilux to those in the back.

"Righto," Shaz replied, grabbing hold of the vehicle.

"Hold on, Sammy." Malik pushed himself into a crouch and moved alongside the young man. He patted him on the back. "Just try and relax, kid. When this is over, I'll give you some pointers on some things."

"Thanks," he muttered. Malik could see the boy was shaking with fear and looked paler than before.

"And we'll zero that damn weapon!"

If he survives the shit storm about to happen.

Malik gripped the vehicle. Soon, the Hilux would be accelerating behind the supply convoy to provide further protection.

Several other four-wheel drives nearby roared to life, all packed with Guardian Angel fighters.

The small side street down which they remained parked provided only a small outlook over the highway from the Port of Brisbane, down which the Unimogs were travelling.

Almost losing his balance as the Hilux nudged forward, Malik adjusted his footing as their vehicle, taking the lead, advanced out of the side street so the whole highway became visible to their left and right.

"There they are!" shouted Shaz, pointing to the left.

Malik followed her finger and watched a large convoy of Unimogs accelerating towards them. A number of Humvees drove in front of the convoy, another group in the middle, and a third at the rear. As the vehicles drew closer, the fifty-cal mounted on top of the lead Humvee tracked around until it was pointing directly at Malik's vehicle.

"Convoy to our front, convoy to our front. We are friendly. I repeat, we are friendly." Malik listened to the driver talking into the radio.

Silence.

Malik craned his neck and watched the driver bringing the handpiece back to his mouth in preparation to make another call, when static exploded from the speakers. *Go ahead with code word, over."*

"Blue dragon, blue dragon."

Malik touched Shaz on the shoulder. "What's going on?"

"Convoy's just checkin' we're who we say we are. The US Navy send a text to our head honcho specifying what the code word will be in advance. He then disseminates it amongst us, so we can identify ourselves." She shrugged. "Just standard procedure, mate."

He nodded, impressed. *Smart. Although, bit of a risk if one of the Guardian Angels gets captured.*

"Our head honcho never comes out on convoy missions, and the code word changes for every single convoy as well," Shaz said, as if reading his mind. "So, if one of us got taken prisoner, the code word would be useless to those fuckers."

"Basic, but effective." Malik nodded. "I like it."

"Glad to have you with us, welcome to the party. Out."

The fifty-cal gun tracked away from them and a weight lifted from Malik. *One short burst from that gun and we would've been toast.*

The convoy passed, gradually building speed. Eventually they would be travelling well in excess of one hundred kilometres per hour as they headed towards Brisbane city. Speed was safety. As the Unimogs departed, Malik's Hilux began accelerating. The fifty-calibre machinegun of the rear most Humvee turned to face them, keeping a close eye on the small group of four-wheel drives following in their wake. Malik knew the convoy escorts were being careful. But in addition, they'd be able to provide fire support to the Guardian Angels if they became involved in a fight.

"Here we go!" said Shaz, a slight smile playing at the edge of her lips.

Malik remained silent, clasping onto a hard point with his left hand, bringing his rifle into shoulder and resting it on top of the Toyota's roof. He pointed the weapon's barrel towards the ocean, showing the Humvee at tail-end-Charlie that they were still no threat.

He nudged Sammy. "Good luck, kid."

Sammy nodded but remained silent.

If those fuckers attack, they'll wish they hadn't. He smiled through tight lips.

The group of four-wheel drives had spread out into an inverted V formation two hundred metres behind the supply convoy, with Malik's vehicle taking the lead. Malik relaxed, leaning on the roof of the Hilux. The wind whipped past his face, massaging his skin. Watching the road slide by beneath them was somehow satisfying. He looked out to sea and admired how the sun glinted across the mirror-like surface. On the horizon, the small silhouette of the aircraft carrier *USS Ronald Reagan* sat proudly upon the ocean.

He took a deep breath of fresh sea air and smiled again. After all Jayla and he had been through, some semblance of normality was beginning to edge its way back into their lives. It had been too long. The invasion of Australia had left them permanently scarred, both physically and mentally. But Malik hoped that with Jayla now safely at home, and the Indonesians on the run, boring routine might become the norm.

It'd make a nice change. He stared at the tiny aircraft carrier anchored in the distance. When hostilities came to an end and consulates reopened, it wouldn't be long before they were back in the USA. *I think we've seen enough of Australia,* Malik chuckled at his private joke. He turned back to face the convoy, the rear most Humvee's turret continuing to track them occasionally, before turning away to patrol its arcs.

Malik looked across at the young man, the fear was still strong in his eyes. He slapped Sammy on the shoulder and gave the boy a wink and thumbs up. He returned a tight smile and looked away. As for Shaz, she was sitting down, back to the Toyota's cabin, smoking a cigarette, watching their six. Movement to their front caught Malik's eye, and he watched a blue car pull out of a side street and accelerate parallel to the convoy. Following in rapid succession came another seven vehicles.

"Oh shit!" he heard Sammy cry.

"You see them?" shouted Malik, slamming his hand down upon the roof of the vehicle.

"Yeah, mate, on `em!" the driver replied, although his words were almost inaudible over the noise of the vehicle's engine and wind blasting through Malik's ears.

The Hilux and majority of Guardian Angels changed direction to follow the newcomers, while a single four-wheel drive remained on track, following the supply convoy. As they closed the distance, he saw the lead vehicle of the newcomers was a blue Ford Falcon sedan. *Is that the same vehicle involved in Jayla's capture?* He ground his teeth and snarled. *Looks mighty familiar!* But there must have been hundreds if not thousands of similar vehicles in Brisbane. *Not many of those would be involved with the looters, though.* He argued with the little voice of reason in his head. *I hope it's the same fucking car.* A wide grin spread across his face, his eyes wide with fury. *Show me what you got, motherfuckers!*

Directly behind the Ford, the driver of the Toyota began beeping and signalling for the sedan to slow down and pull over. Malik noticed the older woman was knelt up once more, weapon pulled into her shoulder, cigarette dangling from the side of her mouth. The young man remained unchanged, other than his eyes were now the size of dinner plates.

"Pull over!" the driver roared, leaning out the window.

Malik flicked off the safety catch as he noticed the driver's side window of the sedan descend. Pulling the assault rifle into his shoulder, he allowed his index finger to gently caress the trigger.

The driver of the sedan gave them the finger and sped off, aiming for the convoy.

"Shit," Malik muttered to himself, watching the departing Ford through the scope of his weapon. The Toyota Hilux accelerated to give chase, but it was no match for the sedan making a beeline for the middle of the convoy. Malik's first thought was a possible vehicle borne improvised explosive device (VBIED.) Leaning against the Toyota's roof and stabilising himself, Malik fired several shots. The bullets ricocheted off the bitumen directly behind the speeding car. Readjusting his aim, Malik fired again, his rounds slamming through the back window, wounding the rear passenger. The Falcon swerved to throw Malik's aim off. The American noticed, as the car moved from side to side, the passenger he'd shot slumped to one side, held in place only by his seatbelt.

One down.

Malik lost his balance and almost fell out of the tray as a car following the sedan slammed into them, in an attempt to slow them.

"Hold the fuck on!"

He grabbed Sammy by a shoulder and dragged him to the floor.

"Stay low, son!"

The boy lay prone. Shaz opened fire as the car swerved towards them again, the rear passenger window descending to allow a man to lean out and bring a rifle to bear. A bullet *cracked* past Malik's ear, sending him diving to the floor. He heard Shaz open fire once more.

"Hold on!" she shrieked.

The car slammed into their four-wheel drive, doing

more damage to the enemy vehicle than it did to the sturdy Hilux. Malik pushed himself into a crouch and stepped over Sammy. Squatting by Shaz, he wedged himself in as stable firing platform as possible and saw the gunman still leaning out the window, preparing to open fire again. Malik shot him. The round drilled a hole through one eye and exited the back of his head in a fine spray of blood and several small chunks of brain matter.

Time to play.

Shaz looked across at him. "I'm out of ammo, mate." She ducked from sight as she began reloading.

The enemy vehicle slowed and steered away from them.

Not that easily! He fired several short bursts, the bullets peppering the windscreen. When the vehicle suddenly swerved and drove aimlessly away from them, he knew he'd hit the driver. With one vehicle out of action, he returned his attention to what was happening around him.

Three cars had followed the blue sedan after the convoy and were well out of range. As for the remaining two enemy vehicles, they'd been all but destroyed by the Guardian Angels. One was on fire and the other spewed steam from under the bonnet. Both were stationary and rapidly disappearing into the distance.

Four cars left.

Malik knelt beside Sammy. He tapped the young man on the shoulder. "Are you okay, son?"

He looked up. "I think so, yeah."

He could hear the fear in Sammy's voice. *The boy should never have been here. Dang stupid allowing him on this mission. He needs training.*

Training, rehearsals, familiarisation with one's personal weapon, and more training, provided confidence and the ability to act in a flexible, fluid environment. Placing a young man with no training at all, clutching a weapon with which he'd never fired, was a recipe for disaster.

Stupid. These guys should know better. They've probably never had formal military training either, I guess.

He sighed. *Not their fault.*

He glanced at Shaz, who approached and hunkered down beside Sammy.

"Sammy, we're fast approaching the remaining vehicles chasing the convoy! You've gotta fight, mate! Got it?" Shaz shouted over the noise of the vehicle's engine and the wind blasting around them.

The boy nodded but remained silent. He was still terrified.

No way, man. This ain't gonna fly.

"Yo, Shaz!"

She looked at Malik. The big American placed a hand on Sammy's shoulder to let the boy know he had his back.

"Sammy's not fighting. No way, man! He's gonna stay low and wait it out. You got that, son?"

Sammy nodded, looking between Shaz and Malik with wide eyes.

"What the bloody hell's the point of that, mate? We're here to fight! That's what we're here for. If we all lie down and hide," she locked eyes with Sammy, "then we may as well give up, right now."

"He's never fired a weapon. He ain't never been in a fight."

"There's always a first——"

"He's had no training. His God-dang weapon isn't even zeroed!"

Shaz clamped her mouth shut and glared at Malik.

Mind you, she fired a couple of magazine's worth of ammo and didn't hit a damn thing.

"Is yours?"

Shaz shifted and looked away. "Is mine, what?"

"Is your weapon even zeroed?"

She closed her eyes and clenched her jaw.

I didn't think so. Malik's shoulders slumped and let out a sharp breath. *How are these guys supposed to put up a fight, when it's amateur hour?*

"Sammy," Malik squeezed the young man's shoulder. "We're gaining on them fast now. You stay low. Okay, son?"

"I don't wanna hide, though! I'm not a coward."

"You're no coward, Sammy. You fight smart, you pick the fight you can win or you wind up dead. Clear?"

Sammy nodded and remained silent.

"Without no experience, or training, you're not getting involved. It's not a game, and these looters aren't here to fuck about. They'll kill you inside thirty seconds."

"You're makin' a mistake, mate."

Malik ignored Shaz. "You stay low, Sammy. When we're back at base, I'll take you through a few drills and rehearsals." He looked at Shaz and stared at her. "And we'll zero our weapons."

"Remember, you're a newbie here, Malik. Best you wind your attitude back a notch."

He ignored her and pushed himself up so he was looking over the roof over the Hilux's cabin.

"Here we go!"

They were fast approaching the convoy and the fifty-cals of all the Humvees driving tail-end-Charlie had swung around to aim at the approaching threat. The mighty guns had already destroyed two vehicles, one engulfed in flames, the other sitting still, blood oozing out of the small gaps in the doors to drip onto the road in puddles. Malik's vehicle roared past the disabled vehicles and continued the chase.

The driver steered their vehicle away from a direct line behind the enemy cars. This allowed the fifty-cals to fire upon the adversary without fear of hitting any Guardian Angels behind the looters. The fifty-cals fired in long bursts, trace rounds bouncing high into the sky as they ricocheted from the road directly in front of the looters' sedans or passing inches above them. Having served in the Navy SEALs, Malik knew how difficult it could be firing from a moving vehicle at a moving target. It took great skill, not to mention a degree of luck.

The driver of the Hilux brought them parallel to the pair of vehicles chasing the convoy, and Malik moved into a sitting position, crossed his legs, and pulled his weapon into his shoulder. He pushed his elbows into the crease behind both knees and stabilised his weapon.

He could aim for the driver, in the hope of hitting him, but decided against it. Every second counted, and he chose a larger target. Firing a few shots, Malik watched with satisfaction as a bullet punctured the rear, left tyre. The sedan immediately began to slow, pieces of rubber flinging clear of the damaged wheel. Eventually, the whole tyre disintegrated, leaving chunks scattered all over the highway behind the vehicle. The bare rim began to spark upon the road.

Malik changed his point of aim and fired again, hitting the left front tyre. The car spun out of control and was soon out of range. The fifty-cals thundered at the last vehicle giving chase, the blue Ford Falcon. Deciding it was a bad idea, the Ford turned away from the convoy and headed for the closest side street.

Malik knew what was coming and grabbed for a

strong hold. "Hold on!"

Sammy clenched his teeth and did likewise. The Hilux swerved suddenly to give chase and Shaz stumbled backwards. As she was about to depart the ute's tray and crash onto the bitumen below her at one hundred and sixty kilometres per hour, Malik lunged forward with one hand and caught a fistful of her shirt. Praying the fabric didn't tear, he pulled her towards him until she was able to regain her balance. She scuttled forward and grabbed onto a strong point.

"Thanks!" she shouted, her voice was even, but her eyes betrayed the fear coursing through her body. She'd known just how close to death she'd come.

Malik smiled and winked.

The Hilux gained on its target slowly, eventually cutting the Ford off. Without waiting for the four-wheel drive to come to a complete stop, Malik leapt clear, closely followed by Shaz. The passenger of the Toyota flung his door open and stepped out, weapon in shoulder. They surrounded the blue sedan. The driver held up his hands.

The game's up!

Malik moved around the opposite side of the vehicle and froze, a chill passing up his spine, causing the hairs on the nape of his neck to stand on end. But the chill soon disappeared as the heat of anger swept through him.

He snarled. "Motherfucker!"

In the centre of the front passenger window was the small hole where a bullet had passed. The bullet *he* had shot the day Jayla had been taken. It *was* the same vehicle that had carried Jayla away that terrible day! Holding his weapon stable with his right hand, Malik opened the passenger door with his left and stepped back, the barrel of his weapon hovering over the passenger's head.

Make a move, bud, I fuckin' dare you!

The man's face was not familiar. He was pale and in pain. The Ford's passenger wore a sling on his left arm and a claret tinged bandage was wound around his left shoulder, where he carried a wound.

Possible gunshot wound? Malik's eyes narrowed. *Was this the man who'd been driving the day my girl was taken?*

The man looked up at Malik, and he flinched. Fear and realisation entered the man's eyes. It was the only confirmation Malik needed.

"Get the fuck out!" the American shouted.

The wounded man didn't move. He sat frozen, continuing to hold his hands up, eyes wide as dinner plates.

Malik stepped forward and spoke through clenched teeth. "You stupid or just deaf? Get out. *Now!*"

He dragged the man clear of the vehicle.

"Hey, whoa! Whoa!" Shaz yelled at him from the opposite side of the blue sedan. "What are you doing?"

"Shut up, Shaz, and stay out of this. This doesn't concern you."

"The hell it doesn't, Malik!"

Malik ignored her and forced the man into a kneeling position, pushing down on his injured shoulder, causing the wounded man to cry out in agony.

"Stop!" Shaz called, moving around the vehicle towards Malik. "You can't just kill an unarmed man in cold blood!"

"This man took my wife hostage, then tortured and beat her! Trust me, Shaz, the world's not goin' to miss him."

Shaz stopped short and dropped her rifle to her

side. "This man?" she pointed at the kneeling looter.

Malik looked down at the back of the man's head and nodded. "This man." He looked up at Shaz.

Fury flickered across her eyes and her mouth tightened. "He's a piece of shit, Malik, the scum of the fucking earth," she held out one pleading hand, "but you can't just execute him!"

"No?" Malik nodded again, then pushed the barrel of his weapon against the looter's head. "Fucking watch me."

CHAPTER EIGHT

Four hours later, Greg pulled over in a bustling Indonesian city.

"Wow, that didn't take long," said Skippy.

Ethan looked out the window, glanced at shops and watched the passing traffic with disinterest. "Doesn't look like Jakarta, mate."

"That's `cause it's not Jakarta," said Greg, applying the handbrake. "It's Tjiandjur. We're about halfway to Jakarta."

"Thought it'd be somethin' like that." Ethan observed, wedging an elbow against the arm rest and placing his head in his hand.

Greg remained silent, watching Ethan. "You alright?"

"Me? I'm fine, Greg. I know two things, though. The first is, we ain't in Jakarta, and the second is Christmas is coming."

"Good observations." Greg grinned.

Ethan glared at the younger man and decided he needed to be less subtle. "Okay…so what's happening now? You need a piss or something?"

"Nah, I'm right, thanks."

"What the fuck's going on out there!" Bob's muffled voice roared from the boot.

Greg flinched. "Forgot about him," he muttered.

"He has good point." Skippy leaned forward. The big Russian tapped Greg on the back of the head. "You need toilet? Or you just stupid?"

Mark chuckled.

"Right, no more jokes." Hayche slammed a knee into the back of Greg's seat. "We've gotta long way to go, the less fucking about the better. What's going on, Greg? You need a break?"

Greg pushed himself forward in his seat and rubbed the small of his back. "Jesus, guys. Relax. Patience is a virtue."

Hayche leaned within inches of Greg's ear. "And death is final. Or so they tell me, anyway. You keep fucking about and we're gonna find out."

Greg's pleading eyes darted to Ethan. "Ethan, I just need a few more minutes, and we'll be underway, I promise."

A string of incomprehensible sounds boomed from the vehicle's boot.

"Give him a break, fellas," Ethan said, trying to keep the amusement from his voice. "I don't know what the hell you're up to, Greg, but don't take too long." He tapped the younger man on the shoulder and leaned close to him, cupping a hand to Greg's ear. "If you're looking to fuck us over, you'll be the first to die." He grinned and slapped the younger man on the shoulder.

Greg swallowed and nodded. "Wouldn't dream of it. Trust me." He flung open his door. "Just give me a second, I'll be right back."

Before Ethan could reply, Greg had jogged across the road, deftly dodging scooters and cars.

"Shit, dunno about rest of you, but I need to piss," said Skippy, stepping out of the vehicle and disappearing behind a nearby building.

"Yeah, righto, but hurry up!" Ethan called after him.

Mark departed the car and walked swiftly to the driver's seat. He slammed the door behind him, started the engine, and waited, one hand on the steering wheel, the other on the gear stick.

Ethan never allowed Greg out of his sight. If it ended up being some kind of elaborate ambush, at least Mark would be able to accelerate away at short notice.

This'd be the perfect ambush location. If he's a traitor, we're as good as dead.

"Fuck's he doing?" muttered Hayche, watching the young man standing on the other side of the street, sharing a cigarette with an Indonesian man outside a Kawasaki service centre. They were chatting amiably.

Ethan's hand tightened around the pistol grip of his assault rifle. "Not sure, mate."

It wasn't long and Bob's muffled voice began protesting from the boot, demanding to know what was going on.

"Calm your farm!" Hayche shouted back at Bob. "We'll be out of here shortly."

The worn shock absorbers protested with loud squeaks as Skippy lowered himself onto the rear seat. He slammed the door behind him. "That's better."

"This isn't quite going to plan is it, boss?" Mark asked quietly, glancing at Ethan.

Not quite, no! If Greg doublecrosses us, then we're cut off and alone in the middle of some strange Indonesian town with no support. Best case scenario, we might last forty-eight hours. Fuck!

"I wouldn't worry too much at this stage, mate." Ethan leaned back in his seat and rested his head. "I don't think Greg's a traitor to his country." He watched as Greg shook the Indonesian's hand and headed back towards them.

"Looks can be deceiving. I was born in Russia.

Trust me when I say this." Skippy's words tore the thought from Ethan's mind.

Mark opened the door and stepped out of the vehicle.

"Why're you in the driver's seat?" asked Greg as he jogged across the road. "What, you don't trust me?"

"Not really, no," Mark replied. The tall soldier gestured at the vacant seat from which he had recently departed. "Get in, and hurry up about it."

Greg held up his hands. "Alright, alright. Keep your knickers on."

Mark turned back to him and half-raised his assault rifle. "Get the fuck in!" he said softly, fury lending menace to his eyes. "If you've done some deal with the Indonesians, trust me, your body will never be found."

Greg swallowed but remained silent, sliding in behind the steering wheel.

"Oh, nice of you to join us," Ethan said with cheery sarcasm. "What was that all about?"

"He's actually an Aussie," said Greg gesturing at the Indonesian, who flicked the spent cigarette out onto the street and walked back into the motorbike service shop.

Ethan stared at the younger man. "That's not what I asked."

"Look, Ethan, he's an ASIO field agent, alright? I needed to link up with him so he can pass on our progress to his handlers. This whole scenario is so much larger than the Special Air Service, you realise that?"

"Okay, understood. But aren't you ASIO as well?"

"No, mate, I'm ASIS, I have my own hierarchy I have to answer to. Like I said, whilst you guys are important, with all due respect, you're only one tiny cog in a much larger machine."

"Ah, okay. I was told you were ASIO," said Ethan as they pulled away from the curb and accelerated into the traffic.

"You heard wrong."

"So how long have you been operating in Indonesia?"

Greg ignored him, swerving around a slow moving moped and slotting in behind a small bus.

"No comment then?" asked Ethan.

"This operation you're doing in Jakarta, what's it all about?" asked Greg with an innocent tone, glancing at Ethan.

"Yeah, righto. Point taken." Ethan nodded. He was reluctantly starting to warm to Greg. The young man seemed a bit of a friendly, unassuming airhead, but more than likely, that was simply a façade to hide a cold, calculating and intelligent field agent. It was exactly those personality types who won hearts and minds.

Not to mention wars.

"How long to go, son?" Hayche boomed from the back seat.

Greg looked at the soldier in the rear view mirror. "Probably another three hours or so, maybe four, depending on traffic." He braked hard and leaned on the horn as a moped pulled out in front of them. There were three people crammed onto the scooter, the man driving, his wife sitting behind him, arms wrapped around him, and their small daughter, sitting in front of her father.

In Australia, if someone honked at another driver, more than likely someone would be presented with the finger or a few choice words. But in Indonesia, even though the beeps were constant, there was no hostility. People just ignored each other and drove the way they wanted, anyway. There seemed to be some kind of order amongst the chaos.

"Three or four hours?" Hayche swore. "An hour is a bloody long time! So which is it, three or four?"

Ethan heard Greg swear under his breath. "It all depends on traffic, Hayche."

Hayche shifted in his seat and swore again. "The whole journey is less than three hundred kilometres! We'd be there by now if this was Australia."

Greg glared at Hayche in the rear-view mirror. "Guess what, Sherlock?"

"Yeah, I know, dickhead, this ain't Australia," replied Hayche.

"Shitty roads and lots of traffic mean travelling takes time. Blame your boss," Greg said, smirking sidelong at Ethan.

Ethan shrugged. "Better to arrive in some dodgy, old, inconspicuous car than getting shot down aboard a Blackhawk flying into Jakarta, like the head shed wanted us to do."

"True," Mark chimed in.

"Well, you can swap with me then, Mark!" Bob's voice shouted from the boot. "I'll take the bloody Blackhawk any day!"

"Alright, mate. Oi, Greg! Pull over. Me and Bob'll swap."

"Nah, I'm right!" Bob's voice boomed.

Mark rolled his eyes. "Dickhead," he muttered.

"Righto. Well, let's get crackin'."

The young man nodded and pulled away from the curb, holding his hand on the horn and forcing his way back into the traffic.

"The chopper might have been quicker," said Hayche, sighing.

"I'd be surprised if the pilots would have even

agreed to the mission, just quietly," Ethan said, stretching his back.

"Dunno, there's crazy pilots around," Skippy said with a chuckle. "Probably be a handful willing to fly."

Ethan raised his eyebrows and nodded. "True."

They drove on for another three hours, swapping stories, banter, and backseat observations of road users around them, often resulting in raucous laughter, or Hayche leaning out the window, shouting at a driver. To the credit of the Indonesians, however, not once were they met with hostility, just stares and the occasional shake of the head. Every half an hour, Greg was forced to pull over, apologising profusely as he ran off to open his bowels in some alley or side street. On one occasion, an old lady holding a broom, chased him back to the car, shouting a string of Indonesian words and shaking her fist.

As they approached the outskirts of Jakarta, the traffic came to a screeching halt.

"What's the go?" Ethan asked.

"Checkpoint," replied Greg, elbow on windowsill and head resting on the palm of his hand.

"What?" Ethan turned in his seat to glare at the younger man. "What do you mean a checkpoint?"

"Relax, Ethan," Greg continued staring idly out the window. "There's no drama."

"What, you mean apart from five white boys sitting pretty in a car, armed to the teeth, not to mention one in the boot? Oh yeah, we should be fine!" Ethan clenched his jaw as anger swept over him. "Fuck!"

"Trust me, mate, it's all sorted. Nothing to worry about," said Greg, edging the car forward until the bumper was almost touching the rear tyre of the stationary moped in front of them.

We'll see. Ethan watched the traffic nudge forward at a snail's pace. *Bloody hell! We could be in the shit here.* He glanced at the younger man, concentrating on driving. *If he's betrayed us, I'll shoot the bastard myself.*

"You know what they say about best laid plans, boss," said Skippy as if sensing Ethan's concern.

"Yeah I know." Scratching his chin. "Right! Here's what's going to happen, you're going to back off and allow some space between us and the motorbike in front," he turned to Greg. "Got it?"

"Yeah, okay." Greg shrugged. "But as soon as I open up a gap, some bike or car from another lane will just shift across."

"Do it!"

"Righto, righto!" Greg said, shaking his head. "Sheesh."

As soon as the gap began to expand, a small Hyundai forced its way in.

"See?" Greg said gesturing at the car in front of them.

"Okay, get to the outside lane," said Ethan.

After close to ten minutes, slow progress and incessant beeping, Greg managed to move across to the lane closest to the buildings and away from the centre of the eight-lane highway.

"Actions on compromise," Ethan turned to address his soldiers. "Exit either side, Hayche and Skippy provide covering fire. Mark, get the boot open for Bob, then we break contact. Get to the cover of the buildings, then we'll sort out how we exfiltrate. Okay?"

"Roger," replied Hayche, bringing his assault rifle up to rest across his lap.

"You got that, Bob?" Ethan shouted.

"Yeah, mate," came the muffled reply.

"You're overreacting." Greg looked at Ethan. "We'll be fine."

"No offence, but I'm not taking your word for it. I'd prefer to be prepared for the worst and be able to react than be taken by surprise."

"And what am I supposed to do if all turns to custard?" asked Greg.

"Not sure about that yet." Ethan glared at the young man. "Who knows, maybe you're leading us deliberately into an ambush. Maybe the Indonesians are paying you to bring them Australian soldiers? That'd be pretty damn easy cash. Maybe you don't have the shits at all and each time you run away to empty your guts, you're updating the Indonesians on our progress."

"Don't be ridiculous." Greg frowned and sighed. "Why would I do that, Ethan?"

"Money, mate. Cold hard cash can speak any language."

"That's not what's going on here, mate. It's just a checkpoint, purely routine. But like I asked before, if on the extremely unlikely chance it does turn to crap, what do I do?"

"Who gives a shit!" Bob's muffled shout erupted from the boot before Ethan could answer. "You're best mates with the Indonesians running the checkpoint, remember?"

Mark snorted.

"Ya little shit!" Bob added.

Greg chuckled, grinning. "Man, that bloke hates me."

Even with all the angst, Greg shook it off like water off a duck's back, to his credit.

"You're all worrying for nothing. You'll see."

Traffic began moving faster as they approached the

checkpoint. Eventually, they were next in line. An Indonesian guard strolled to the vehicle in front of them, leaned down and began talking to the driver. After a brief, nonchalant conversation and a cursory glance around the vehicle, he waved the car through. Greg began rolling forward.

"Weapons out of sight," muttered Ethan, pushing his assault rifle down into the foot-well and hiding it with his knees. Withdrawing his pistol, he pushed it in behind Greg's back, between him and the driver's seat.

"What are you doing?" Greg asked, flinching.

"Fuckin' relax." Ethan growled.

If all turned to shit, Ethan could withdraw the pistol and fire a bullet straight into the guard's face, prior to his patrol decamping the vehicle.

The guard, completely relaxed, signalled for Greg to stop and wind down his window. While his weapon was slung across his chest, the Indonesian didn't even have a hand on the pistol grip, meaning he would be unable to react and return fire with any speed.

Good. At least that's something in our favour. He smiled and nodded at the guard as he leaned down to speak to Greg.

Greg spoke Indonesian fluently. He held up some kind of card while having a joke with the guard. Ethan may have been mistaken, but he was sure the Indonesian's eyes bulged slightly as he scanned the card. He took a respectful step back, bowed his head, presumably thanked Greg, and waved them through. They accelerated through the checkpoint and continued towards the capital.

"See? You were worried for nothing," said Greg.

Ethan ignored him and holstered the pistol.

"Well done, boy." Skippy patted Greg on the

shoulder. "I was expecting a shit fight." The big Russian laughed. "Was ready to kill you."

Greg laughed, obviously oblivious to the fact the soldier wasn't joking.

Ethan had been concerned when Greg had initially introduced himself to the soldiers. The young man seemed grossly out of his depth and had the potential to put them in real danger of compromise. Happily, Ethan had been completely wrong and had utterly misjudged the civilian.

And that doesn't happen too often. Usually Ethan obtained an overall feel of a person's personality within the first few minutes after meeting them. Matching speed with the traffic around him, Greg managed to push his way into the middle lane, which seemed to be moving faster than the others.

"We'll be there before sunset," said Greg.

"I fuckin' hope so," replied Ethan. "I thought we'd bloody be there by *now*."

"Doesn't help when I have diarrhoea, I guess. Can't help it, I'm afraid."

"No worries, Greg, I know you can't. No shame in that. You been drinking much water?" Ethan looked across at the civilian.

"No, not really. My guts feel a bit off. I think I'd spew if I tried to drink water."

"Mate, you need to try. You're gonna end up dehydrated the way you're going. You're shitting out a lot of water."

"True."

"We gotta be there soon!" Mark shifted in his seat to gain a more comfortable position.

"Wanna swap?" Bob shouted from the boot.

"I offered!" yelled Mark, grinning. "You said you

were fine."

Bob replied, but the words were indistinguishable over the constant beeping, not to mention the roar of the old car's engine. Although Ethan was sure he heard a string of expletives amongst there somewhere. As promised, Greg brought them into the outskirts of Jakarta as the sun touched the western horizon.

"Well, we made it, fellas!" said Hayche.

"Yeah, not quite," said Greg.

"Waddaya mean?" asked Mark softly. "You takin' the piss?"

"Another hour or so before we reach our destination." Greg kept his eyes on the road and refused to look at Ethan.

"What?" roared Bob. "An hour! Is that what he said?"

"No, mate, you misheard," said Hayche, nudging Skippy.

"Oh, thank Christ," replied Bob.

"He said two hours!"

"Right! Pull over!" shouted Bob from the boot. "PULL…THE FUCK…OVER!"

"Happy to oblige." Greg pulled over with a screech of old brakes. "Oh shit. I dunno if I'm gonna make it this time!" The young man vaulted out of the vehicle and sprinted out of view, one hand firmly holding the seat of his pants.

* * *

Malik lost his balance as the woman shoulder-barged him. He almost lost the grip on his weapon. Even as he fell to the ground, he disengaged his index finger from the trigger and pointed the barrel up at the sky so

171

no friendlies were inadvertently shot should the rifle fire.

Man, she can hit hard! She'd be a good line-backer.

Pushing himself back to his feet, he glared at the woman.

"No, mate. Not today. Not ever! We have rules!" She jabbed a finger into the centre of Malik's chest. "You can't just execute an unarmed man."

Malik gestured at the man kneeling on the road. "You don't know who this is!" He snarled.

"I don't care if he's the prime minster of America. We don't execute people!"

"President."

"What?"

"It's the president of the USA. Not the prime minister," Malik corrected, looking down at the prisoner.

"Fuck, mate. Whatever! I don't care if it's the queen of America. You get the point I was trying to make?"

"Yes, Shaz. Crystal clear." He growled.

I'll find another way to kill him. One way or another way, I will kill this man.

"Good, Malik. To tell the truth, I thought I'd bounce clean off you. You're a big prick." She grinned and slapped the American on the shoulder.

His face softened. "You can certainly pack a punch, ma'am."

"Right, you," Malik tapped the kneeling looter on the shoulder, "hands behind your back."

When he complied, Malik turned to the small group of Guardian Angels. "Anyone got any tape, string, or rope? Let's secure these prisoners."

"What? We can't take these people hostage, Malik." Shaz slung her weapon and placed her hands on her hips.

"Shaz, I'm not going to argue with you on this one. We're not taking them hostage, they are prisoners. You don't get to wage war on allied soldiers and civilians for months on end and then get to walk free. It doesn't work like that, Shaz."

"But we've never taken hosta— I mean prisoners, before! This is all new territory for us. In the past, we have either killed the fuckers outright or chased them away from the convoys."

Malik shrugged. "Always a first time for everything, Shaz. I wanted to kill these cowards," the American sighed and leaned against the ute, "and you stopped me, rightly so. I know I was wrong, but this is a good compromise. We can't just let them go because we are the good guys."

Shaz swore and pulled out a fresh cigarette. "Why not?" She lit it and took a long drag.

"You know exactly why, Shaz. You're not that dumb." He took a step towards her. "It's time to stop being the sheep and to become the sheep dog, instead. You understand?"

Shaz grunted and crossed her arms. "Not really, no."

"We protect the herd against all odds. Sometimes that means making difficult decisions."

"I'm with the yank!" the Hilux's driver spoke.

"Shut up, Chris!"

"No, Shaz," Chris continued, taking a step forward to stand beside Malik. "You've had your say, and you're wrong. These fuckwits have given us enough of a headache in the past, including being responsible for killing our own people." Chris took a deep breath and let it out fast. "Christ, Shaz, have you forgotten that! You already forgotten about Andy, Slim, Jen, Fran?

Remember Kath? What about John? I'll tell you what," Chris pointed at the kneeling man, "those fuckers killed them all in cold blood. Now you wanna let `em go? No way, mate. Not a fuckin' chance in hell."

Finally, I get some backup. Shaz isn't going to win this one.

"So, anyone got any rope?" Malik looked around.

"Fuckin' oath," said Chris. "Give me a sec." He climbed into the ute's cabin and began rummaging around.

"This can't be right," Shaz whispered. "We're not soldiers."

"I am," said Malik. "And this is how we do things. If we release them, who knows, they might kill more people tomorrow, or the day after, or next week."

"Here." Chris slapped several lengths of rope into Malik's hand.

The tall American walked behind the kneeling looter. "I said hands behind your back."

"Fuck you, you black prick!"

Chris barged past Malik and kicked the man face down upon the road, air blasting from his mouth. Malik knelt beside the Guardian Angel and forced the looter's hands behind his back. Chris held them in place while Malik bound them. He made sure the rope was extra tight.

"Not too tight?" Malik asked.

"Way too tight, you idiot," muttered the prisoner, taking a deep breath.

"Good!" said Chris, slapping Malik on the shoulder. "Next!"

Within minutes the prisoners, three in total, were secured. The team of Guardian Angels searched the car with thorough, methodical patience. When the boot was cleared and no evidence of explosives were found, Malik climbed into the vehicle. He started the engine and left it idling before stepping back out onto the road.

"Let's get these fools loaded," he muttered, striding towards the trio of bound, kneeling men. "You got anything to cover their heads?"

"What?" asked Shaz, perplexed.

"A hood or a blindfold." Malik moved to the ute and leaned in. After a brief search of the cabin, he came up empty-handed. "Wait! Of course we do!" he grinned like a Cheshire cat and advanced on the prisoners. "Give me a knife."

Chris slapped a pocket knife into Malik's open palm and the African-American sliced through the first prisoner's shirt, pulling the fabric free. "Oh shit, boy!" Malik laughed. "You need to lose some weight, chubby!"

"Whatever," the prisoner grunted.

Still chuckling, Malik folded the shirt into a long, narrow band and pulled it tight around the man's eyes before tying it in a knot at the back of his head. He passed the pocket knife to Chris, who started cutting the second man's shirt off.

"Okay, Buddha, on your feet, pal." Malik pulled the man to his feet.

"Oi! Don't be so fuckin' rough!" the man complained.

Malik slapped him on the back of the head, hard. "Shut up and get moving." He shoved the man in the back and guided him to the empty tray of the ute. After some extended instruction and not so gentle coaxing, the blind-folded, bound man was sitting cross legged in the back of the vehicle.

"Now, hold on, because Chris is a rough driver!" Malik's teeth flashed. "Oh yeah, you can't hold on. Just do your best, Buddha."

"Haha," growled the prisoner. "Very, fucking funny, yank!"

Shaz chortled as she pushed her prisoner towards the back of the ute. "Gee, you're a cheeky bastard." She glanced at Malik. "You're growing on me, mate."

Malik threw her a quick salute and helped Chris package up the last looter. When all three were sitting in the back of the ute, Malik strolled to the waiting sedan and lowered himself into the driver's seat.

The convoy had long departed and there'd be no chance of catching them now.

In fact, they've probably reached their destination.

"You look right at home there," said Shaz.

Malik placed a forearm on the steering wheel and grinned. "Suits me, hey?"

She smiled, the cigarette almost slipping out of her mouth in the process. "Sure does, mate!"

"I'll follow you guys back to base."

Shaz patted Sammy on the shoulder. "We're comin' with ya."

"Alrighty then, jump in!"

* * *

Dave sat on the concrete floor of the warehouse, back against one of the many shipping containers. He idly munched on a sandwich and watched a small group of looters in the near distance. They seemed more agitated than normal.

Somethin's up. Good. Might mean we can get out of this shit hole soon.

He missed Bob's banter, Hayche's larrikin attitude, and Skippy's Russian drawl. It'd been more than two months since he and Charlie had been separated from their unit. But most of all, he missed Beth. He'd proposed to her on Cottesloe Beach before the invasion. He still remembered the day, her tears of joy as the sun kissed the western horizon. The way the orange-tinged afternoon sky silhouetted her face as he knelt before her staring up at the love of his life. It'd been such a wonderful day. So many good memories.

Can't wait to see you again, babe.

Embedded with the looters had been interesting and exciting to begin with, but that wore off inside the first week. When the first large engagement had occurred near the docks, they'd lost Hayche and Mark, who'd made the best of a bad situation and returned to Ethan's patrol, helping to neutralise the looters present that day.

He and Charlie hadn't been on the mission, so he wasn't one hundred percent sure Hayche and Mark had survived, but what he did know was the looters had driven out the following day to collect their dead. Neither Mark nor Hayche were among the corpses.

He shifted into a more comfortable position, finished off the last of his sandwich, and watched Wyatt break away from the large group of looters and approach him. He despised the man. A loud-mouthed coward who could talk the talk but little else. He'd once told Dave he'd been in the Army and tried out for the SASR but had fractured his ankle when he jumped out of a Blackhawk helicopter with a Jerry can strapped to his leg.

As if the Army'd waste time and money on a Blackhawk for a bunch of candidates. He remembered thinking, careful to keep his face neutral as he had listened to the man's bullshit. *More like your personality and attitude were incompatible with serving in Special Forces. Fuck knuckle.*

He looked up at Wyatt as the man arrived and kicked Dave in the leg. "Oi! You heard the goss?"

Anger washed over Dave, but he pushed it away and took a deep, gentle breath, instead. "Depends what the goss is."

If it's that, you're a complete twat. But then, I already knew that.

"Smart arse, cunt! Ya want to hear the goss or not, fuck stick?"

Dave smiled. "Why not?"

"Dozer's probably been captured, everyone else is dead. The entire crew who went out this morning to intercept the convoy have been wiped out!"

Dave's eyes widened, but not for the reasons Wyatt might have thought.

"Yeah, exactly!" barked Wyatt. "Get your lazy arse up. We head out in half an hour on body recovery."

"Is that wise?" Dave pushed himself to his feet. "Why not wait until dark?"

"What, scared are ya?" Wyatt roared with laughter. "Fuckin' coward! Get ready or else you'll be one of the fuckin' corpses. Got it?"

"Sure, why not?" Dave stretched his legs and paused as he noticed Wyatt still staring at him. "Anything else?"

Wyatt hawked and spat at Dave's feet, then stormed away cursing.

He watched Wyatt's departing back. *I'll kill you last.*

"Tell the others!" Wyatt shouted over his shoulder.

"Will do!" Dave snapped off a crisp salute with his middle finger.

He found Charlie in one of the large shipping containers, clasping a clipboard, holding a pen to his lips as he counted stock.

"You doing stock take *again?*"

Charlie looked up and slid the pen into a pocket.

"Yeah, mate. I don't mind it, though. I find it kind of therapeutic, to be honest."

"Fair enough."

Each to their own. Couldn't think of anything more bloody boring.

"We're always missing stock, though, mate. It's almost like one of the guys is constantly stealing stuff on the sly."

"You're taking this stocktaking gig pretty seriously, mate. Remember that we've gotta mission to do."

Ignoring him, Charlie sighed and reached up to move a one litre can of beetroot to see beyond it. "It's not like we don't get fed well enough."

Dave frowned. *Who gives a fuck if someone's stealing rations? Not our problem. It bloody will be for the idiot concerned, though.*

"They wouldn't want to get caught by Wyatt and the other head sheds."

"I know, Dave. That's why I've gotta be careful." He grinned, reached into a pocket and pulled free a king-size Mars Bar. "Here." He slapped it into Dave's hand.

"Fuck, now you're talking!" He ripped the wrapper free and consumed the chocolate in quick time.

He stuck the empty wrapper safely away in a pocket. "So, these missing rations, is that reflected on the stocktake?" He gestured to the clipboard Charlie clutched.

"What do ya take me for, Dave? A friggin' amateur? The books are as smooth as a baby's arse."

"Nice to know. Listen, that convoy that left this morning?"

Charlie paused and looked at him. "Yeah?"

"They were brassed up good. Wyatt reckons they're all dead apart from maybe Dozer and a couple of others. The few survivors have been captured."

"Oh shit, nice! Those Guardian Angels don't usually take prisoners, though. Wonder what's changed?"

Could be Ethan. Charlie's probably thinking the same thing.

"Ethan?" Charlie mouthed, confirming his assumption. To talk outwardly about Ethan and his crew was suicide. Especially in a shipping container in which anyone would be able to creep upon them unseen and mostly unheard, to eavesdrop.

He shrugged.

"Not sure, mate," his voice turned to a whisper, "but I'm not complaining."

Charlie shrugged. "Shit, neither am I. This is our chance to finish these pricks once and for all."

He nodded. "My thoughts exactly." He pulled the clipboard free of Charlie's grip and placed it on a shelf. "You won't be needing this anymore, mate. Grab your weapon, we're heading out shortly on body recovery."

"Let's fuckin' end this and go home," muttered Charlie as the pair strode out of the container.

Mr. Wyatt, you're about to have yourself a very bad day. Dave laughed.

* * *

"Here we are," Greg said, pulling over and bringing the vehicle to a halt and shutting off the engine.

"Thank Christ for that," muttered Hayche.

"Right, get me outta here!" Bob's muffled voice boomed from the boot. "I want out, right now!"

Ethan suppressed a groan as he stepped out onto the cracked, poorly maintained footpath.

God, that's better.

He stretched his legs and walked to the rear of the vehicle, releasing the catch for the boot. With a loud squeak it swung open and Bob pushed himself clear, nodding his thanks to Ethan.

"Ah shit, cramp!" Bob winced as he sat on the edge of the boot, legs dangling to the ground.

"Where?" Ethan took a step towards him.

Bob clutched his thigh. "Right there."

Skippy appeared beside them, cigarette dangling from between his lips. He smacked Bob on the back. "You'll live, my friend. You know the saying. Walk it off."

"Walk it off?" Bob asked through clenched teeth. "Really? I'm gonna ram that durry down your throat in a minute."

"Okay, okay." Skippy held out his hands and backed away. "Just trying to help." He lit his cigarette and strolled away, smoke drifting over one shoulder.

"Want me to rub it?" Greg asked.

"Greg," Ethan turned to the young man, "you're not helping, mate. He just needs to stretch his quad. I'm pretty sure he doesn't want another bloke rubbing his thigh."

"I dunno, he didn't complain last night," said Hayche, smacking Bob in the leg. "Did ya, mate?"

"Oh, fuck off, all of you!" Bob said, hopping up to stand on his one good leg. Placing a hand on the car for balance, he pulled his ankle up to his butt to stretch his cramping thigh.

"Oh shit, that's better." He gently released his foot and took a few gentle steps. He breathed a sigh of relief. "Cramp's gone. Shit, that hurt like a motherfucker!"

* * *

Greg led them to a nearby two-storey building, two apartments on each level. The group piled into one of the apartments on the ground floor. Ethan stood and looked around.

Impressive.

The entire area had been gutted of furniture and most non-weight-bearing walls had been knocked down to make one massive, open room. Against the far wall, upon a huge bench, sat several computers. Behind each, a smartly dressed person was busy tapping away on a keyboard or zooming in on photographs, topographical maps, or perusing satellite imagery.

Greg turned to the soldiers, a proud look glinting in his eyes. "Our nerve centre." He closed the door behind them.

The computer operators stopped work and turned to watch the newcomers. All but one nodded a greeting, or offered a wave of their hand, before turning back to their screens. The last stood and strode towards them.

"Greg! Good to see you back safe and sound, mate!" the man said. He was of average height, bald, and wore thin spectacles halfway down his nose.

"Everyone, this is William Blunt, my boss." Greg gestured towards the well-dressed, gaunt looking man.

"Good to see you all." William nodded. "Your gear is ready to go over there." He pointed towards five black bags against a wall, one beside the other.

They're organised, too. I thought this'd be a circus act. He looked around at his men and noticed they were also pleasantly surprised.

Ethan nodded and thanked him.

"Well, I'll let you get settled. You'll be staying in the apartment beside this one. I'm sure you're all tired so feel free to put your heads down."

"Sounds good," said Ethan.

When William walked back to his computer, Ethan turned to Greg. "Thanks for everything, mate. Hope you feel better soon. Get some Gastro Stop into you!"

"It's at the top of my list, don't worry about that, Ethan. Guys, grab your bags. I'll be over early tomorrow morning to brief you as to the finer details.

"Can't wait," Bob muttered.

Greg didn't hear him, or if he did, he'd chosen to ignore him. "I've organised everything our end so it should be smooth sailing."

"Should." Mark smiled. "Never been a fan of that word."

"You'll see," Greg assured him.

* * *

Ethan stood at the large window, looking out at Jakarta. The morning sun glanced off rooftops, glimmered against the mirrored windows of distant high rises, and shone down upon the traffic-choked roads and highways criss-crossing the capital.

A rapid knock on the door broke Ethan from his reverie. He strode to the door and pulled it open.

"We've been ready two hours." He ushered Greg in.

"I didn't want to come in too early. I thought eight o'clock would be fine."

"Yeah, no dramas. Better late than never, I guess. Want a coffee?" He looked Greg up and down. He saw the young man was already wearing the black Indonesian counter-terror uniform.

Greg shrugged. "I'll be driving you all so I need to fit in."

Ethan nodded. "Fair call. Coffee or not, mate?"

"No thanks."

"How's your belly treating you?" asked Skippy. "Still shitting like hose pipe?"

"No." He pulled a packet of Gastro Stop out of his pocket. "I keep these on me religiously. Feel a hell of a lot better."

"Good to hear, mate," said Mark from the couch. "Not a good feeling when you're crook."

"No way. Alright, Ethan, get your guys ready and meet me in the living room. We have a few things to go through."

"Oi, you lot!" Ethan roared. "Living room. Now!"

Greg shrugged. "Fair enough."

* * *

"Alright, there's been a threat against the Indonesian president," said Greg as the soldiers made themselves comfortable on the large couches set in a square around a glass coffee table in the centre. "Anti-Indonesian insurgents have placed themselves in a building close to the Istana Merdeka, the presidential palace in Jakarta."

Hayche frowned and leaned forward. "Hang on, how do we know this?"

"Because we, that is ASIS, fabricated the threat." Greg flicked through pages of the manifest before him. "Any more questions before we continue?"

Silence.

"Good," he said, finally looking up to scrutinise the soldiers around him. "The Indonesian police are moving in as we speak and are expected to assault the building in question in," Greg checked his watch, "about an hour."

Smart. The boy's not as light on upstairs as we all thought. Ethan had his suspicions that Greg was not quite as dense as he made out, but this complete change of character confirmed his theory.

Greg's definitely got his game face on. Ethan began feeling more at ease.

The young man flicked a page over to reveal a colour photograph taken from a satellite of the target in question. "As you can see, the target building is the white one immediately northwest of Istana Merdeka."

Istana Merdeka, the presidential palace in Jakarta. Ethan scratched his chin. From memory, there were six similar such palaces dotted around the islands of Indonesia.

Ethan looked around at his troops. "Okay, we've rehearsed this. We know what to expect so let's get in there and get the job done." He turned to Greg. "You got the police vehicle ready?"

The young man nodded and jerked his thumb towards the closest window. "Parked out front."

"Nice work. Righto, everyone, get changed. Be back here in ten minutes," Ethan said, standing. "Let's get this done."

Ethan already had the black bag unpacked and the dark Indonesian counter-terror police uniform laid out on his bed. He'd tried the uniform on the night before, as had the others, so adjustments were already made to ensure the uniforms fitted each soldier. Ethan had been forced to swap the black gas mask with Bob's. He pulled the apparatus over his face and tested it once more. It fit well and sealed the way it was supposed to. The eyeholes were tinted, which hid the wearer's eyes from outside observation. A good thing, because if they hadn't been tinted, the Australian soldiers would immediately be noticed by the Indonesian policemen with whom they would be carrying out the assault.

Walking back out into the living room, Ethan was fully dressed. He'd placed the gas mask away in a large pouch over his left hip. The Indonesian assault rifle was slung across his chest. A few minutes later and the others wandered out of their rooms, similarly dressed, although Hayche was still wearing his gas mask.

"Luke, I am your father," he said, grabbing hold of Bob's shoulders.

"Fuck off, you idiot," chuckled Bob.

Hayche pulled the mask off, grinning, and placed it in the pouch.

"Alright, everyone ready?" Greg looked around the group. "Then let's go."

They filed out of the unit and made their way towards a large, grey armoured vehicle, with the word 'Polisi' painted along the side in large yellow letters.

"Everyone in the back. Ethan, you can come and sit up front if you like." Greg, opened the driver's side door.

"Wait, where should I go?" Bob asked, wandering around behind the vehicle. His eyes widened in surprise. "Greg! What the fuck, man! Where's the boot?"

Greg sighed. "There's no boot, Bob, I'm afraid you'll just have to climb in with the others."

"Oh, are you sure?" He stepped within an inch of Greg, eyes locked on the young man. "Because there's far too much room up there." He gestured at the large seats where the others were already settling themselves. "Don't know how I'll survive."

The young man chuckled and shook his head.

"Give him a break, Bob." Ethan stopped alongside the younger man, a glint of humour in his eyes.

Bob grinned and stepped up into the vehicle. "Oh,

if you insist! This is sheer luxury!" He sat down on the seat and reached for the seatbelt. "Sheer bloody luxu—"

Ethan slammed the door closed. "Don't worry about him, mate. He's a good bloke, deep down…very deep down."

Greg shrugged. "Doesn't bother me, Ethan. I know he's only taking the piss."

"Good man. Let's get crackin'."

With everyone mounted, Ethan secured his seatbelt. As the vehicle pulled away from the curb and began to accelerate, he pushed a finger against the transmit button nestled against the base of his throat.

"Radio check, over." The microphone was a small, wireless dot stuck onto the skin over his larynx.

"Loud and clear, over," each soldier replied, their voices almost deafening through the tiny earpiece.

"Loud and clear, out," Ethan replied.

Good, all comms are operational. We're on.

As they made their way onto a major arterial highway, Greg flicked on the emergency lights and siren, forcing traffic out of his way.

"Masks on, we're about two minutes out," said the young man, pulling the gas mask over his face.

Ethan pushed the transmit button. "Get your masks on, we're two mikes out." He pulled the mask over his face, tightening the plastic straps and testing it to make sure there were no leaks.

No sooner had he done so then he saw a small convoy of Indonesian police vehicles ahead. Greg tacked their vehicle onto the rear of the convoy, which snaked its way through the civilian traffic, forcing vehicles out of the way as they travelled in the direction of the presidential palace.

"One minute," said Greg.

Ethan passed on the message.

Greg flicked off the siren but kept the emergency lights engaged to match the police vehicles in front of them. Only the lead vehicle kept its siren engaged. The convoy veered off the highway and swept past the presidential palace. The lead vehicle turned off its siren, and within thirty seconds, the white target building came into view.

Ethan placed a hand on the door handle and pressed the transmit button as they began braking heavily. "Standby, standby, standby."

Ethan launched forward in his seat, the belt locking and stopping further movement as the vehicle came to a screeching halt.

"GO!"

CHAPTER NINE

Before the vehicle had come to full stop, Ethan's boots were on the road, weapon in shoulder, and barrel up in the ready position, scanning doorways, windows, and corners.

Better make it look legit.

The others, having exited the rear of the armoured vehicle, were right behind him, moving fast. But as the Indonesian policemen began dismounting, some of them remained in cover behind the vehicles, weapons pointed at the target building. A large number formed single file, their left hands on the shoulder of the officer in front of them, their weapon held in the right hand, pointed towards the sky.

Reacting as they were trained to do, Ethan was immediately aware that the Indonesians responded a little differently to a possible terror threat. He lowered his weapon and ran forward to tack onto the rear of the line. Grasping the shoulder of the man in front of him, he brought the barrel of his rifle skyward and followed suit. Moments later, he felt one of his soldiers grasp his shoulder as they replicated him.

"Is this an assault or a fuckin' conga line?" Bob's whispered voice crackled into Ethan's earpiece.

"An assault…apparently," whispered Ethan.

Maybe I should start dancing a jig and begin kicking out my leg, one at a time. What a joke. If this was real, those blokes up front could kiss their arses goodbye.

Ethan refrained from rolling his eyes. Even though the eyepieces were tinted, it was not a good habit to foster.

"Half of us'd probably be dead by now," Mark's voice boomed in Ethan's ears. *"These clowns have no idea".*

Ethan chuckled but ignored him.

The lead assaulter breached the front door with a small, but heavy ram, and they began entering the target building.

"Top floor, go!" hissed Ethan once he entered the building.

The Indonesians, to their credit, cleared the building quickly, but with a clumsiness telling of a lack of training and rehearsal. The Australians took the stairs two at a time, weapons up, pointing towards various corners and doorways as they moved, each man's arc differing, ensuring all areas were covered.

The Indonesian Police did not yell, 'Clear,' as counter-terror units of the western world were trained to call out when a room was found to house no threat, but rather, 'Baik,' which roughly translated to 'okay.'

Ethan reached the top floor and yelled, "Baik!"

The others followed suit, shouting the word over and over as they briskly walked along the corridor. Although Mark and Bob remained at the top of the staircase, waiting for Indonesian police to begin moving up behind them.

When Ethan reached a door roughly halfway the length of the building's top-most floor, he tested the knob to make sure it was unlocked and swung the door open.

"Baik!" he roared as he walked through.

According to the building's blueprint he had memorised, the room in which the Australians now stood offered the most comprehensive view of the Istana Merdeka.

When Indonesian Policemen sprang `round the corner and began mounting the stairs towards them, Bob held out his hand and yelled, "Baik!"

He gave a thumbs up and said, *"Lantai atas baik-baik saja."* Roughly translated as, 'Top floor okay.'

The lead policeman gave a sharp nod, his face hidden by his full-face gasmask. Turning around, he gestured for his comrades to retreat down the stairs. Mark and Bob thudded down the steps behind them, but when the Indonesians disappeared back around the corner leading to the lower floor, the pair froze and crept back to the top before padding along the corridor to join Ethan and the others.

The Australians crouched in the Spartan room and remained silent. Even though the room's single window was closed, the men could hear the armoured vehicles below roar to life. A minute later, they began leaving, one after another. If Greg had followed the plan, as the assault came to an end, he would have turned his vehicle around and departed. Being the last to enter the target area, Greg would be the first to depart. Within five minutes, silence enveloped the soldiers as they waited, listening. The Indonesian police had departed.

Ethan crept towards the window and peered out. The courtyard beneath was empty, although part of the low concrete wall on one side had been knocked over, probably where one of the armoured cars had reversed into it. He remained there for some time, slowly raking the area with methodical efficiency to ensure no Indonesians were in the vicinity. When he was sure all police vehicles had departed, he sat with his back to the wall, pulled off the gas mask, and gave a thumbs up.

***

It took several hours of perseverance before Malik spotted Geoff at the markets arrayed along the Queen Street Mall. The large Australian was waiting in line to order fruit and vegetables.

"Geoff!" Malik placed a hand on the man's shoulder.

"Malik, isn't it? How are ya, mate?" Geoff smiled and offered his hand.

They shook.

"Are you still looking for your wife?" Geoff asked, pity glinting in his eyes.

"No, man, I found her. She's safe and sound."

"Oh shit, mate, that's great!" Geoff said, clamping a firm hand on his shoulder. "I'm happy she's safe."

The man's genuine reaction was touching, and Malik felt a lump develop in his throat.

"Thanks, man. Thanks for your help, too. Couldn't have done it without you."

"You're very welcome. It's always good when one of the good guys survive!"

Malik nodded and remained silent for a moment. "Talking about the good guys," he began, "I was wondering if I could borrow your car again?"

Geoff paused for a moment, but to his credit, the hesitation lasted only a few seconds. "Sure, mate. Just bring it back when you're finished."

There was no way the Guardian Angels would allow him to take a vehicle for this mission.

Malik pushed two hundred US dollars into Geoff's hand. "Thanks, man, I appreciate it."

"What? No way, mate," Geoff protested. "I'm not going to accept your money. Just bring the car back and I'll be happy."

Malik shook his head. "That's the thing, Geoff. I may not be back. This'll buy you a good replacement," he said, stuffing the cash into Geoff's top pocket.

He wasn't wrong, two hundred US dollars would buy a vehicle far superior to Geoff's Hyundai Excel.

"Only if you're sure."

Malik slapped him on the shoulder. "I'll be back. But in case I'm not, I'm sure. Alright?"

* * *

Geoff's Hyundai Excel was parked close by. The engine started on the fourth attempt, and Malik pulled away from the curb and accelerated away. It would be much easier to carry out his personal mission without the hindrance of the Guardian Angels dictating what he could and couldn't do. In a country where law had taken a back seat, all he knew was that criminals would walk free if good men did nothing.

First thing on the agenda was to swing by where the firefight had taken place earlier, and if the bodies of the dead were still lying where they fell, to search them for information. Smart phones, notebooks, radios, anything that might garner any new piece of intelligence as to the location of the looter's main base.

Searching the dead should have been the first thing the Guardian Angels did after the fight. But they wouldn't have listened to me no matter what I said. I'm only a newbie to the group.

He smacked the steering wheel. *They're only civvies, I guess.*

As he'd hoped, the corpses were still there. Blood was slick upon the road, and the flies had started their work, buzzing upon the bodies, exploring wounds, nostrils, and lips. He'd seen his fair share of the deceased to grow accustomed. He stepped through the bodies, searching pockets.

What the fuck?

Apart from some spare ammunition, every pocket he'd searched was empty. Not even a food wrapper. Nothing!

These dudes were well prepared.

Obviously, someone somewhere in the looters' chain of command had taught them the importance of cleaning themselves of potential intelligence prior to mission insertion. Or thieves had beaten Malik and already stripped the bodies of anything they deemed valuable.

Of course! Malik stood and sighed. *You idiot, Malik! You ain't gonna find shit.*

So now what?

I'll head to the port. There're supplies being flown in soon. I'll follow the convoy and hope to see the looters make another strike.

You going to take them all on by yourself? a little voice of reason asked.

There can't be that many of them left. They've been at the losing end of several fights. Now their head honcho is captured, they're all but destroyed.

The thought imbued more confidence in Malik. *They're all but destroyed. I'm ending this today!*

He parked in Sandpiper Avenue, which was a side street looking out onto Lucinda Drive, a large street on the ocean side of the Port of Brisbane. Malik switched the engine off and waited. He could see the convoy of

Unimogs ahead. They were facing south so that, once loaded with supplies, they could accelerate straight out onto the highway towards central Brisbane without the hassle of turning around and causing congestion and therefore possible choke points where an ambush could be launched against them.

For the better part of half an hour, Malik waited. Then growing slowly in volume, he heard the distant, rapid *thud* of rotor blades slapping across the sky, telling of incoming helicopters. Squinting, he tried to focus on the growing noise, but was unable to spot the aircraft. A few minutes later, he saw them. They were Chinooks, flying close to the ocean and fast. Five of them, tiny dots to begin with, but growing in both size and volume as they progressed. Ten minutes later, they had landed, two behind the convoy and three in front. The pilots did not shut down the engines in case they were required to conduct a fast exit.

Two Chinooks each carried a forklift, used to carry pallet loads of food and water to the Unimogs. Malik admired the speed with which they moved. Although he couldn't help but notice one Humvee, which had taken an interest in him. The vehicle's fifty-calibre machine gun was turned towards him and had remained so for the past few minutes. They hadn't challenged him for a code word yet, but once he moved out and began following, they'd challenge him for sure. As far as the gunner was concerned, Malik might be checking a map, having a sleep, or may have just broken down.

He picked up the radio resting on the passenger seat and checked the battery status.

Still full. Good.

Within ten minutes, the forklifts were loaded back onto the choppers, and the Chinooks were airborne, ascending, turning and accelerating from the area as one. Malik turned the key in the ignition, and the engine reluctantly turned over but failed to start. A second attempt ended in the same result.

"Come on, baby," he turned the key again.

Finally, the engine spluttered to life. He chuckled and revved a few times to ensure it wouldn't die. Changing into first gear, he saw the convoy in the near distance was already accelerating away. As he began rolling forward, the last escort vehicle disappeared from view.

"Shit, come on now!" he changed into second gear and revved the engine as it began to stall. The motor roared back to life, and the car sped up. Thick blue smoke drifted across the surface of the bitumen in its wake.

"That's better!"

He turned the corner and pulled out behind the fading convoy, struggling to maintain speed with them. The rear escort vehicle was scanning the six o'clock position with its machinegun. As soon as the little Hyundai Excel came into view, the large weapon swivelled to zero in on the vehicle, ready to open fire at a moment's notice.

"Go ahead with code word, over."

Malik reached over and brought the radio to his mouth. "Desert creeper. I say again, desert creeper."

"Welcome aboard, son. Are you American, as well?"

Malik smiled and pressed the transmit button. "Roger that. On honeymoon with my wife when the invasion went down."

"Hell, man, sorry to hear it. That's some shit luck. You guys are a bit light on today."

"The others are still sleeping. Didn't want to wake `em."

"Ha! Their loss. Nice to have you with us. Good luck, out."

Shifting into fourth gear, Malik pushed the car up to eighty kilometres per hour, probably the fastest it had been in a long time. The convoy continued to pull away. At ninety kilometres per hour, he shifted clumsily into fifth gear. Malik was still not only trying to get used to driving on the left side of the road but using his left hand to change gears. It felt alien to him.

At one hundred and ten kilometres an hour, he was matching speed.

"One more push, baby, you can do this!" Malik patted the top of the dash.

The engine screamed as the little Excel nudged one hundred and thirty and the convoy slowly became larger as the distance became smaller with each passing minute. The Humvee at tail-end-Charlie continued to track its arcs with the massive machinegun, although Malik was more concerned in watching for the appearance of a looter column in case they might try and intercept the convoy again.

If I ever get my hands on any of the surviving looters… Malik's knuckles turned white as he gripped the steering wheel.

What? What are you going to do? Execute them on the side of the road? He hadn't even thought it through properly. Anger and a need for revenge had driven him. His SEAL training began to kick in, pushing the emotions to the side. *What's the plan? How am I going to carry it out? What are the risks? Does mission success outweigh the risks?*

"Of course it fucking does," he muttered to himself.

What's the plan? His SEAL mind insisted.

His foot eased off the accelerator.

"What *is* the plan?"

The convoy was within fifty metres of him now. He'd been so furious, the emotion had blinded him, clouded his judgement, and placed him in real danger.

The vehicle slowed, and the convoy began pulling away once more. Malik silently berated himself for not being more clinical and methodical in his thought process.

You want to get yourself killed, son? the SEAL mind asked, which happened to be the identical words shouted at him by his instructor after Malik's boots slammed onto the deck of a Navy destroyer after having almost missed the rope dangling from the door of the Blackhawk chopper hovering seventy feet overhead.

The engine began to purr as the vehicle slowed. The convoy faded into the distance.

A plan began to rapidly formulate in his mind, actions on contact with the enemy, vehicle malfunction, fastest exits from the area, when to abort should the risks outweigh the mission's success, and finally breaking contact and withdrawal from the highway to a safe area.

Better, his SEAL instincts told him.

He took a deep breath and felt in control for the first time in a long while. Pushing the accelerator back to the floor, the car reluctantly picked up speed once more as the engine's revs shrieked. Within several minutes, he slowly began to reel the convoy in, although his eyes constantly swept the highway for any looters.

Malik frowned as he noticed four or five cars and a Unimog parked in the middle of the road ahead.

That's where the last firefight happened. Could be searching the bodies for valuables. He rubbed his chin. *Pretty damn organised crew, though.*

Once the convoy had passed the area, Malik noticed movement and realised people had been taking cover behind the vehicles in case the Humvees opened up on them.

He took his foot off the accelerator and allowed the Excel to slow. As he approached the area, he noticed small groups carrying the dead bodies and loading them onto the truck.

They're collecting their dead!

"Motherfucker!" he roared and slammed on the brakes, bringing the little car to a stop. He exited, ran to the rear, and squatted out of sight. Pulling the buttstock of the assault rifle into his shoulder, he flicked off the safety catch, stared through the scope, and opened fire.

Time to die.

* * *

Dave bent down and grasped one of the corpses under the arms, Charlie lifting the legs. He ignored the putrid smell. The aroma brought images flashing into his mind of the massacre in Rwanda, where he had served in the Australian Army as a teenager. He closed his eyes and forced the images away.

"You right, mate?" Charlie asked.

"Yup, all good." He swallowed and, together, they carried the body to the Unimog, where a small team took over and lifted it up onto the rear tray of the vehicle, placing it neatly beside the others already lying supine.

The smell had soaked into his clothes, hair, nostrils, not to mention his mind. That last one was the most dangerous. He heard a high-pitched screech of old brakes engaging and turned to watch an old Hyundai Excel come to an abrupt halt in the near-distance. A well-built African man stepped clear, ran to the rear of the little car, squatted, and opened fire.

Two men were already dead as Dave ducked. "Cover!" he shouted, dropping to the floor.

"We're on, mate!" Charlie called. "Let's do what we came here for!"

This is a good a chance as any. The enemy of my enemy and all that.

He rolled onto his side and unslung his weapon. The looters' reactions were slower than that of the soldiers, and they were still running for cover when Charlie and Dave opened fire.

Dave nestled the metal sights over a looter sprinting away towards one of the vehicles and sanctuary.

I think his name's Will. Fuck knows. Who gives a shit, anyway?

He fired a shot, the round taking the looter between his shoulder blades and dropping him to the road, lifeless.

Charlie's weapon cracked to life beside him.

Where are you, Wyatt?

He looked for the man but couldn't see him. The looters were so disorganised and surprised by the ambush that, as they reorganised themselves, they neglected to notice that two of their own were firing upon them.

Dave fired, changed aim, shot again. He killed looter after looter with smooth, repetitive skill. Half of the crew who'd departed on body recovery that morning had soon joined their bloated, stinking comrades.

Shooting the last round in his magazine, Dave pulled the empty magazine clear, shoved it down the front of his shirt, and grabbed a fresh one from his chest webbing. Slamming it into the weapon, he cocked the rifle, stared down the metal sights, and continued the murderous onslaught.

A bullet ricocheted off the bitumen next to Dave's head. He flinched and rolled away, realising the looters were returning fire.

The game's up!

"Oi, Charlie! I'm moving. Cover me!"

"Yeah, mate, go!"

✳ ✳ ✳

Malik scuttled around the far side of the Excel as bullets peppered holes in the vehicle's skin or drilled through the windscreen. Tiny shards of glass littered the bitumen around the car.

Shit! More looters here than I thought.

He reloaded the weapon.

Too late, there's no way I can get outta here safely now. Fight or die, man. Fight or die!

As adrenaline thumped in his veins, he ran in a crouch to the far side of the car, and with weapon at the ready, peeked around the edge of a front tyre. Rapidly shifting his point of aim, he fired several shots in quick succession, watching two men drop lifeless to the road. The air around him came to life as bullets hissed by his head.

Fuck!

A round ripped through the window nearby, shattering the glass and spraying shards across the bitumen. Malik dropped out of sight. Clenching his jaw, he squeezed his eyes shut as bullets pinged off the road or thudded through the Excel. Fuel glistened upon the bitumen, pooling under the Hyundai from the punctured gas tank.

It might be fight and *die, Malik.*

"Fuck that!"

Get that thinking out of your head. It ain't an option! He released a breath in a rush, rolled to his feet, and ran for better cover. He crept in behind a concrete barrier resting on the curb of the road and pushed himself as close to the ground as possible. Even though the intensity of fire continued, he noticed fewer and fewer bullets whizzed over his head.

He slid along to the corner of the barricade and carefully looked around the edge.

What the hell?

He pushed forward a little more to gain a better look at the battle and realised the looters were firing upon each other. One, closest to Malik, had his back to the American, providing covering fire for his friend, who pushed himself clear of cover and ran across open ground.

I could drop 'em both right now. Like shooting fish in a barrel.

But why would he? They were thinning out the ranks of the looters by the second. Soon, they'd be the only two left alive. Then he could shoot them. Malik grinned and slid backwards out of sight.

***

Skidding to a halt behind a four-wheel drive vehicle, Dave pushed himself to his feet and opened fire.

"Got ya covered, Charlie!"

Charlie sprinted and was knelt beside him within a few seconds.

He looked over at Dave. "Well, fuck me, this is going well!"

Dave laughed and flinched as a bullet hole appeared in the skin of the vehicle near his arm.

Shit!

He saw a looter standing up, leaning his rifle upon the roof of a car, and aiming at them. Dave aimed and shot. The bullet took the man through the throat and sent him tumbling to the ground. He released the weapon and clutched the terrible wound in his neck instead.

Dave changed his aim, fired again, altered aim, and opened fire. The looters fell in quick succession.

* * *

These boys know what they're doing!

Malik nudged forward to gain a glance at the firefight. *Definitely military trained, probably former grunts. Gotta be!*

He almost felt sorry for them, outnumbered as they were, but something confused him. *Why the hell are they shooting up their own dudes? There has to be a reason.* The actions of the pair seemed too well rehearsed and instinctive for their sudden disloyalty to be some sudden rogue decision.

Malik cursed and crept into view. He nestled the crosshairs over a looter running between cover, gave him a slight lead, and fired a single round. The bullet slammed into the looter's chest just under his left armpit. He was dead before his body crumpled to the ground.

Malik cupped a hand to his mouth. "Hey, you two! Fall back here. Fall back now!"

* * *

Dave heard a voice shouting from behind them. He glanced around and saw the African man yelling at them.

"Can't hear ya!" Dave roared back. Deciding the man was no longer a threat to he and Charlie, he turned away and opened fire.

The voice persisted.

Dave felt a sharp slap on his back and looked across at Charlie. "He wants us to withdraw to his position!" Charlie shouted over the noise of the gun battle.

"You go, mate. I got you covered."

He fired a shot and his weapon went silent. "Stoppage!"

Charlie ducked back into cover.

Dave ripped out the empty magazine, pushed a fresh one into the weapon's recess, and cocked the rifle. He knelt back into view, saw a muzzle flash from behind a concrete pillar in the near distance, and returned fire. "Go!"

Charlie sprinted clear towards the position of their new friend.

* * *

Ethan sat by a window, holding a pair of binoculars to his eyes as he stared at the Istana Merdeka. Occasionally, he dropped the binos so they dangled from the strap around his neck and allowed his eyes to rest for a minute or two.

The others were spread out around the room behind him, sleeping. It had been an exhausting twenty-four hours and Ethan had elected to take the first watch so the others could get some much-needed shuteye.

Sweeping the president's building, nothing of note was evident. All windows were closed, and apart from the front entrance where two guards stood, the place seemed abandoned. The Indonesian president had similar luxurious buildings on several of the islands of Indonesia from where he could carry out his political duties. He could be staying at any one of them, but intel had indicated he was currently located at Istana Merdeka.

He brought the binoculars back to hone in on the guards. Sometimes there were dignitaries arriving and departing, but in between these seldom occasions, the guards were slumped against the wall of the building, chatting and laughing. Ethan allowed the binoculars to drop and scribbled several sentences in his notepad. Leaning over, he picked up a digital SLR with a tinted lens to reduce the chances of the sun shining off the glass and attracting attention of unwanted outside observation.

Carefully focusing in on the guards so that their faces filled the screen, he snapped several photographs, then zoomed out to take in their general demeanour before taking another few photos. They were bored, he noticed, their weapons slung across their chest, hands in pockets, one talking while the other laughed. Placing the camera down, his hand fell to the binoculars and raised them back to his eyes, where once more, he allowed himself to sweep the building. The flash of sunlight on glass flared for a fraction of a second from an upper window halfway along the Istana Merdeka. Ethan brought the binos across and focused upon the area where he thought he saw the anomaly.

Replacing the binoculars with SLR, he focused in on the area and saw a man standing in the window, staring out at the world, a drink in his hand. He brought the glass up to his mouth, and the sunlight glared off the cup again for a moment. Ethan zoomed in on the face and clicked the silver button. Drinking the last of the contents, the Indonesian turned away from the window and disappeared from sight.

Ethan brought the photograph up on the SLR's five-inch LCD screen and concentrated on the face. It wasn't the president. Leaning over, he dragged a small laptop to him and tapped the keyboard to bring it out of sleep mode. With a few keystrokes, several mouse clicks and a lot of scrolling, he found himself staring at the same man. He held the camera up against the laptop's screen to compare them. Definitely the same man.

Not the president, he thought, *but it* is *his head of personal security detachment*. Ethan smiled. Why would the president's personal security detachment be in the Istana Merdeka if the president himself wasn't there? It was a smoking gun as far as Ethan was concerned.

"Bingo," he whispered and brought the binoculars back up to his eyes.

* * *

Bullets slammed through the skin of the vehicle behind which Dave took cover.

This is gonna end in tears!

He crawled to the far end of the car, looked around the completely flat, rear tyre, brought weapon to bear, and took another life. The empty cartridge somersaulted through the air and coming to a rest near his elbow with a metallic *clink*.

He heard the intensity of fire from Charlie and the African intensify behind him. Within moments, Dave was receiving very little incoming fire as the looters began attempting to neutralise the new threat.

"Dave, withdraw! Withdraw!"

Nope. This is too good an opportunity.

He looked over his shoulder. "I'm gonna flank `em!"

"What?" Charlie shouted.

"Cover me!"

He sprinted clear of cover and made for the Unimog.

"Dave, for fuck sake!"

Dave ignored his comrade and leapt over a body oozing life blood across the highway. The air around him came to life with hisses and cracks as bullets narrowly missed him. He went to ground behind the large tyre of the truck. Looking back at Charlie in the distance, he gave thumbs up. But Charlie was too busy providing cover fire to notice.

He crept forward, ran in a crouch to the front of the Unimog, and looked around the mighty bulbar. A small group of looters had been shooting from behind the cover of a nearby concrete pillar. He couldn't see them as they had gone to ground. Self-preservation was a strong instinct, after all.

The game's up fellas.

He sprinted clear of the truck and made a beeline for the pillar. Relief washed over him as he heard Charlie's fire increase again. He ran around the far side of the pillar and opened fire from the hip.

No need to aim at this range.

Seven looters died on the bitumen together. But no Wyatt.

Where the fuck is that piece of shit?

The gun battle drifted to silence as the looters' numbers dwindled to nothing.

"You okay, Dave?"

Dave jogged back to the Unimog, ignoring the stench wafting from the corpses resting on the back of the truck's tray.

"Yeah, mate. I'm moving to you."

"Oi!" Charlie's voice boomed. "Halt! Halt or I shoot!"

Dave nestled against one of the truck's large wheels and craned his neck in an attempt to see who Charlie challenged.

Can't see shit.

No weapons had been fired so maybe the looter had complied.

"Last warning, mate!"

Nope, old mate is still on the run. You're gonna cop a bullet, buddy.

A car door slammed nearby, and the engine roared to life. Charlie opened fire.

What the hell's goin' on?

Dave pushed forward beyond the Mog's tyre and the scene came into view. One looter remained and was accelerating away from Charlie but towards Dave. He stood up, sprinted to a nearby car, and rested his weapon on the roof to provide a stable platform. He took aim at the driver of the vehicle, and as he focused on the face, his blood turned ice cold.

Wyatt!

He fired a short burst, the rounds slamming into the vehicle, peppering the windows and doors, but missing Wyatt. He fired again, bullets ricocheting off the road with loud whines. But the car continued to depart the area.

"Let him go, mate. No point chasing him, he's the only one left!" Charlie called, grinning like a Cheshire cat. "How much damage can one bloke do?"

Dave snarled and slammed a hand onto the car's roof. "Like bloody hell, he's getting away!"

"I'm with your friend," said the African. He spoke with an American accent. "One man can do more damage than you think."

What the fuck's a yank doing here amongst all this?

"Let's go!"

He ran to Charlie's position.

"Alright, Dave, let's get after him. This is Malik, by the way."

Dave nodded at the American. "Thanks for your help, Malik."

"My pleasure, man. My pleasure. Now, let's take out this one last guy." He gestured at the rapidly departing vehicle. "Take my car."

"We finish this right now," Dave said.

The trio jogged to the Hyundai excel. Moments later, Malik had them in chase of Wyatt.

* * *

Malik pushed the little car as hard as possible and was soon gaining on the sedan in front of them. He altered course so he was approaching from the vehicle's left side. His reasoning being that most people were right-handed, and if shots were fired, the occupant of the car would be stretching the weapon across their body.

The Excel continued to accelerate beyond one hundred and forty kilometres per hour. The speedometer stopped just short of one hundred and fifty, the engine letting Malik know it was giving all it had. He kept a close eye on the temperature gauge.

"Good car!" the Australian beside him shouted.

"She is, sir. She's seen me through a couple of problems."

Dave, that's his name, I think.

"Bring us up a bit closer and I'll see if I can hit a tyre."

Malik nodded and patted the dashboard.

Come on, girl, just a bit longer and it's done.

The Hyundai wouldn't be able to keep such a pace up for a prolonged length of time. They were gaining fast on the car.

* * *

Dave wound down his window, air blasted into the vehicle, throwing empty food wrappers clear of the car.

"I'll try from the other side," said Charlie, who was sitting on the right, rear seat.

"No worries, mate."

Leaning out with weapon in hand, he struggled against the wind, which hit him in the face like a train. He'd have to shoot left handed. Although he'd trained extensively firing from either side, like most people, Dave was more comfortable firing right handed. Gritting his teeth, he ignored the wind as best he could and pulled the rifle into his shoulder.

Dave's first round drilled through the rear window but missed its target. The car they chased began to swerve in an attempt to throw off their aim. Dave fired again, the bullet pinging from the road directly behind the rear tyre.

Almost.

Wyatt slammed on the brakes so he was driving parallel to them and turned into them.

"Shit!"

Dave ducked back into the Excel and shifted as far away from the door as possible. The vehicles collided, but aside from a small inward dent, there was no major intrusion to Dave's door.

Bloody lucky, mate.

He pushed himself back out, bringing weapon to bear, and aimed at Wyatt . Focusing the weapon's sights, he rested his finger on the trigger and squeezed. The weapon bucked and the bullet missed.

By a bee's dick.

He smiled and fired another shot, the round ripped through the panel just above the front tyre. It was wildly off course, but Wyatt ducked away all the same. Malik braked hard, allowing the target vehicle to move in front.

"Take out his tyres!" shouted the American. "It's a bigger target. He's only got a small head!" Malik grinned.

Dave laughed.

I'm beginning to like this yank.

He fired several rounds at the rear tyre. The third bullet perforated the rubber, and it wasn't long before the second tyre was deflated, decelerating the vehicle against the wishes of the driver.

Malik slowed in conjunction with the car in front of them, making sure he steered off to the side in case any pieces of rubber tore free of the deflated tyres and in turn damaged the Excel. Eventually, the brake lights illuminated, and the target vehicle decelerated violently. Malik braked hard and brought the Excel to a halt.

Dave ran clear, closely followed by Charlie. Wyatt stepped clear of the car, hands held high in the air.

"Please, don't shoot. oh Christ, please, don't shoot."

Dave smiled as he strolled towards the surrendered man. "Morning, Wyatt. Do you know why we pulled you over today?"

Charlie chuckled.

"Don't shoot." Wyatt stretched his arms towards the sky as far as they would go.

Can't kill a man who's surrendered.

Dave sighed and clenched his jaw. As much as he wanted to end the looter's life, shooting a prisoner of war brought with it extremely harsh penalties. It would be something that caught back up with him once the invasion was over and order was restored.

"You gonna kill me?" asked Wyatt.

Dave shrugged. "All depends on you, Wyatt. If you cooperate, then no. But if you try on any kind of fancy shit, I'll put a bullet in you."

"Jesus," Wyatt began but fell silent. He looked at Dave, then glanced at Charlie. "Why'd you turn on us, mate? You killed a lot of good men back there."

Dave laughed with genuine humour. "Good men? Is that what you said?"

Wyatt nodded, his mouth clamping shut, lips disappearing in a tight line.

"Ambushing food convoys destined to feed the innocent people of Brisbane? Killing soldiers protecting those convoys? Selling off the food at extortionate prices? You keep telling yourself you're a good man, Wyatt." Dave gestured in the direction from which they'd come. "Those corpses lying on the road back there were not good men. They're fucking criminals. Like you!"

Malik appeared beside Dave's side. "You forgot to add kidnapping to their list of *skills*."

Dave turned to the American. "What do you mean?"

Malik explained what had happened to Jayla.

"Shit, I had no idea about this," said Dave. "Did you?" he glared at Wyatt.

Wyatt shifted uncomfortably and looked away.

"You *did*!" Dave snarled. "You fuckin' piece of shit! How could you ever think you were amongst good people?"

"You were one of us, weren't ya?" Wyatt shot back.

"Wyatt, mate," he gestured at Charlie, "we were never one of you. We were placed there to kill you all. You really think you could kill civvies and soldiers in their scores and steal tonnes of food destined to hungry Australians without reprisal?"

Wyatt swore. "You're looking at it wrong! What's the problem with trying to better yourself? Or making good out of a bad situation? That's all we were doing."

"Selling stolen food provided by the UN at extortionate prices to desperate people isn't bettering yourself. Now put your bloody hands behind your back!"

"What are you going to do?"

"I'm going to tie your hands together. What are you, simple? Charlie, you got a Zip Tie spare?"

"Yup, here's one I prepared earlier."

He took it from Charlie without taking his eyes from Wyatt. "Thanks. I said put your hands behind your back!"

Wyatt closed his eyes, nodded, and dropped his hands behind him. "Fine."

"Just wait until you meet my wife," Malik said with a chuckle. "She's going to *love* you."

Wyatt looked up at the big American. "I've already met her once before." He smiled. "She didn't like me much then, don't see why she'll like me now."

* * *

"Motherfucker!" Malik strode forward and slammed a fist into Wyatt's jaw.

I'm going to tear you apart, you coward.

The prisoner fell to the road, his head striking the bitumen with a dull *thud*. He spat out a tooth and looked up at the trio standing above him, eyes glassy.

"Get the fuck up!" Malik said, taking a grip of Wyatt's shirt and dragging the man to his feet. He slammed an open palm into Wyatt's solar plexus, the breath leaving the looter's lungs in a rush. As Wyatt bent over, Malik brought his knee up, smashing it into the nose of his wife's tormentor. Blood exploded from the crushed nose, and the man hit the ground again for the second time in less than a minute.

Wyatt wiped blood from his eyes with a shaking hand and climbed back to his feet with a groan. Wisely, he remained silent.

"Hands behind your back," the Australian said.

I think his name's Dave.

Nodding slowly, Wyatt 's hands disappeared behind him and came back out clutching a pistol. He pointed it at Dave. "Get the fuck back!"

"Now, come on, mate. Don't be stupid."

Malik almost laughed at the lack of fear in the Australian's voice.

"I'll shoot, I swear. Get back, all of you!"

The Australians casually stepped back and dropped their weapons to their side. "Fair enough, Wyatt."

"You too, you black fucker!" Wyatt began to swing the pistol towards Malik.

No chance, son.

Malik stepped forward, slapped the pistol away, disarmed him, and hammered a fist into Wyatt's throat. He felt the cartilage of the trachea disintegrate beneath his knuckles.

Wyatt lay writhing on the ground, clutching his throat, and struggling desperately to inhale air into his lungs that would never make it past his mouth. His eyes bulged in terror.

Malik knelt beside the dying man, tapped him on the shoulder to gain his attention and spoke four words.

"Her name is Jayla."

CHAPTER TEN

The advance of night's dark blanket was gradual, but incessant, as the sun retreated towards the western horizon. As darkness slowly descended upon them, Ethan felt more at ease. Night was their greatest ally. Ethan ensured the laptop was closed so that no white light inadvertently leaked out. Even with such a small amount of light, their position might be compromised by prying outside eyes. Ethan sat, glaring down a night vision scope at the Istana Merdeka.

"All good, boss?" Skippy asked softly, crawling up beside him.

"Yeah, mate," he whispered. "They've changed guard twice so far."

The ear-piercing shriek of jet engines roared through the sky, followed by several blinding flashes across the horizon. Moments later, the explosions rolled across the city like some toddler clumsily bashing a bass drum. Both men ducked from sight, taking cover.

Thank fuck we got the French involved in this mission. With the French aware of the presence of Ethan and his soldiers on the ground in the area around the Istana Merdeka, the fighter-bombers would not drop ordnance anywhere near them.

Crouching up, he peaked over the window sill to see tracer streaming into the night sky from all areas of the city closely followed by the dull chatter of the machineguns responsible. The gunners were hopeful if they thought they had any chance of hitting the fast jets. More than likely, the aircraft had flown over the city and departed from the area before the bombs even hit their targets. The northern sky was glowing a dull orange as, in the distance, the target of the bombing mission began burning.

"Wish they could strike president's palace," whispered Skippy. "There be no need for us to be here."

"Yeah, I know, mate. Against the Geneva convention according to the Froggies. They're allowed to strike facilities directly involved in the support of the occupation of Australia. But any buildings or structures related to domestic governance are—"

"Strictly off limits," Skippy finished. "I know, boss, I was at briefing." He sighed. "I need cigarette."

Ethan shifted into a more comfortable position.

"I'm awake," Bob whispered, sitting up and stretching.

There was movement to Ethan's left, and he glanced to see Mark beside him.

"What the fuck was that?" grumbled Hayche, failing to suppress a yawn.

Ethan ignored them all, silently watching the machinegun fire continue to strafe the darkness. He guessed it was more to reassure the Indonesian civilians that their military was fighting back than it was to actually defend against fighter jets blitzing across the sky twice as fast as the speed of sound. Several much smaller flashes illuminated thick, low clouds in the far west, followed seconds later by the dull *thuds* of explosions. The French were busy this evening, it would seem.

Almost as soon as the machineguns ceased fire around the Istana Merdeka, tiny streams of distant tracer rose up into the cloud cover in an attempt to shoot down the new threat. Although this time, the machineguns responsible remained inaudible to the Australian soldiers silently observing the lightshow.

"Orders at midnight," whispered Ethan when silence reluctantly fell upon the immediate area.

"Roger," replied Skippy.

"Yup," said Bob.

"Okay," muttered Hayche, stretching back out on the floor.

"I'll take over, boss. You get your head down, hey?" Mark spoke softly, tapping Ethan on the shoulder.

"Righto, mate. Give me a nudge at twenty-three thirty."

"No worries," Mark replied, taking the night vision scope from Ethan. "Speak to ya soon."

Ethan held back a groan as he lay flat out upon the floor, allowing the muscles of his back to relax. His eyelids closed and sleep swept over him faster than he expected.

* * *

He stretched out on the couch, hands behind his head, eyes closed while a gentle breeze, provided by the ceiling fan, brushed against his skin. Taking a deep breath, he let it out slowly, completely relaxed.

"Ethan?" Sally's voice was soft, almost fearful, he realised.

"Mmm?" he responded, opening his eyes and glancing over to see his wife sitting on a nearby chair. She was blindfolded. A tall, grim looking man stood behind her, the barrel of a pistol touching the hair above one ear.

"Sally?" he said, coming fully awake, adrenaline pumping through his body.

"Ethan!" she pleaded.

"Sally!" he shouted.

* * *

Ethan was roughly shaken awake.

"Boss!" hissed Mark. "You alright?"

"Yeah." He rubbed his face and yawned. "Why?"

"You were dreaming about your missus. You were shoutin' her name, and not in a good way," whispered Mark, the grin evident in his voice. He slapped Ethan's shoulder and moved away. "It's almost twenty-three thirty," he added as he sat near the window, bringing the night vision scope to his eyes.

"Righto, thanks." Ethan sat up slowly.

He stood, moving to the closest sleeping form. Nudging the shadow formed in a half-foetal position upon the floor, he knelt.

"Orders," Ethan whispered when he felt movement.

A sigh, and then a whispered, "Yup, okay." It was Bob.

Ethan moved from one sleeping man to the next until all were awake and preparing for the coming mission. Within minutes, the soldiers sat in a semi-circle around Ethan, listening intently as their commander went methodically over the plan. They had discussed the mission at some length on many occasions and had already rehearsed several times upon the French aircraft carrier *Charles de Gaulle* prior to their insertion onto Indonesian soil.

When he was sure the cobwebs of slumber had departed the minds of his soldiers and each man knew what he was to do, Ethan asked for questions, offering each the opportunity to raise a query or concern. When none were forthcoming, Ethan stood.

"Time to move."

He pulled on his helmet and tugged the night vision goggles attached to the front of the helmet so they rotated down to sit just in front of his eyes, casting the world in front of him in a thick, grainy green. Cradling the Indonesian assault rifle across his chest, Ethan walked out the door, along the hallway, and descended the stairs, listening as his soldiers followed behind.

The men moved slowly, but sure-footed, and inside five minutes, they were outside, hugging the shadows as they patrolled towards the Istana Merdeka.

Powerful jet engines filled the silence and blinding flashes rippled across the city. The men instinctively went to ground. Silence reigned for some seconds before the explosions rolled across them. Machineguns began speaking from all directions, tracer streaming into the vacant night sky.

Not a hope in hell, Ethan thought as he watched the machinegun fire seeking the flesh of French fighter-bombers, which had long departed. When his vision, blinded by the sudden bombing mission, had returned to normal, he stood and turned to the others, signalling for them to follow.

The patrol was on the move again, making progress towards the target building and, ultimately, the Indonesian president. Stopping by a large tree, Ethan pointed at Hayche and signalled the soldier to him before indicating for him to setup his position.

* * *

Hayche settled down behind the tree. He rolled onto his side and looked into the canopy. It was a stinging tree, he was certain of it.

Great. Just fuckin' great!

Setting up a position within the building they so recently departed would have been more favourable. Not to mention far safer. However, if the mission turned to custard, and the patrol were required to break contact and make a rapid withdrawal, being out in the open and not hindered by being inside a building several stories above the ground reduced both the complexity of the plan and the possibility of complete mission failure.

Moving slowly to reduce sound, he pushed a Claymore anti-personnel mine into the ground behind him, protecting the approach to his rear. The initiation device, commonly known as the *clacker*, lay by his right hand. The Claymore had the potential to wound or kill enemy moving up from behind, but it was also to serve as a distraction. Combined with the smoke grenade sitting on the ground beside his left hand, it would be enough for him to break contact and relocate to cover in order to return fire. Hopefully he'd need neither devices but preparing for the worst-case scenario was always a smart move.

Nestling into a more comfortable position, Hayche brought the stock of the sniper rifle into his shoulder. Detaching night vision goggles from his helmet, he switched them off and placed them on the ground beside him. Using the night vision capability of the scope attached to the rifle, he watched the progress of his patrol. Spaced well apart, they walked slowly, covering their arcs and staying in the shadows.

"In position," Hayche whispered, pushing on the transmit button built into the weapon, just above the trigger guard and connected to his throat mic via Bluetooth.

A single *click* was Ethan's response as he depressed and rapidly released the transmit button to confirm he had received the message.

Focusing beyond them, Hayche moved the rifle slightly so that the crosshairs rested upon the chest of an Indonesian guard leaning against the wall next to the entrance of the Istana Merdeka. The second guard sat with his back to the wall, one leg bent, a hand resting upon the knee, cigarette clasped between index and middle fingers. Occasionally, the bored guard brought the durry to his lips, his face glowing for a moment, before he exhaled the smoke. Moving the scope up, Hayche noticed a small neon light illuminating the entrance. Beside the light was a small bubble, which he assumed was a camera.

Reaching forward, he clasped a hand to the silencer attached to the barrel and checked it hadn't loosened. It was tight and fully engaged to the muzzle. Taking a deep, gentle breath, Hayche returned his attention to the Australian patrol, watching their quiet advance towards the entrance.

Touching the ground beside him, he found the night vision goggles, switched them on, and brought them to his face. Sweeping the length of the Istana Merdeka, he watched for any extra guards or new threats. Nothing. Turning the NVGs off, he placed them down and returned his attention to the Australian patrol.

They had stopped and were crouched, waiting. He heard the radio click to life as Ethan pressed and released the transmit button. Dash, dash, dot, dash, dash, dash. In Morse Code, the clicks spelled 'GO.'

Hayche pulled the sniper rifle tight into his shoulder and nestled his cheek against the buttstock, glaring down the night vision scope. He watched the

Indonesian guards, shifting the crosshairs smoothly between the two. The one sitting had lit a new cigarette and remained complacent. The second guard, who stood, leaning against the wall, had a two-way radio clipped to his belt, Hayche noticed.

However, the first priority must be the camera, followed by the guard with the radio on his belt. The ability to communicate via radio or other such technology remained the most powerful and efficient weapon on the modern battlefield.

Hayche gently pressed the transmit button and whispered, "Standby."

Smoothly bringing the crosshairs to hover over the small glass bubble attached high on the wall near the neon light above the entrance, he fired a silenced shot and altered his aim. Less than a second later, the neon bulb exploded into a thousand tiny shards as the bullet ripped through the glass. The more alert of the two guards flinched, reached for his radio, and died as small shards of his skull, chunks of brain and blood splattered across the wall. He dropped to the ground without a sound. The second guard managed to shout a warning before a bullet hammered through the side of his face, passed through his skull, and ricocheted off the stonewall with a loud whine.

"Fuck!" Hayche snarled.

* * *

Hayche's sniper rifle was no more than a dull *thump* behind them, the rounds cracking over their heads in quick succession. Within several seconds, both guards were dead.

"Go!" Ethan hissed, pushing himself up and

dashing towards the front door of the president's palace. He didn't turn to see if the others were following. He didn't need to. Their boot falls were a soft staccato behind him as they advanced. Ethan gently tried the doorknob, but it was locked.

"Shotty!"

Mark slung his weapon, and then withdrew a shotgun holstered on his back. Stepping forward, he pressed the barrel to the top hinge and pulled the trigger, leaving a hole in the door, beyond which hung the tattered remains of the hinge. Shooting out the bottom hinge, and then the lock itself, Mark took a step back and kicked the door in. Without hinges or lock to support it, the door flew inwards and landed on the carpeted floor with a heavy *thud*. Mark stood aside, his back to the wall, and allowed Ethan to lead the others through the breeched entrance and into the Istana Merdeka.

Ethan ran down the hallway, weapon at the ready, finger gently touching the trigger. He removed his night vision goggles and placed them away. The lower floor was well-lit with banks of neon lights providing more than enough illumination. For the third time in as many minutes, he checked the safety catch was disengaged. The president's master bedroom was located deep in the bowels of the building on the third floor and positioned centrally.

Ethan came to a stop, back to the wall near the staircase leading up to the next level. He slowly peered around the corner and checked the stairs were clear. It would have been a perfect place for the Indonesians to setup an ambush. All clear. Sprinting up the staircase, controlling his breathing and ignoring the burning beginning to make itself known in his thighs, he stared down the sights of his weapon.

Reaching the second level, Ethan stopped, allowing the others to pass him. A single door led from the stairwell to the second level. He locked it and taped a grenade onto the wood just above the handle, ensuring the adhesive strip reached the wall into which the door was recessed. Gently pulling the pin clear of the grenade, he placed it away in a pocket. A simple, yet devastating booby-trap for the unwary.

Turning from the locked entrance, he ascended the stairs and saw the others waiting just short of the door leading out onto the third level. Ethan was just about to give the thumbs up signal when the deafening roar of low-level fighter jets screamed above the building, causing the walls to shake. The explosions that followed were close. Far too close for comfort. If the Istana Merdeka was on the target list of French pilots tonight, it would all be over in a matter of seconds. At least they'd have no idea what hit them. *Small consolation, but better than nothing.*

He gave another thumbs up, and Skippy turned away from him, stepped through the doorway and disappeared from sight, closely followed by the others. Moments later, the ripple of gunshots echoed, followed by silence. Ethan bounded up the stairs and glanced round the corner. Mark was hugging the wall of the corridor, facing right in a kneeling position, staring over the scope of his weapon.

The others were facing left, Bob kneeling on one side of the corridor, Skippy standing on the other. Both held their weapons at the ready. Beyond them lay the corpses of two guards, the soft, cream carpet beneath them slowly turning claret.

Ethan pressed the small transmit button attached

to the skin of his throat. "Move up."

Skippy and Bob walked briskly forward, Ethan following. Mark trailed behind the group. Once beyond the door leading to the stairwell from which they had originally appeared, he knelt down once more, facing away from the others, protecting against any enemy advance from behind.

There was little doubt the pair of deceased guards had been protecting the entrance to the president's room.

Here we go.

Ethan ordered the pair in front to stop, drop prone, and provide cover.

Once they were in position, one either side of the corridor, Ethan padded forward, weapon up, staring down the battle-sight attached to the top of the weapon's scope. The door in front of which the dead men lay was reefed open and a hand appeared, flicking out a small, dark object towards them. Ethan's brain analysed what the threat was before it bounced off the carpet.

"COVER!"

It was a ridiculous order he knew, as there was nowhere to go, and no cover behind which to hunker. He dropped to the ground and rolled to one side, waiting for the grenade's blast. But it never eventuated.

After a few seconds, there was a loud pop followed by an incessant hissing. Smoke filled the corridor. Within seconds, the dead guards and the doorway they had given their lives to protect disappeared from sight.

The Australians waited in silence. Weapons ready to engage any threat. Ethan flinched as several bursts of gunfire ripped towards them. The muzzle flashes were only faintly visible through the haze. Aiming at the muzzle flash and ignoring the crack of bullets above his head, he shot several times. The gunfire stopped.

Another burst of gunfire interspersed with Indonesian shouting erupted. The Australians returned fire instantly, and within seconds, the once peaceful corridor turned into a loud and confusing fight for survival.

Ethan saw a couple of humanoid shadows pass through the smoke and run in the opposite direction. He took aim and fired, but couldn't be sure if he hit his target. Then as fast as it started, the fight was over. Silence reigned supreme. The smoke grenade continued to hiss with innocent consistency for more than a minute before it began to splutter. Seconds later, it died and the cloud slowly began to disperse.

Ethan signalled his soldiers to provide cover while he pushed himself to his feet, weapon up and ready, finger brushing against the trigger. Ignoring the acrid smell of smoke, he stopped at a dead body and gave it a gentle kick. Nothing. Ethan sent the weapon once belonging to the deceased Indonesian sailing down the corridor with deft flick of his wrist. It landed with a loud clatter. Advancing, he disarmed another lifeless form in a similar manner.

Creeping into the room from which the Indonesians had recently exited, Ethan walked in a brisk crouch, taking cover behind a dressing table. Hearing the soft noise of footfalls, he turned his to see Mark enter the room behind him. They cleared the area with lightning efficiency, but found nothing.

He left the room, noticing the smoke had almost vanished. Skippy had rolled the two dead over, searched them, and dragged them to one side. He looked up as Ethan approached and shook his head. Neither of the

Indonesians was the president.

"Hayche, you on air?" Ethan whispered.

"Roger."

"We got possibly the president and a few guards leaving the building. Standby and engage if possible."

"Roger."

"We're withdrawing. Your loc three mikes."

"Okay, boss."

The Australians departed the way they had approached. At least that route had been cleared of any ambushes or booby traps. Ethan also had no idea how many guards and soldiers were stationed in the building. But one thing was for certain, the whole building would be aware that an assault was underway, and their immediate response should be to secure both the president and the building, before calling in backup.

"This has all the signs of a royal fuck-up," whispered Bob as the patrol descended the stairs.

Fuckin' oath, it does. Although Ethan had better sense than to voice his concern.

* * *

"Okay, boss." Hayche released the transmit button.

"What a shit fight," he muttered. Bringing the night vision goggles to his eyes, he scanned the ground around the building, searching for movement. Nothing.

Letting a breath out through pursed lips, he persisted. A flicker of movement brought his concentration towards the rear area of the building, then he saw them. Three men, two armed guards and a civilian man sandwiched between them. They were fleeing from the area and making for a nearby parked car. Faint shouting began issuing from all areas of the building as the occupants began to waken.

Dropping the goggles, he swung himself around so his body was pointing at the distant figures, brought the sniper rifle around, stabilised it, pulled the buttstock into his shoulder, and stared down the night vision sight.

"Tunguu! Tunguu!" roared Hayche. In English, the word translated to 'wait.'

The civilian in the centre slowed and turned towards the Australian. Hayche managed to obtain a good look at the man's face. It was definitely the president. If not for the guard behind him, the Indonesian president would have come to a complete halt. But he was forcefully pushed on with a rough shove in the back.

The confirmation was all Hayche needed. Judging the speed the men were running, he aimed slightly in front of his intended target and released a single shot. It missed. Relaxing, he tracked the moving targets, pushed doubt from his mind, and fired again. The president dropped to the ground, silent, still and lifeless. As best as Hayche could judge, the round had taken the man through the centre of the chest, just below his left shoulder.

The rear guard stopped, knelt by the man he was sworn to protect and died as half his face disappeared in a swathe of blood, bone, and tiny chunks of grey matter. The guard leading the trio was oblivious to what had taken place behind him. He reached the escape vehicle, unlocked it with a click of a button, opened the driver's door, and turned to see the two bodies upon the grass behind him. He hesitated, unsure what to do now seeing as their escape plan had failed. A moment later, his lifeless corpse slammed onto the bitumen, a bullet having drilled its way through his forehead.

"Target down," said Hayche.

"Roger. Your loc one mike."

Hayche picked up the eight empty cartridges, placed them away in a pocket, pushed himself into a kneeling position, and packed away the Claymore mine. In less than a minute he was ready to move. Shouting from the Istana Merdeka was becoming more intense but still sounded as confused as it had been earlier. Once the inhabitants worked out exactly what was taking place, the Australians, vastly outnumbered, would be overrun and killed within minutes. Time was of the essence.

* * *

The soldiers descended the stairs as fast as they dared, ignoring the muffled Indonesian voices erupting around them. Ethan allowed his soldiers to lead the way down to the ground floor. When he reached the second floor, he saw the grenade he had attached to the door was still in place, although the handle was being tested from the other side.

Nice!

A cursed shout and dull *thuds* began as the kicking started. It would not be long before they had the door open. The plan had gone to shit, and with a quickly narrowing window of opportunity to withdraw safely from the area, Ethan and his soldiers were in real danger. He dropped a smoke grenade, waited for it to sputter to life, and then followed the others down onto the ground floor.

Inside one minute, breathless, adrenaline pumping, and in a small circle of defence, they were back with Hayche.

Ethan pulled a small radio out of his webbing, switched it on, waited for it to self-test, and then lifted it to his mouth.

Hayche looked at Ethan. "Well, that went smoothly, boss."

"Yeah, went off without a fuckin' hitch." Ethan swore. "Let's get outta here."

"Bali belly, Bali belly, this is bravo one four, do you copy? Over," he said.

"Bali belly?" asked Bob. "Really?"

Ethan shrugged. "He insisted."

Bob muttered some choice words under his breath.

"Bravo one four, this is Bali belly, roger, go ahead, over."

"This is Bravo one four. We're compromised, target is down, we need immediate extract, do you copy? Over."

"On our way."

"Thanks, one four out."

"Alright, let's move to—" Ethan was interrupted by a powerful *thump* as the grenade on the second floor exploded, followed closely by screams of both fear and agony.

"Time to move," muttered Ethan. "On me."

The patrol withdrew from the area towards the building they had originally departed. Two soldiers were always static, facing the Istana Merdeka, weapon in shoulders and ready to engage potential targets. When another two went to ground to supply cover, the original pair picked up and withdrew as fast as their legs allowed.

Ethan knelt behind a tree and brought his weapon up. "Go!"

Bob set down behind another tree twenty metres way.

Skippy and Hayche pushed themselves to their feet

and sprinted towards them. Ethan kept a sharp eye on the target building, watching and waiting for enemy soldiers to come streaming out from all sides. So far, there was no sign of movement, although the building itself was now lit up like a Christmas tree as flood lights streamed out at all angles.

Breath caught in Ethan's throat as several distant figures sprinted into view. As they stepped into the beam of one of the floodlights, he saw they were Indonesian soldiers. Four more came into view, followed by another group. Hayche and Skippy pounded past Ethan, their breathing loud and rapid. The Indonesian group began to slowly grow until a veritable army stood around the Istana Merdeka, watching and listening.

A frenzied shout and the corpse of the president was located. A small crowd gathered before he was lifted and carried to the nearby building. The pair of dead guards were moved in a similar fashion.

"Covering. Go!" the breathless voice of Hayche hissed over the radio.

Ethan stood, ensured Bob had heard the message and was also moving, then began running back towards the soldiers covering them. He heard a distant shout, several gunshots, more yelling, the voices quickly building in intensity and anger. As more Indonesian voices joined the throng, the gunshots increased, fast becoming a barrage of fire. Rounds snapped and whipped past Ethan. There was now no doubt the Indonesian soldiers had spotted the Australian patrol.

"Cover!" Ethan roared, diving behind a nearby tree.

Bullets bit into the tree's trunk, sending small chunks of bark and wood in all directions. He remained still, waiting for the rounds to find interest elsewhere.

When the incoming fire became less intense, Ethan slowly shuffled to the right-hand side of the tree so he could garner a look at the enemy. Staring down the scope of his weapon, he lined up a soldier kneeling and firing. Releasing the round and watching him fall, Ethan adjusted his aim and continued to fire single, deliberate, well-aimed shots.

"Moving!" Ethan said into the throat mic. "Cover me!"

"Roger, go!" it sounded like Bob.

Ethan stood and sprinted away from his position of safe cover, his brain berating him for a fool. However, to become bogged down, especially against such overwhelming odds, was death. He repositioned behind another tree.

"Bob, go!"

"Moving!"

Bob appeared, dodging and weaving as he ran before finding cover nearby.

Rounds cracked, snapped, and whipped through the air near the Australians as fast as a hail storm.

Christ, only a matter of time before one or all of us is hit. Ethan stared down the scope at another enemy soldier and shot him through the chest. *Only a matter of fucking time.*

Ethan pulled the handheld radio out of a pocket. "Bali belly, what's your ETA?"

"Two minutes." The response was almost instantaneous.

"Moving!" Ethan ran, darting through knee high shrubs, dodging trees, and settled behind a small concrete wall near the building from which they had originated. "In position!"

"Moving! Cover me!" It sounded like Bob again.

Moments later, Bob vaulted the wall and hunkered down beside him.

He pushed the transmit button. "Hayche, go!"

Ethan rested his cheek on the buttstock of his weapon and firing a shot, the bullet finding its mark in the head of an enemy soldier.

Within minutes, all five men were in cover behind the wall. Only a short bound and they'd be clear of the fight on the far side of the building and ready for extraction by Bali belly. They kept low and returned fire sporadically as the numerous enemy bullets snapped over their heads or ricocheted off the wall.

"This is Bali belly. We're thirty seconds out!"

About bloody time.

"Right, we're extracting," he shouted. "Get to the far side of the building, I'll cover you. Go!"

Ethan knelt up and began firing towards the enemy position. Bob and Hayche both threw smoke grenades, before sprinting away with the others. The green and yellow smoke began drifting across in front of Ethan, protecting him from enemy view. He dropped another smoke grenade at his feet, waited until it hissed to life, spewing blue smoke all around him, then ran back to the building and hoped for the best. He flinched as a bullet cracked beside his head. Another several rounds thudded into the ground beside him.

Only a matter of fucking time.

"Bali belly, what is your ETA, over?" Ethan shouted into the radio, hunkered down against the wall of the building.

"Thirty seconds!"

"You said the same thing three minutes ago, over!" Ethan slammed the handheld on the ground. "Fuck!"

Are we gonna die here?

It was the first time Ethan had doubted the survival of his patrol. Although the mission had been accomplished, to a point, their extraction might be a complete failure.

"Fuck this, boss." Mark sprang up and ran to a nearby car.

The radio crackled to life, but the response was washed out in static.

"Bali belly, you are broken and unreadable, say again words twice, over," Ethan spoke through clenched teeth.

No reply.

Mark tried the driver side door; it was locked. Smashing the window with the butt of his rifle, he flung it open and sat on the seat, ignoring the crunch of broken shards of glass. Tearing off the plastic cowling enshrouding the keyhole of the ignition, he ripped clear the wires, located the pair he needed, and wound the wires together. The engine sputtered to life, a blast of smoke erupting from the exhaust pipe.

"Let's go," said Ethan, leading his soldiers in a foot race to the vehicle. Waiting any longer for Greg's arrival would be too risky.

The men piled into the car. Ethan knelt on the back seat in the centre, facing the six o'clock position, weapon ready, pointing towards the rear windscreen. Bob, sitting behind the driver, had his weapon pointing right. Skippy, sitting behind the passenger, pointed his weapon left. Hayche sat front passenger, weapon pointed forward, finger gently touching the trigger.

"We're all in. Go!" Ethan lifted the radio to his lips. "Bali belly, Bali belly, this is bravo one four, over."

"Bravo one four, this is Bali belly, send over."

"We're located in an old Mitsubishi Lancer heading

away from area of contact, acknowledge over."

A pair of headlights came tearing into sight around a distant corner, following them.

"Acknowledged. You are in sight, keep driving, we'll follow you! Over."

Several figures came sprinting around the corner of the building beside which they had so recently been taking cover. They stopped, a few standing, others dropping into a kneeling position and opened fire together. Rounds hammered into the Mitsubishi, puncturing both rear tyres and battering holes through the rear windscreen. Bullets exited the roof near Ethan's head, and a few others cracked past him, slamming through the front windscreen, making Mark flinch and swerve across the road.

Ethan aimed and returned fire, the noise deafening in the enclosed space. Deftly turning himself around, Bob leaned out the window, weapon aimed towards the enemy figures growing ever smaller, and opened fire. A blinding flash from the top of the much larger vehicle following them illuminated the familiar armoured police car, and the powerful, dull *thump* of the fifty-calibre machine gun joined the fight. The enemy were obliterated by the machine-gun, which continued to suppress the area long after the enemy soldiers were corpses upon the concrete, to persuade any further potential Indonesian advance to rethink their plan and remain in cover.

"This car's fucked," said Mark, looking at Ethan in the rear view mirror. "She ain't gonna last much longer."

Ethan nodded and brought the handheld to his lips. "Bali belly, this is bravo one four, we are immobilised. I say again, we are immobilised. Nil wounded. Prepare to cross-deck, over."

"Roger, preparing to cross-deck, over."

Mark pulled the car over to the curb and pulled the two wires apart, causing the engine to immediately die.

"Standby," said Ethan, glaring at the fast approaching Indonesian police vehicle. "Standby." The nose of the armoured vehicle dipped as it began to slow, blue smoke drifted from the rear tyres accompanied by the screech of rubber. "Standby." With a loud hiss of brakes, the armoured vehicle came to a halt beside the beleaguered car. Ethan flung open his door. "GO!"

He exited the car, ran to the much larger police vehicle, darted to the furthest side, and went to ground, facing the six o'clock position. Staring through the night vision scope attached to the top of his weapon, Ethan watched several Indonesian soldiers come running around a distant corner. He opened fire, dropping the first like a rag doll. Leaving their comrade in a messy heap in the middle of the road, the other soldiers ran for cover.

Ethan adjusted his point of aim and was about to re-engage when the mighty fifty-cal machinegun on the top of the police vehicle roared into life. Tracer rounds flew in a steady stream down the road, ricocheting off the bitumen and arcing skyward. As the gunner watched the fall of shot and adjusted his aim, the trace rounds became more accurate, slashing through the air near the Indonesians desperately sprinting for cover. One, too slow to avoid the onslaught of the heavy machinegun, fell lifeless to the concrete footpath.

With ears ringing as the fifty-cal gun ceaselessly continued to suppress the area, Ethan pushed himself to his feet and ran to the rear of the armoured vehicle. The heavy armoured door was wide open, and he ran to it just in time to see Bob, who, apart from himself, was the last man to climb inside.

Heaving himself up into the rear compartment, he turned and swung the door closed with a grunt. The steel door slammed shut with a solid metallic slap, and with a swift turn of the locking mechanism, Ethan's patrol was safe.

"Cross-decking complete! I say again, cross-decking complete," Ethan said into the radio. "Go! Go!"

"*Roger!*" replied the crackled voice.

The engine revved, the gearbox *crunched*, and then they were underway, rapidly accelerating. Inside the cabin, the fifty-cal was no more than a dull *thump* above them. Only after had they turned a corner did the heavy machinegun fall silent.

"Well…that went well!" shouted Bob over the engine's powerful roar.

Ethan leaned back in his seat and laughed, tension beginning to leave his body.

"*Hey, bravo one four, or whatever you call yourselves these days, do you read?*" it was Greg's voice.

"Yeah, mate," responded Ethan, lifting the radio to his lips. "Go ahead."

"*Word's already out that the Indo president has been assassinated. It's all over the local radio and television stations. In a few hours, it'll be splashed all over the front covers of the newspapers.*"

"Didn't think it'd take long," replied Ethan, allowing the radio to drop to his lap. After a moment's contemplation, he brought the radio back to his mouth. "Hey, Bali belly?"

"*Yeah?*"

"Who they laying the blame on?"

All he received was a protracted, genuine, and contagious laugh over the radio. "*You wanna know who they hold responsible? The British SAS!"* More laughter.

A wide grin spread across Ethan's face.

How ironic, he thought. The British could take the blame for the time being. Long enough for them to leave Indonesia, anyway.

"We've organised your exfil. Later this evening, a French chopper will be landing on the outskirts of the city. We're heading there now."

Ethan lifted the handheld and pressed the push-to-talk button. "Thanks, mate."

"Too easy. I'll miss you blokes, it's been fun," Greg replied.

"Not sure fun's the right word of choice, but I know what you mean. Where are you, by the way?"

"Driving the bloody car!"

"Ah okay, explains the rough ride," Ethan said with a grin. "Now I know what Bob was talking about!"

"Yeah, yeah."

* * *

After more than an hour on the road, the armoured police vehicle rolled to a stop and shut down. The rear door opened, and the soldiers quietly exited, spreading out upon the thick, weed-riddled grass to provide cover for both the armoured car and the fast approaching helicopter.

"Chopper's inbound, two minutes out," Greg whispered into Ethan's ear.

Ethan nodded. Walking in a crouch to the closest man, he tapped him on the shoulder. "Two minutes."

"Copy."

Ethan moved from one soldier to the next, discreetly passing the word. No sooner had he informed the last man, the distant, almost inaudible chatter of an approaching chopper drifted over the position. As the gentle breeze disappeared, so did the sound of the helicopter. Movement beside him made Ethan turn. Greg knelt beside him.

"Listen, if you blokes ever get in the shit and need technical advice, or a hacker, I'm your man, okay?" Greg said softly. "Even from here—" he hesitated as the powerful sound of rotors slapping against the night sky returned, this time louder. "Even from here in Indonesia, I can hack into any computer or device anywhere in the world."

"A handy skill to have," Ethan observed.

"This is my mobile phone number. It's setup for international calls so you can reach it no matter which country you're in."

"Thanks for that, Greg," Ethan replied, accepting the piece of paper and carefully placing it away in a pocket. "If we ever need ya," Ethan's voice was at normal volume to compete against the rapidly increasing volume of the French helicopter, "I'll give you a call."

"Okay. Well, we're outta here. I've run out of Gastro Stop again!" Greg said, holding out his hand.

Ethan chuckled and shook the man's hand. "Seeya, mate," he said, slapping the young man on the shoulder.

"Tell the others I might see them again sometime. *Especially* Bob."

Ethan laughed as the helicopter flared to bleed of speed and began rapidly descending towards the open field.

"Will do!" he shouted with a grin.

Minutes later, they were aboard the helicopter and scudding south towards safety.

*** * ***

When the Indonesian coast lay behind them, and they roared above the safety of the vast ocean, Ethan slapped Bob on the shoulder and passed on Greg's message.

Bob's eyes widened as fury entered them. "If I see that little shit one more time…" A large vein in his neck threatening to burst. He clenched his fists and fell silent.

"Don't be like that, mate," Ethan shouted. "He's gonna miss you the most."

"I'll fuckin' kill him," yelled Bob, his eyes wild. "If I lay eyes on him one more time…" he held up a finger. "*One* more time, and I'll put a bullet in his head. Fuck!" Bob punched his own leg in frustration.

"Jesus, Bob, you're gonna have a stroke, mate. Relax!" Ethan clapped him on the shoulder.

The others watched on with amusement but wisely remained silent.

"Get fucked!"

"Sorry, what'd ya say?" Ethan shouted, holding a hand up to his earmuffs.

Bob's head snapped up, and he glared at Ethan, clenching his jaw.

"Alright, alright," said Ethan, balancing his rifle between his legs and holding out his hands in appeasement. "I'm sorry."

Bob seemed to relax.

"Hey, Bob?" Ethan asked.

Bob looked at him.

"He gave me his phone number if you want it?"

"RIGHT!" Bob screamed. "That's fuckin' IT!"

CHAPTER ELEVEN

The chopper slammed onto the deck of the French aircraft carrier just after midnight. Groggy, tired, and lethargic, the Australians clambered out of the helicopter and walked clear, waving their thanks to the aircrew. The mission hadn't quite unfolded as planned, but the end result was acceptable. By the time they made their way below-decks, word had reached Australia that the Indonesian president had been assassinated at the hands of the British SAS.

Exhausted as he was, Ethan strolled through the cramped hallways of the aircraft carrier. He squeezed past sailors and clambered up ladders until he reached a bank of satellite phones placed neatly beside each other on a long table. Only two phones were free, the rest being used by sailors talking to loved ones back home. Clamping a hand on the back of an empty steel chair, he pulled it away from the table and sat.

God, it's nice to just sit and relax.

Ethan ran a hand through his hair and sighed, his eyes heavy as sleep beckoned. He reached for the satellite phone. Dialling the numbers, he pressed the cold plastic against his ear and waited for the connection to be made. A few seconds later, he heard a *click*, followed by an ear-piercing tone, and then it began to ring.

He checked his watch. *Shit, might be too late. She'll be asleep.*

Click.

"Hello?"

He smiled. "Hey, babe. How are ya?"

"Ethan!" her voice perked up. "I haven't heard from you for ages, how are you sweetie?"

It was so good to hear Sally's voice.

"Good. A bit tired, but good. How're you and Ashlyn going, love?"

"Well, we had a nice day today. We went for a walk on the beach, and then had an ice cream by the beach." Sally went quiet for a moment, and he heard her sigh. "We were going to watch some cartoons on TV, but Ashlyn got her cranky pants on so I put her down to get some sleep."

They're the kind of days I miss the most, cranky pants and all.

He cleared his throat and swallowed. "How is she sleeping, now?"

"She woke up screaming again."

Ethan closed his eyes. "Okay, I'm sure it's something she'll move through, love. Just give it time. She'll move through it."

"That's easy for you to say when you're not here, when you're God knows where. Try getting up in the middle of the night to it, Ethan! You don't know how—" she stopped short.

Christ, don't do this Sally.

"I'm sorry, sweetie," she breathed.

"It's okay, babe," Ethan reassured her. "I'll be home before you know it."

"I hope so."

"So do I. But stay strong, okay?"

He heard her sniff.

"You're doing a wonderful job with Ashlyn. She's going through some hard times right now, and you're being a great mum for her."

"I love you, Ethan."

"I love you, too, sweetheart. Listen, I won't be away for too long, I promise. I'll give you a ring within the next few days, and I'll try to call during the day so I can speak to Ashlyn. Sound good?"

"Sounds good, sweetie." He could hear the smile in her voice.

He glanced across and noticed there was now a line of sailors and Marines waiting one behind the other for their turn to ring loved ones.

"Okay, Sally, I gotta go. I love you, I miss you, and I'll speak to you soon."

"Love you, sweetie."

He ended the call and placed the phone back on the cradle. Pushing the chair back from the table, he stood.

Time to sleep.

* * *

When the sun came up the following day, the world media had run the same story and Indonesia was in disarray. Indonesian media outlets quickly blamed the death of their president on his personal security team and their supposed lack of training. They pointed the finger at the British Ministry of Defence's disregard for Indonesia's sovereignty and alluded to the matter being taken further through the International Court of Justice. Australia's limited media outlets reminded Indonesia the same course of action was not only open to Australia, but would more likely garner far more traction with the International Court of Justice than Indonesia's complaint. But as expected, Indonesia's national media conveniently ignored the rebuttal and maintained their grievance.

After a long flight, the French helicopter landed on the deck of the *USS Ronald Reagan*, patrolling the coast of southern Queensland. The Australian soldiers climbed clear, weapons unloaded and slung.

Thank Christ that's over and done with.

Ethan watched an F-18 slam onto the deck and come to a skidding halt as the arrestor hook caught the cable. The Australians were ushered forward and escorted to the nearest ladder, where they could descend below decks. Ethan nodded at the ground crewman, who turned away and went back to work.

Ethan stepped through a door and was met by a sailor clutching a clipboard.

"You guys just came in on that French helo?"

"Sure did."

She glanced down the clipboard, her index finger tracing a vertical line downward until she saw what she was after. Her finger then moved across and she muttered to herself.

"Okay, you guys are allocated bed spaces on deck five, troop's mess six alpha. You want me to write that down?"

"No, I got it. Thanks for that."

"You'll be outbound to Brisbane tomorrow morning at zero seven-thirty on a Blackhawk. Any questions?"

"No, all good th—"

"Yeah, I got one question," Mark barged forward, a lopsided grin adorning his face. "What's your name?"

She raised one eyebrow. "Thank you, gentlemen." She turned and strode away, disappearing through a nearby doorway.

"Wow, real smooth, mate," said Hayche. "You'll have to teach me that one day."

Mark shrugged. "Worth a crack."

Ethan checked his watch. "Right, let's go get settled. It's almost dinner time and the mess'll be open soon."

"Scran hall, remember?" corrected Skippy.

"Shut the fuck up, Skip," Bob growled. "Fuckin' Navy."

* * *

Malik opened the door and strode through, feeling satisfied.

"Where the hell you been?"

Jayla stood before him, hands on her hips. "Boy, you been gone for hours! You said you shopping." She gestured at his empty hands. "Where's the food?"

She noticed the dried blood plastered all over his knuckles. Then began relaxing as she noticed his blood-stained shirt. Her anger disappeared instantly.

Her hands dropped by her side. "What happened, Malik?"

"Jayla, there's something I need to tell you."

She turned away, holding her face in her hands. "I can't hear this right now!" She sat on the old sofa. "Not now, Malik."

"I've joined the Guardian Angels." He sat beside her and draped an arm around her, pulling her to him.

She flinched away and jumped to her feet. "Boy, you go wash yourself first. I don't want no blood on me! Is that even your blood?"

He sighed. "No, baby. It's someone else's."

Several other people's if truth be told. She don't need to know that, though.

"Malik, I know why you joined the Guardian Angels. You care about me and it's your way to try and protect me." She sat back down beside him and placed a hand on his knee. "But, baby, I need you here." Her voice began to tremble. "With me."

"They're all dead." The words tumbled out of his mouth. "All the looters are gone. They'll never touch you again."

"What!" She took a deep breath, tears cutting lines down her cheeks. "All of them?"

"Well, most of them are dead. The others have been taken prisoner. You're safe, baby."

"Malik," she took a shuddering breath and wiped tears with the palm of her hand. "Baby, are you sure?"

Malik looked down past his blood-soaked shirt at bloodstained hands and nodded. "Oh, I'm sure."

She threw herself into his arms, sobbing into his neck. He held her to him tightly, listening to her cry tears of relief.

They'll never touch you again, baby.

He stroked her back and for the first time in what seemed like an eternity, Malik smiled.

* * *

Ethan and his soldiers awoke early the next morning. With breakfast eaten, they returned to collect their equipment prior to negotiating the narrow corridors and ladders towards the upper deck. At one point, they were forced against a wall as a small team of sailors rushed past, clearly on an urgent mission. The last man offered them an apology.

"No worries, mate," Ethan said, pushing off the

wall and strolling onward. He stepped over the lip of an open door and jogged up a ladder to reach the deck immediately below the top deck. He could faintly hear the flight line humming from above. Ethan pulled on his hearing protection, unhooked the latch, and pushed through one last steel hatch to be rewarded by the refreshing sea air, mixed with a blast of aviation fumes and noise. He held the door open for his soldiers, and once they had stepped through, slammed it closed and latched it securely.

Within minutes, they were standing on the top deck of the carrier in a small huddle off to the side, accompanied by a tall American sailor wearing a bright white jacket. As always, the flight line was buzzing with activity. Sailors dressed in varying-coloured jackets were carrying out their appointed tasks, refuelling aircraft, re-arming fight/bombers, or marshalling jets out onto the main runway.

Ethan felt a powerful thump reverberate up through his feet and watched an FA-18 catapulted clear of the deck, afterburners glowing red as it departed on another endless assault upon the beleaguered Indonesian forces.

Within a minute, a Blackhawk flew into view, flared, and landed in the near distance. Soldiers ran clear, carrying a stretcher on which lay a wounded and bandaged soldier. Behind them ran a female combat rescue medic. She was followed by a small group of bewildered civilians, looking upset, relieved, and unsure of themselves in the new environment. A hand tapped Ethan on the shoulder, but he ignored it as he recognised the soldier running behind the group of civilians. He carried a girl in his arms.

Is that Craig?

Ethan cupped his hands around his mouth. "Oi, Linacre!"

But he didn't hear Ethan.

Shit I'm sure *that's him!*

"Crackers!"

But Craig disappeared from sight behind the group of soldiers as they made their way towards the hospital below decks.

He felt a hand on his shoulder, and then a voice near his ear. "That's gotta be Craig!" It was Hayche's voice.

"Yeah, I'm sure it was, too."

Another Blackhawk landed beside the first, and a loadmaster jumped clear and pointed to the group, gesturing them towards him. The tall sailor in the white jacket turned to them.

"Okay, hustle up!" he shouted.

No shit, stretch!

Ethan nodded at the tall sailor and led his team out onto the flight line towards the waiting chopper. They clambered aboard, and no sooner had they strapped in, the helicopter was airborne, accelerating towards the coast and Brisbane. As the Blackhawk ascended, Ethan saw the distant horizon tarnished an unhealthy stain of black. An enormous bushfire somewhere to the west was wildly out of control.

He waved his hand and gained the attention of one of the loadmasters. Ethan pointed at the distant, dark pall. The loadmaster reached above him, opened a pouch attached to the ceiling of the helicopter, and took out a headset. Plugging it into a vacant communications jack, he threw the headset to Ethan. He deftly caught it, placed it over his ears and pulled the boom mic down in front of his mouth.

"*Hell of a sight, ain't it, man?*" the American voice blasted in his ears.

Ethan pressed the transmit button. "Yeah, what's the go? Bushfire?"

"*Kinda. People way outside of my paygrade thought it'd be a good idea to carpet bomb the Indonesian positions with B-52s. Now the forests and mountains are burning.*"

How the fuck did they ever think that was going to work? Ethan passed a hand across his face.

"Are you joking, mate?"

"*Wish I was, pal. Wish I was.*"

Do the idiots not know how bloody massive Queensland is? The Indonesians would be concentrated in only small areas as well. What a waste of money and resources.

Ethan leaned forward, elbows on knees. "What's the result been?"

"*Of the carpet bombing?*"

He nodded.

Laughter boomed into his headset. "*I think you know the answer to that one, bud. The fifty-twos did take out some encampments. But from what I hear on the grapevine, most of the Indonesian positions are unscathed.*"

"Not surprised, mate. Inland Queensland is massive."

"*We can only hope the fires do the job the bombs didn't.*"

"Doubt it."

"*I hear you, pal. I think they were going for a quick fix to get the war over and done with in one hit. Didn't work.*"

"Shit, I could o' told 'em that and saved them a few billion dollars. Jesus."

More laughter blasted into his ears.

"*Unfortunately, I think we're here for the long haul.*"

Yup, the yank's right, we'll be here for a while, yet.

Ethan's thoughts turned to Sally and Ashlyn, and

his heart sank. How long before he saw them again? One month, three? A year? He sighed.

"Yeah, mate, I think you're right." He tried to keep the disappointment from his voice.

He felt a tap on his arm and turned to see Skippy lean into him so his mouth was only centimetres from the headset. "What's smoke all about?"

Ethan explained.

The Russian roared with laughter and slapped his thigh. Ethan watched the big man pass the word on to the others. Bob rolled his eyes and released what Ethan could only assume was a sentence of expletives. Hayche grinned and slapped a palm to his forehead. Once he'd heard the news, Mark looked away, his alert eyes raking the distant smudge on the horizon.

Typical Mark, he wants to get in amongst it already. Ethan smiled. *Patience, my son. We'll be out in the middle of those fires before you know it, I'm sure.*

"So what's the plan once you get back, bud?" the loadmaster asked.

Ethan looked at the American, smiled, and pressed the transmit button. "I'm gonna have a few beers and sleep for a month."

* * *

Within hours, Ethan and his soldiers were back at the house in which they'd held Tony Bell prisoner.

Ethan walked towards the kitchen. "Coffee anyone?"

Bob nodded. "Yeah, mate"

"Please," said Hayche, sitting down at the table.

Mark declined and headed for the 'Personal' phone to make a call home.

Skippy flopped into a chair beside Hayche and looked up at Ethan. "Why not? I need caffeine in my system."

Right, let's see here, mine's a flat white, Skippy's is NATO standard, Bob likes black and one sugar, and Hayche is white and one sugar. Pretty sure that's right. He grinned. *I should have been a bloody barista.*

"Mine's black and three sugars, remember?" Bob spoke.

Fuck!

Ethan smirked. "All over it, mate."

The soldiers sat around the table, sipping their coffee and relaxing. It had been a long few days, with little sleep and a lot of tedious travelling.

Ethan looked out the nearby window at the cloud-riddled sky. *What's next?* He turned his attention to the 'Work' phone and willed it to remain silent. *Well, at least for a day or two, anyway.* He downed the last of his coffee and placed the empty cup upon the table.

Having finished on the phone, Mark wandered over to the table and sat. "Well, I'll be stuffed! The Guardian Angels knocked off what was left of the Fat Cats."

Hayche leaned back in his chair and laughed.

Ethan looked at Mark. "Really."

The soldier shrugged. "That's what Sarah reckons the newspaper is saying." He jerked a thumb at the phone marked 'Personal' sitting silent behind him. "Something about an American turning the tide."

Ethan smiled and nodded. "Gotta be Malik."

"Probably," Bob agreed.

Skippy stood, pushing his chair back. "Time to get pissed." He placed a cigarette between his lips and lit up, striding from the room.

Hayche grinned. He downed the last of his coffee, slammed the cup down on the table, and stood. "Now *there's* a plan."

Ethan nodded. "You blokes go ahead, I'm just going to give Sally a bell and I'll catch up."

Bob pushed his empty cup away. "Tell her we said g'day."

Ethan picked up the 'Personal' phone. "Will do, mate."

He dialled the numbers burned into his mind, waited for the connection and heard silence. Eventually there was a click followed by the chime indicating a satellite connection had been made, a long pause, and then it began ringing.

The third ring cut short followed by Sally's voice. "Hello?"

"Hey, babe!"

"Sweetie! How are you?"

"Good. How are you and Ashlyn going?"

"We're okay. We had a normal day, really. We had toast for breaky, didn't we, chicken? And I have some good news for you."

Ethan heard a faint voice in the background. "Is that Daddy?"

"Yes, chicken."

His smile widened. "Is Ashlyn there?"

"Here she is."

There was a *clunk* and a *bang* followed by a small voice. "Daddy?"

"G'day, my Princess."

"I miss you, Daddy."

Ethan ignored the lump in his throat. "I miss you, too, Princess. What happened today?"

"I played in the street with some other kids. We

played tag. Have you played that before, Daddy?"

"I have, a long time ago, though."

"Well this was only yesterday! And I tagged a tall girl from down the street. She didn't even see me coming!"

"You've always been fast."

"I *was*, Daddy, I was faster than fast!"

"I bet you were. How have—"

"I love you, Daddy. Here's Mummy."

"I love you too, Princess."

The phone went quiet briefly. "You there, sweetie?"

"Yeah, love. She sounds happy."

"She is, Ethan. She misses you badly, though. She asks about you each morning, but yes, she's happy, sweetie."

"That's good to hear. How are you going?"

"I'm okay. Although I can't wait for you to get home."

Sally had been an Army wife long enough to know not to ask a question like, *"How much longer will you be over there?"*

"Can't wait to get home, babe. You'll wish I was gone again within a week!" He laughed.

She giggled. "Never, sweetie. You're missed here, let me tell you. But I'd better let you go, Ethan. I love you heaps."

"I love you, too. Before you go, though, how's Ashlyn been sleeping?"

"Oh, I totally forgot, I meant to tell you before. The good news was that last night was the first night she slept all the way through without a single nightmare."

Ethan closed his eyes. *Thank Christ.*

"Shit, that's good news, love. Tell my Princess I

love her.”

“I will, sweetie. Love you, and speak to you soon.”

“Love ya.”

He waited for the *click* to signify the call was disconnected before hanging up the phone.

In the wise words of Skippy: “Time to get pissed.”

He walked out the front door and closed it behind him. He noticed Skippy leaning against a wall nearby, enjoying a cigarette.

“I expected you’d be at the pub by now, mate.”

Skippy exhaled smoke through his nose. “Thought I’d wait for you, boss. If shit hits fan on the way to pub, two soldiers better than one. How’s Sally?”

“Yeah, good, Skip. It’s all good on the home front.”

The big Russian nodded, dropped the spent cigarette to the ground, and crushed it with a boot. “Good to hear.”

They strolled down Queen Street Mall, casting their eyes over the wares on display. Nothing had changed in the short time they’d been away. Ethan noticed the familiar faces of the storekeepers and nodded or smiled when he caught their eye. It might have been wishful thinking on his part, but the atmosphere seemed more relaxed than it had been before when the looters were more active.

Skippy wandered over to a stall, paid for two oranges, and tossed one to Ethan. “Good for you,” he said.

“Thanks, mate.” Ethan peeled the skin free and dumped it in a nearby bin before pulling the fruit apart. “Shit, that’s good!” he slurred through a mouthful. When he’d finished eating, he rubbed his palms against his jeans to dry them of orange juice.

The shops of the mall were long behind them, and the people they passed looked grim and less innocent than the families going about their shopping in the distance. The far end of Queen Street Mall belonged to the darker side of Australian society, the fighters, those who'd resisted, those men and women who'd stood up and fought, and more often than not, killed multiple times, to protect their way of life. Although they may have been innocent Aussies before the invasion, their lives were forever changed.

For the better? The unanswered question drifted around Ethan's mind as he cast his eyes over the groups of people sitting, standing, or walking to and from the bar.

"How are you, Chris?" Ethan asked the security officer standing guard at the front of the public bar.

"Good, mate. Haven't seen you blokes for a while." He turned and pointed to the far corner. "Your boys are over there."

Ethan followed Chris's finger, and his eyes came to rest on his crew, sitting in a tight group, laughing at some story Bob was telling. But he looked beyond Bob to the two soldiers sitting on the far side of the table. He hadn't seen their faces in some months.

Holy shit, it's Dave and Charlie!

"Cheers, Chris."

"You have durry." Skippy offered Chris a cigarette.

"Don't smoke."

"You have durry," Skippy repeated, pushing the cigarette into Chris's hand. "Good for bartering later on." The Russian brushed past Chris, following Ethan.

"He's Russian, mate. He won't take no for an answer!" Ethan shouted over his shoulder.

Ethan came to a stop behind Bob, but Dave and

Charlie had already seen him and moved around to greet him. He shook their hands, grinning like an idiot. "Bloody hell, fellas, it's good to see ya!"

"Likewise," said Dave.

"What you drinkin'?" asked Charlie.

"This is my shout, mate. You fellas have been through enough. I take it the Fat Cats are on the bones of their arses?"

Dave roared with laughter. "That's one way to put it!"

Ethan took note of the drinks held by Dave and Charlie. He turned to the rest of his soldiers.

"Who needs a drink?"

Hayche held up an empty cocktail glass. "I'll have an Adios Motherfucker, Boss!"

He turned to Skippy. "What are you drinking, mate?"

"Whatever you're drinking, boss."

Ethan took the empty glass from Hayche and made his way to the bar, filing through the crowd. He was relaxed but was acutely aware of those immediately around him and was comforted by the feeling of the pistol wedged down the back of his jeans. Knowing Chris and his colleagues meant that he had his soldiers remained armed while the vast majority of the patrons had been forced to turn in their firearms at the front door.

He shouldered his way to the bar, forcing aside a man who'd been standing at the bar drinking. The man glared at Ethan, but he ignored him. Eventually, the bartender approached, and he placed his order. The beers would take but a moment to serve, but the cocktail would take a few more minutes. Ethan placed his forearms on the bar and waited, relaxed. It had been a long few days, and they'd very nearly not returned home at all.

If there was still a lotto, I'd buy a fuckin' ticket. He smiled.

"Excuse me, sir, you mind if we order a drink?" an American voice asked.

The man Ethan had barged aside nodded and slurred something incomprehensible before stumbling away. He threw a glance at Ethan and snarled, speaking another string of incomprehensible words.

Ethan looked across at the newcomers but knew who'd be standing there before he laid eyes on them. He grinned. "G'day, Malik!" He looked at the woman. "Jayla, how are you?"

She looks nervous. But who can blame her with what she's been through?

"I'm good, thanks to you and your soldiers." She smiled.

A chair scraped on the floor nearby, and Jayla flinched, her eyes widening.

Malik draped an arm over her shoulder, and she seemed to relax a little.

"Well, you're in a safe place, Jayla, and you're amongst friends." Ethan turned to face her. He swept his arm around the pub. "There's no way any looters would dream of coming into a place like this. They'd be hung out to dry inside a minute."

"See?" Malik kissed the top of her head. "Not that there's any of them left," he added.

Ethan chuckled. "So I hear, mate."

"Apart from the couple of prisoners the Australian Federal Police are holding, take it from me, there are none of them left walkin'."

He nodded. *Thought so. Old Malik, the Guardian*

Angels, and my two lads have gone through them like a hot knife through butter.

Ethan thanked the bartender as the drinks were served. He picked up his beer and took a sip. "You guys want to come and join us?" He pointed at his soldiers sitting in the near distance.

Malik looked at Jayla. She nodded and smiled again.

"Thanks, man, we'd love to. Yeah, those looters are done. It's over!"

Ethan placed his beer down and laughed. "Yeah, the looters are done with, but it ain't over, Malik. We got a long way to go yet."

"You sure about that?"

"Oh, I'm sure, mate."

Ethan carried the drinks across to his soldiers and handed Hayche his cocktail and Skippy his beer. Minutes later, Malik and Jayla joined them. They were warmly welcomed, and Ethan noticed Jayla visibly relax.

Finally, she feels safe. He caught her eye and gave her a thumbs up.

Jayla laughed and held her thumb up.

"Oi, Malik!" Skippy called.

The American looked at the Russian.

"Soon, we head out to fight bushfires."

Ethan leaned back in his chair and looked at the Navy SEAL. "Yeah, Malik, you ever been in a bushfire before?"

"Can't say I have, no."

Ethan nodded and leaned forward, placing his hands on the table. "Always a first time for everything. Want to join us?"

THE UNFORESEEN SERIES

The Reckoning: The Day Australia Fell (Book 1)

Aftermath (Book 2)

STAND ALONE NOVELS

Tour To Midgard

Tasked with a mission in Iraq, an Australian SAS patrol deploy deep behind enemy lines. But when they activate a time portal, the soldiers find themselves in 10th century Viking Denmark, a place far more dangerous and lawless than modern Iraq. The soldiers have no way back. Join the SAS patrol on this action adventure and journey into the depths of a hostile land, far from the support of the Allied front line. Step into another world…another time.

www.ingramcontent.com/pod-product-compliance
Lightning Source LLC
Chambersburg PA
CBHW070438120726
47910CB00003B/842